"What are people saying?"

Finn weighed his stupid idea, quickly racing through a mental list of pros and cons. Since the list was pretty evenly matched, it was only his desperation to find a killer that tipped the scales toward the pro.

With that goal in mind—closing this case and catching a killer as quickly as possible—he opted to go for broke.

"Bo Gage was killed the night of his bachelor party. Michael Hayden was killed the night of his rehearsal dinner. One thing the victims had in common—they were grooms-to-be. And in a matter of weeks half the town has called off any and all plans to get married or host an engagement party."

"I still can't see what this has to do with me."

"If you're as innocent as you say you are, surely you'd be willing to help me."

"Help you do what?"

"Pretend to be my fiancée, Darby. Help me catch a killer."

Addison Fox is a lifelong romance reader, addicted to happily-ever-afters. After discovering she found as much joy writing about romance as she did reading it, she's never looked back. Addison lives in New York with an apartment full of books, a laptop that's rarely out of sight and a wily beagle who keeps her running. You can find her at her home on the web at addisonfox.com or on Facebook (Facebook.com/addisonfoxauthor) and Twitter (@addisonfox).

Books by Addison Fox

Harlequin Romantic Suspense

Midnight Pass, Texas

The Cowboy's Deadly Mission
Special Ops Cowboy
Under the Rancher's Protection
Undercover K-9 Cowboy

The Coltons of Grave Gulch

Colton's Covert Witness

The Coltons of Mustang Valley

Deadly Colton Search

The Coltons of Roaring Springs

The Colton Sheriff

Visit the Author Profile page at Harlequin.com.

DEADLY TRAP

ADDISON FOX

Previously published as *Colton's Deadly Engagement*

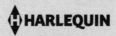

Special thanks and acknowledgment are given to Addison Fox
for her contribution to The Coltons of Red Ridge miniseries.

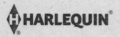

Recycling programs
for this product may
not exist in your area.

ISBN-13: 978-1-335-47376-9

Deadly Trap

First published as Colton's Deadly Engagement in 2018.
This edition published in 2022.

Harlequin Enterprises ULC
22 Adelaide St. West, 41st Floor
Toronto, Ontario M5H 4E3, Canada
www.Harlequin.com

Printed in U.S.A.

DEADLY TRAP

For Aunt Bonnie

Godmother. Aunt. Friend. Cheerleader.
You've always been that to me and so much more.

But would I be me if I didn't memorialize
our oldest joke in your dedication?

Bonnie really IS a nickname for Angela.
(Even if my 1st grade teacher still believes I'm wrong!)

I love you!

Chapter 1

Cold air pierced Finn Colton's lungs as he ran hell-for-leather beside his faithful and loyal partner, Lotte. Although she was trained specifically for attacking and guarding her quarry, the German shepherd was a mighty fine tracker and Finn followed in her wake as she pounded over the hills and valleys of Red Ridge, South Dakota.

In February.

Damn, it was cold.

As soon as the thought registered, Finn pushed it aside as he pressed on toward the fleeing figure about seventy-five yards ahead, weaving in and out of shadow. Was it possible they were this close to the suspect dubbed the "Groom Killer"?

Although he'd put little stock in the sensational and lurid depiction the local press had been dreaming up for nearly a month, he would cop to concern over the safety of his town. A police chief's duty was to his people and that was a mighty challenging job when everyone he spoke to admitted to walking around in fear.

Tonight's discovery of a second dead groom was going to turn subtle unease to full-on terror.

Lotte's bark pulled him from his dismal thoughts as she put on another burst of speed, leaping forward into the night. Finn ignored the cold air and kicked it up a notch, digging deep for the stamina to keep moving.

In an apparent burst of speed of his—or her—own, their quarry put on the juice and zagged out of view. Finn kept going, trailing Lotte so close he could feel her tail slapping against his thigh, but in moments it was clear they'd lost the trail.

Lotte whined as she slowed, running in a circle as she fought to pick up a fresh scent on the ground before letting out a sharp cry.

The distinct odor of bleach, especially piercing in the bitter cold, hit his nostrils as he narrowed the distance to his partner. He came to a solid halt and bent to settle his hands on his knees. He quickly stepped back, ordering Lotte with him, out of range of the harsh scent.

Years of consistent training and the deep love and

affection they'd built had her backing up immediately and she moved to his side.

"We were set up, girl. That bleach was laid down only a little while ago. Bastard wasn't running from us. He was running to his own version of the finish line."

Finn cursed again and stood to his full height, willing his other senses into action as he searched the darkened night. A wash of stars lit up the sky, made even brighter by the thick halo of a nearly full moon, but revealed nothing. Whomever they'd chased was gone and the night held no clue as to where.

He toyed with following, anyway, heading in the last direction he'd seen his quarry, but knew it was a lost cause. If the killer was smart enough to put down the bleach in advance, he or she was smart enough to change direction once out of sight.

Lotte edged toward the chemical, backing away when the scent hit her nose once more.

"Clever," he muttered. *And dangerous*, he added to himself. Very dangerous if the killer had enough sense to prepare like that.

Red Ridge's K-9 unit was famous across the state and even farther on than the boundaries of the Black Hills and the South Dakota border. The killer would have known they'd use every resource at their disposal, including well-trained K-9 dogs who needed relatively little scent input to hunt their quarry.

He patted Lotte's head, burying his fingers into the thick pelt of her fur. She was lean and fit, but winter had brought her thicker fur and he loved the way his palm seemed to sink into the warmth. She was a beauty and he scratched behind her ears as he praised her, reassuring her of her successful tracking even if the perp did get away. Finn Colton loved his sweet girl and he always made sure she knew she was appreciated and important.

He also talked to her like a partner. While he harbored no delusion she understood the differences in the gauge sizes of guns or the headache of late-night paperwork, she understood her role in their partnership and always sat and listened, staring up at him with large, soulful eyes. They shared an amazing bond and he never took her or her training for granted.

His wealthy uncle, Fenwick Colton, had seen to it that his investment in the unit and its cofunded training center—one of the largest in South Dakota—was well publicized. His uncle was an old bastard, Finn thought, but a crafty one. Man could get three dollars out of one and was always looking for an angle. If there was an opportunity to put Colton Energy in the paper, on TV or splashed all over the internet, he leaped at the chance.

The K-9 unit and training facility had given Fenwick that and more. Not only did they receive more than their fair share of local news coverage and even the occasional spate of national attention, but the unit had been a tribute to Fenwick's late first wife. Dubbed "the only one he ever loved" by Fenwick's own admission, he'd continued the funding long after he'd assuaged his grief with a string of generously endowed younger women.

The training center was one of the few reasons Finn tolerated his uncle. While his appreciation had a solid core of selfish motivation for the continued support of his precinct, a small corner of his heart liked the fact that Fenwick might have been a decent human being once upon a time.

Since he'd gotten Lotte as well as his entire department from the deal, Finn could hardly complain. But it did mean his uncle came calling a bit too often at police headquarters. His recent rant over the need to catch the Groom Killer had been a world-class tirade.

The fact that his uncle believed it was his niece and Finn's cousin Demi Colton who was responsible, had added an uncomfortable edge to the proceedings. He knew how to deal with his uncle—he wasn't a man who backed down easily before anyone—but the determined rant that Demi had gone so far off the edge she'd started killing men was a tough pill to swallow.

If asked, Finn would have said it was ludicrous. But after finding her necklace at the first crime scene and her name drawn in blood beside the body, he could hardly ignore what was in front of his face. Given her strong motive—she'd been engaged to Bo Gage before he'd dumped her for another woman he'd quickly proposed to—and the circumstantial evidence, Demi was their prime suspect. Yet the man who'd known her since she was an infant wanted to believe in her innocence.

The police chief had to work every angle, run down every lead and needed a great deal of objectivity. Especially with Demi on the run and seeming uncomfortably guilty when he'd questioned her after Bo Gage's murder.

With their race toward answers lost, he gestured Lotte to follow him. It was time to head back to review the crime scene they'd abandoned—a celebration turned tragedy—to chase a murderer.

He still saw it in his mind—had already begun the mental walk through the details of the crime. The second groom lay outside the back door of the kitchen at the Circle T Steakhouse. The man had been murdered in the midst of his rehearsal dinner, his body discovered only when one of the line chefs had run outside for a quick break. The man's scream had been heard all the way inside the restaurant and it had taken the foresight of the head chef to keep everyone away from the body. There was no way anyone could have helped Michael Hayden, even had they tried.

Not with a bullet hole seared clear through his heart and a black cummerbund shoved deep into his mouth.

Darby Gage patted the cushion beside her and tried to coax Penny onto the couch. Darby had lived in the same house with the stubborn female for the past two weeks and had been unsuccessful in getting Penny to share any common space. She refused to share the couch, the bed or even a small chaise longue on the back porch.

Since it was February in South Dakota, the chaise experiment hadn't lasted long—it was too damn cold to sit waiting for a stubborn dog to join her on the rattan recliner—and Darby had taken some small measure of pride in the fact that she'd tried.

But enough was enough.

The German shepherd was the crown jewel in the dismal inheritance from her ex-husband and it was high time they came to some sort of grudging truce. Bo wasn't coming back courtesy of the bullet in his chest and Darby was in charge now.

Which seemed to have no impact on Penny. None whatsoever. Nor had it stopped striking Darby with that strange combination of surprise and sadness.

Bo was really gone. And the manner of his death...

She still shuddered when she thought about how he'd been discovered, shot and left for dead, a tuxedo cummerbund shoved into his mouth. It was dark and macabre. She'd tried to avoid thinking about it, but that was difficult when you considered how the *Red Ridge Gazette* had run with a new story every day, each one more lurid than the last. Everything from Groom Killer on the Loose to Is the Groom Killer One of Red Ridge's Own? had graced the paper's headlines. More than that, it was as if a fever had gripped the town and no one could stop talking about it.

Was it a local like Demi Colton? The press had picked up on her as their favorite suspect and had been writing story after story on her background and her brief engagement to Bo before he'd dumped her for his new intended bride, Hayley Patton. Although she supposed anything was possible, as Bo's former wife Darby could hardly understand a woman committing a crime of passion over the man.

He was good-looking in his own way, but she'd learned too quickly that he'd also used those good looks to coast by in life. He'd carried little responsibility, preferring to dump his troubles on others. And other than his dogs, there was little he'd seemed to truly care about.

In the end, it had been his cheating that had killed their marriage. She'd come to realize that even had he been faithful, theirs wasn't a union that would have lasted. It had taken a while, but Darby had finally reached the point where she could accept that without the immense guilt that had initially accompanied the thought.

Which made her current circumstances all the more puzzling.

While she and Bo had ended things amicably enough two years ago, why had her ex seen fit to leave her his German shepherd breeding business? She knew and loved dogs—and she spent more than a few hours of each work week at the K-9 training center making a few extra dollars—but that didn't make her a fit breeder. Neither had her fourteen-month marriage to Bo. He was a responsible breeder—he loved his dogs and he took good care of them—but she hadn't involved herself in the business during their marriage.

Yet here she was. The new owner of Red Ridge's premier breeding business for the town and the county's K-9 units. They sold to assorted others besides the RRPD, but had a reputation to uphold with one of the state's primary K-9 departments.

The PD down in Spearfish had attempted a K-9 unit of their own a few years back and had trained a few of Penny's puppies. The cost of keeping the program had grown too much and they'd ultimately sold the dogs to a good security firm known for its excellent treatment and handling of their dogs.

Bo's other customers, the Larson brothers, were also good for a few puppies in each litter. A fact that settled uncomfortably on her shoulders. It was unfair of her—they doted on their dogs and treated them well—yet something creeped her out about the way the twins, Noel and Evan Larson, strutted around Red Ridge like they owned the town and everyone in it. They'd been raised by their kindly grandmother, Mae, after losing their parents, and Darby knew she should cut them a break.

But she never liked when the Larson boys came around.

Penny's light yip startled her and pulled Darby from her thoughts. The pretty German shepherd had dropped down to her belly, head on her front paws, and was even now staring at Darby.

"You don't like the Larsons, either, do you?"

Penny's dark eyes seemed to bore into hers. Even as she knew it was a silly thought, Darby could have sworn the dog agreed with her.

"You really can sit next to me. I won't bite and I'd like to get to know you better."

Penny's gaze never wavered as she considered her from her spot across the rug. The couch wasn't that comfortable, but Darby had to believe the threadbare carpet was even less so. She was still adjusting to her surroundings. She'd moved her few possessions in from the one-bedroom apartment she'd rented in town and the addition barely made a dent in Bo's small house.

It was so odd to be back in the house. Their marriage had been brief but she'd made some improvements when she'd lived here with Bo. She'd freshened up the curtains and had insisted they paint the living room and kitchen to brighten things up. Now those improvements simply looked garish, like the rest of the house had aged around them, an old woman wearing her years despite the heavy makeup she used to try to hide the lines.

Since the house was hers, she'd like to make a few changes, but the inheritance hadn't come without its challenges. One of which was a stifling mortgage that Bo had overextended himself on and a mountain of debt for the breeding business. She'd spent the past two weeks trying to get her arms wrapped around it all and was still puzzled by just how far into debt her ex-husband had gone. She didn't think he was in that deep when they were married, but in the end, who really knew.

All she knew now was that she had a hill of debt and very few options.

She was also worried about Penny. The dog had kept her distance but Darby wasn't blind to Penny's increasing age. She was the conduit to more puppies though Darby had real reservations about attempting to breed her again.

Which only made the problems she had since the reading of Bo's will grow even bigger.

Why had he chosen her? Was it punishment for a marriage gone bad instead of a gift?

Or was there something else at play?

Hayley Patton was his fiancée, yet she'd gotten nothing of his except the car they'd leased together and the rings they'd purchased in preparation for the wedding. She was flashing a mighty large rock on her left hand but Darby had no idea how Bo had paid for it. She could only be grateful the bill hadn't showed up on her list of debts on the property.

Whatever else he was, Bo Gage hadn't been a saver or a money manager. And now it was up to her to clean up his mess.

Lost in her thoughts, she was surprised to feel the

heavy sway of the couch frame when Penny leaped up. The dog still kept her distance, curling at the opposite end of the three-cushion couch, but Darby smiled anyway.

Maybe they might figure their way out of this, after all.

Finn dropped into his desk chair and glanced at his watch: 4:00 a.m. It had taken them that long to secure the scene, interview the witnesses and take as much detail from the Circle T's property as they could. Only after they'd done that had they been able to move Michael Hayden's body.

The guy had snuck out the back of the kitchen to grab a smoke, his fiancée's legendary distaste for the practice sending him skulking out a rear exit to escape the rehearsal dinner festivities unnoticed.

Only someone *had* noticed.

They'd shot him.

Finn reviewed his notes, typing them into his report to ensure his thoughts were as fresh as possible. What he avoided including was the observation that sneaking cigarettes at your rehearsal dinner because your soon-to-be wife hated the practice likely wasn't the most auspicious start to happily-ever-after.

Not that he was exactly an expert.

His own marriage had crashed and burned in a fiery pile of ash after his ex-wife had grown fed up with his hours and the danger of his job. Mary was a good woman and he'd heard through the grapevine that she was remarrying. She'd left Red Ridge after their divorce, picking up work in Spearfish, about thirty miles away, as a digital designer for a local firm. He was happy that she had moved on with her life and wanted nothing but good things for her.

The fact that he'd felt nothing—not even the slightest tug—when he'd heard the news bothered him more than he could say. Wasn't a man supposed to be jealous if his ex moved on? Even a little bit? Yet here he was, content and maybe even a little relieved that she'd picked up her life and found someone new. He'd never worried much about his reputation as a cold, work-focused leader, but maybe it was time he started.

After, he promised himself. He'd worry about it all after he got through these reports and the inquiries and found out just who was killing men in his town.

The report practically wrote itself. The men and women on his team were well trained and good at their jobs. Between their notes and work, as well as his own, he was able to paint a quick, succinct picture of the crime and Michael Hayden's unpleasant death.

Shutting down his laptop, he caught sight of a note scribbled by Carson Gage and left in the small wooden box he kept on the corner of his desk.

Carson was one of his best detectives on the force and the brother of the first victim, Bo Gage. Finn picked up the note, curious to see what, if any, details Carson had added to his already-robust case file.

Unsuccessful visit to Darby Gage. Persists in saying she had no idea why Bo left her the business and the house. Has alibi for Bo's murder but could have someone covering for her?

Despite the personal connection with his brother, Carson had been invaluable on the case. But that last question didn't sit well with Finn. He knew Carson had worked long and hard to find justice for his brother, but it wasn't like him—or anyone on Finn's team—to question a person's alibi simply for the sake of wrapping up a case and pinning a crime on a convenient suspect.

Was there something behind Carson's concern? Or was he so frustrated by the lack of leads that he'd begun grasping at straws?

Yes, it was suspicious that Bo had left his business to his ex-wife. But Finn had known Bo Gage and the man hadn't been the most responsible soul. It could be as simple as the fact that Bo had never had his will changed after his divorce.

Or there could be something else there.

He made a quick note to himself to go talk to Darby Gage. He'd spoken with her a few weeks before when suspicion had first landed on Bo Gage's ex-wife and hadn't come to any conclusions. Nevertheless, if something about the woman was nagging at Carson, then Finn would talk to her again.

His detective had a lot on his plate, including his

own conflicted feelings about his brother's passing. Perhaps this case needed a bit more objectivity.

Up until their last meeting, Finn had known Darby Gage as he knew most of his constituents, by sight and a vague recollection of a conversation a time or two. She was pretty, with shoulder-length dark hair and vivid blue eyes, her figure petite and waifish. If he hadn't seen her at the K-9 training center a time or two, carrying pails of water to scrub out the dog facilities, he'd not have believed her capable of the work. The slender lines of her body belied a strong, capable woman.

One capable of murder?

He shook off the thought, unwilling to take the same leap as Carson simply for the sake of having a suspect besides Demi Colton.

Fifteen minutes later he was still thinking of her when he stepped into his ground-floor condo and peeled off his gun before climbing into bed.

Was it even remotely possible Darby Gage was the Groom Killer? She had a potential motive for killing her ex-husband—he'd left her the house and business, after all. But Michael Hayden had been killed with the same MO as Bo. And why would Darby kill Hayden?

The thought of her as the perp didn't sit well, but for some strange reason, just as he was fading off to sleep, he felt a shot of interest light up his nerve endings. There was something about her that caught a man's notice.

Something that had caught his notice, even as he'd been forced to remain professional and disinterested.

He hadn't given Darby Gage more than a passing thought over the past five years, but now that he *had* given her a passing thought, he couldn't deny his interest in talking to her.

So he'd go see her for himself.

And try not to notice if she was as pretty as he remembered.

Chapter 2

The hope that had carried Darby through the prior evening when Penny had opted to join her on the couch met an untimely end about ten minutes into breakfast. It had started with Penny's stubborn refusal to eat. Darby had tried to coax her with dry food and, when that hadn't worked, some wet food Bo had kept in the pantry. When neither met with success, she'd even gone so far as to cook the dog some rice and heat up some plain chicken she'd cooked for her lunchtime salads all week. All to no avail.

Penny wouldn't eat.

This had resulted in a call to the vet and a panicked round of "What did she eat the day before?"

before the dog had shamed her into embarrassment by diving into her breakfast after fifteen shaky, fear-filled minutes. The only saving grace was that Darby hadn't called the vet out to the house, only to have paid for an unnecessary visit.

What the call *had* turned up as the vet probed on Penny's age and overall health was his concern that another litter would put Penny at serious risk. On some level, Darby had known it, but she'd told herself she needed a professional opinion.

And now she had it.

That dismal news and the breakfast battle of wills had been followed by the news of another murder in Red Ridge, this one eerily like Bo's. While the RRPD hadn't released all details of how Michael Hayden had been murdered, the fact that it was another groom-to-be—this one celebrating at his rehearsal dinner—was too coincidental for Darby's comfort.

After fielding three calls from concerned friends in town, along with two more she'd sent to voice mail, unwilling to engage in the expected idle gossip that would have resulted, Darby headed out to the backyard and the property beyond.

The day was sharp and cold, but the winter sun was bright in a blue sky. Penny had reluctantly followed her outside and had skirted the property, seeming to take comfort in her perusal of the perimeter before settling on the rattan recliner on the porch, apparently content to watch her.

Darby shot the dog the gimlet eye but was pleased to see Penny's reluctant interest in her activities. "Chalk it up to a silent victory that she's interested enough to hang out here and move on," Darby muttered to herself before heading toward a large shed.

She dug out a bucket and some disinfectant and went to work on the large cage she'd pulled out of the garage the day before. The roomy nest served as Penny's private area when she was preparing for her litter and Darby wanted it clean and fresh.

Penny might not be able to use it any longer but the activity and the bracing air gave Darby purpose and something to do.

It also kept her mind away from the subject of just how far off the rails her life had traveled.

She'd believed her savings would be enough to carry her through the next litter of puppies. But the problems kept mounting and there was no way she could take care of the business, the house, the taxes and the need to purchase a new dog for the breeding program on the small amount she had in the bank.

Bo's once-thriving business with quite a few quality dogs was now down to Penny. Darby knew how much Bo had loved the dog and he'd obviously kept her even after he had to sell all the other German shepherds to keep things afloat.

Bo's father, Edson, had begged Darby to keep the business going in his son's memory, and she'd promised she would. It was only after seeing the degree of Bo's debt that she was fast coming to understand she shouldn't have made that promise.

What a mess.

Settling the thick padding from the base of the cage and the disinfectant on the porch, Darby headed inside to retrieve the water she'd left heating on the stove to mix with the cleaner. She'd nearly wrestled the heavy pot off the stove when the doorbell rang. Resettling the pot and narrowly avoiding the slosh of hot water against the edges, she headed for the front door. The house wasn't large, but she prayed with each footfall that one of the nosy voice mails still waiting on her phone hadn't decided to drive across town to strike up a conversation.

Offering up one more silent prayer, Darby pulled open the front door.

Just when she thought her day couldn't get any worse, she came face-to-face with Finn Colton, the Red Ridge chief of police.

Finn appreciated the authority that came with his position and he made it a point to behave in a way that earned him respect. He'd met a few cops over the years who'd forgotten that the trust the public imbued in them was as important as honoring that trust. He'd never wanted to behave in a manner that disregarded that bond.

His surprise visit to Darby Gage was both deliberate and purposeful. *Respectful*, but deliberate all the same. While not quite full-on disregard for her trust, he was doing a bit of bearding the lion in its den.

Aka surprising the pretty divorcée. On purpose.

"Mrs. Gage. I was hoping you could find a few minutes to speak with me."

"Chief Colton." She nodded but made no move to let him in. "What can I do for you?"

"I wanted to talk to you about Bo for a bit."

Resignation settled in her blue-violet gaze before she nodded her head. "Of course. Come in, please."

He followed her into the small house, surprised to see how run-down the place was. He'd grown up well aware of the long-standing Colton-Gage feud but had always believed the Gages lived well enough to afford the basics. Though he had little interest subscribing to something as antiquated—and decades old—as the town family feud, his reaction to the state of Bo Gage's home only reinforced that he'd never been particularly close with any of the Gages.

Fortunately, working with several members of the family on the force had changed that and he was grateful for it. Carson had his full respect, as did Carson's younger half sister, Elle. Although still a rookie on the K-9 team, Elle handled herself with poise beyond her years and had a keen ability to partner with her K-9 charge.

In Finn's estimation, the Gages weren't so bad, even if his uncles, Fenwick and Rusty, as well as his father, Judson, continued to perpetuate the ridiculous notion of a feud. He'd been called to more than one heated incident between members of the two families since joining the RRPD and knew it was only a matter of time before there'd be another.

Truth be told, he was surprised there hadn't been a skirmish yet, especially with a Gage murdered and a Colton as one of the suspects.

Even with his better understanding of the Gage family—or maybe because of it—Bo Gage's home was unexpected. He might have been a slacker, but Bo was still the son of one of Red Ridge's wealthier individuals, Edson Gage. Somehow Finn had expected Bo's fortunes to be a bit more robust than the shabby decor suggested. Even as his gaze roamed the place, Finn had to give Darby credit. The furniture might be worn and run-down, but it was clean. He didn't see dust on the end table or the TV and he could still see the outline of sweeper marks on the carpet.

Were murderesses that clean?

A quick scent memory of the bleach from the crime scene filled his nose and he struggled against the thought. Bo had been dead long enough that there would have been some accumulation of dust and dirt by now. Yet here she was, cleaning up and making the place her own.

"What would you like to discuss, Chief Colton?"

Darby's question pulled him from his musings, but Finn had to admit the angle wasn't one he'd considered. Perhaps it was time he started.

"You seem to be settling in."

"I didn't have much to move in with me."

"Clean, too." He stated it as an observation and was surprised when she just smiled back, her grin bright and proud.

"My mother raised me to believe cleanliness was next to godliness. Add on the fact that I'm keeping up with a seventy-pound German shepherd and my OCD kicks in hard."

"Does the dog hate the mess?"

"No, Chief. I do. And the endless piles of hair a dog sheds." She turned toward the kitchen. "Can I get you a cup of coffee?"

"That'd be nice."

Finn followed Darby into the back of the house, smiling when the purported mess maker—a German shepherd with the same coloring as Lotte— came through a doggie door and trotted toward him. He extended his hand, keeping an easy smile on his face. "Hey there, girl."

The dog slowed but continued forward, her tail wagging gently.

Finn kept his hand extended, pleased when she allowed him to pet her head. "Hi, sweetheart. What's your name?"

"This is Penny." The slightest grimace crossed Darby's face before she shot an indulgent smile at the dog. "She sure seems to like you."

He dropped to a knee and continued to level praise and affection on the dog. "Why do I sense that irritates you?"

"Let's just say Penny and I have come to a grudging truce since I moved in."

"How grudging?"

"I keep trying and Penny keeps her distance."

Finn stood to his full height. "She's a good girl. She's just had a lot of upheaval lately. Bo loved this dog."

"That he did. Which is why, when I was married to Bo, Penny and I had a reluctant truce, as well."

"She didn't like another woman in her territory?"

He saw the moment the idea struck, Darby's eyes widening. "I never thought about it that way, but I guess I can see that."

Finn had spent enough time with Lotte to know that she was deeply protective of him. And while that hadn't extended to the women he dated—mostly because Finn made a solid point not to bring them around his partner—he knew it was something he'd likely deal with should he ever get back in deep enough in a relationship.

An image of Lotte meeting Darby struck him, the thought out of place for the job he was there to do. He needed to talk to Darby Gage about her potential involvement in a murder, not imagine her making friends with his dog.

So why had the image struck?

Darby handed over a mug, oblivious to his wayward thoughts. "What would you like in your coffee? I have cream, milk and sugar."

"Cream would be fine."

She retrieved the small carton from the fridge and handed it over.

Penny watched her before backing away to take a seat beneath the kitchen table.

"Yep." Darby nodded as he handed back the carton. "She hates me."

"She's just trying to get used to you. Give her some time."

"I suppose."

Finn took a sip of his coffee and gestured to the table. "Mind if I take a seat?"

"Sure."

She fixed her own mug and took a seat opposite him.

"Do you know Michael Hayden?"

"No, I'm afraid I don't," Darby said. "But I've had several calls this morning telling me something terrible has happened to him."

"You could say that."

"Was he murdered like Bo?"

"It appears so."

She shook her head. "What makes people do such horrible things? I know Bo had his shortcomings, but to hurt him like that? It doesn't make sense to me."

Something weird bottomed in his stomach, fluttering beneath the caffeine hit, and Finn had to admit that he wanted to believe her. More than that, the sincerity in her eyes seemed legitimate. He had significant experience reading people—the wacky branches of his family ensured he had to be constantly on his toes—and he'd only further honed that skill with his job in law enforcement.

But the desire to believe her didn't change the fact that her alibi on record was a bit weak for the night of Bo's death. Nor did it keep him from having to ask where she was yesterday when Michael Hayden was murdered.

"Murder makes little sense."

"And here in Red Ridge, of all places. I know people deal with this in large cities. But here?" She shuddered. "It doesn't seem possible."

The fact that she still hadn't tracked to his line of thought was another checkmark in her favor, but none of it changed the point that she was one of the few who'd gained with Bo Gage's murder. "You've benefitted from Bo's death."

The distracted blue gaze, focused on the small circles she drew around the lip of her mug, snapped to attention, fire heating their depths. "This again?"

There she was. Defensive. Because she was guilty?

"This house. His business. Penny." Finn listed them all. "You're the one who profited by Bo's death."

"I was interrogated by your detective after the reading of Bo's will. I did not kill my ex-husband. But is that what you are suggesting, Chief Colton?"

"I'm just asking questions."

"No, you're not." She settled her mug on the table, her gaze direct when she next looked at him. "So I'd like to know if I'm a suspect before I ask you to leave."

* * *

Darby fought the waves of nerves that mixed her few sips of coffee into a dark sloshy brew in her stomach. Even with the subtle feeling that she was going to be sick, she refused to stand down.

How dare he come to her home and ask her questions like this?

She wasn't a murderer. More than that, she'd been so busy since Bo's death, she'd barely kept her head above water. What did he possibly think she was about?

And why?

Unbidden, images of the past few weeks' front pages of the *Red Ridge Gazette* filled her mind's eye.

Groom Killer on the Loose.

The Red Ridge Groom Killer—Crime of Passion or Premeditated Murder?

Love or Revenge? Does the Groom Killer Want Both?

One after the next, the headlines had grown more and more lurid as each day went by without any leads. The reporters at the *Gazette* had been having a field day with the biggest thing to hit Red Ridge since a four-month gold rush helped establish the town in the late nineteenth century. Now that a second groom had been killed, the headlines would only get worse.

Because it was worse, she reminded herself. There *was* a groom killer on the loose.

"You think I'm doing this? First Bo. Then this poor Michael Hayden, a man I didn't even know."

"I'm asking a few questions."

"No, Chief Colton. You're not."

When he said nothing, she continued. "Can you honestly sit there and tell me you think I murdered my ex-husband to get my hands on this?" She gestured to the kitchen at large, stopping when her gaze landed on Penny. "Other than Penny, the man has left me with less than nothing."

He seemed to soften a bit at her mention of the dog, his hard gaze softening as it grew speculative. "I'm not sure his fiancée sees it the same way."

The comment was enough to respike her ire and Darby let out a heavy exhale. "Don't think Hayley hasn't been by a few times to make that very point."

"Miss Patton's been here?"

"Sure. She came to get her things. Made a point to prance out of the bedroom flaunting a small red negligee like it was going to hurt my feelings."

"You were married to Bo Gage," Chief Colton pointed out. He didn't even blink at the mention of a red slinky number. "Presumably she thought it would upset you?"

"Bo and I parted on amicable terms. The best thing I can say about the day I signed my divorce papers was the sense of relief."

"You weren't upset?"

"I spent the majority of my marriage upset. By

the time I reached that day, I was just happy to be out, free to go about my life."

As the words settled between them, hovering somewhere over the sugar bowl in the middle of the table, Darby couldn't deny their truth. She'd had no desire to be a divorcée at the age of twenty-seven, but in the ensuing two years she'd come to accept the fact that ending her marriage to Bo had been the right thing to do.

She might not have found anyone to move on with, but she had moved on. There was strength in that, and a deep sense of pride that she'd been willing to make the tough decisions and stand up for herself.

It had also toughened her up and she knew she didn't have to sit there and answer Chief Colton's questions, no matter how attractive the questioner.

And darn her stupid feminine awareness for picking up on that fact.

Whatever she'd expected when he'd arrived, Finn Colton wasn't there to help her any more than any other gawkers who'd been by over the past few weeks. She was on her own.

Just like always.

But it was his next words that proved it.

"Would you be able to tell me your whereabouts for yesterday between the hours of seven and nine?"

Chapter 3

Finn poured himself another cup of precinct coffee, well aware the caffeine wasn't going to do any favors for the slick knot that still twisted his gut. His interview with Darby Gage hadn't gone well and after securing her unprovable alibi for Hayden's murder—an evening in with Penny—he'd left her in a fine pique.

Although he'd been hoping for confirmation that she'd been out with girlfriends or even on a date, her pronouncement that she'd spent the cold winter night in with her obstinate new roommate hadn't gotten him any nearer to removing Darby Gage from his suspect list.

He headed back to his desk from the small kitchenette the RRPD secretary, Lorelei Wong, maintained with the same ruthless efficiency with which she manned the front entrance. He'd deliberately used the single-cup brewer instead of making a pot so she wouldn't come in Monday morning and razz him for making a mess. She'd probably still find an infraction, but at least he wouldn't risk leaving a coffeemaker full of coffee grounds or stale coffee gone cold in the pot.

The case bothered him. He knew himself well enough to know that not only would it require his full concentration, but that that same concentration would likely reduce a few brain cells for the next few days.

Who was killing grooms-to-be in his town?

What makes people do such horrible things?

Darby's question haunted him, nagging at the back of his sleep-deprived mind. After his visit to Bo Gage's old residence, he'd headed back to the Circle T to review the latest crime scene with fresh eyes. The visit hadn't turned up much, other than the fact that the town was shaken. The restaurant had reported that nearly all their Saturday night reservations had been canceled before the owner was even able to make the calls that they would be closed that evening.

But it was the comments the proprietor, Gus Hanley, had fielded from those canceling guests that had Finn concerned.

"If someone's killing men who are about to get married, can I risk even going out on a date?"

"Big-city crime has come to Red Ridge. Maybe I need to try staying in for a while."

"Should we reconsider our spring wedding?"

Along with the canceled reservations, Gus had lost two events for early March—one for an engagement party and one for a rehearsal dinner.

No doubt about it, Red Ridge was in a panic. As a lifelong resident, Finn found that sad. As chief of police—it was unbearable. He'd become a cop because he'd wanted to make a difference. The fact that he was good at it was an added bonus that kept him focused, determined and dedicated. The *added* added bonus of working with Lotte had sealed the deal.

He hadn't always been a K-9 cop. His first few years on the force had been focused on learning the ropes and endless hours of traffic detail. But he'd showed promise and the old chief, Clancy Macintyre, had taken him under his wing. Chief Macintyre had been a good influence, balancing his innate ability to teach with the patience and care Finn's own father had never exhibited.

Judson Colton was a rancher and a damn fine one. But he'd never understood his oldest son, a quiet kid with an unerring eye for detail. That had always been true and, whether by choice or by habit, he and his father maintained a respectful distance. His father's second wife, Joanelle, had made that even easier to accomplish with her cold ways and dismissal of Judson's first child as a burden she was forced to carry.

But there was one thing ranch life had taught Finn

and that was his love of animals. His opportunity to move in to the K-9 unit and work with a trained canine partner had taken his love of police work and made it his life's calling.

He was good at his job and he was good to the men and women who worked for him. They all kept Red Ridge safe and took pride in their role as protectors. And someone had come to their town and violated all they'd built.

Suddenly tired of it all, including the need to question petite women with silky hair and what read as determined—but innocent—eyes, Finn headed for his desk. The case weighed on him and he'd be no good to anyone if he didn't clear his head. It was time to wrap up the little paperwork he'd come in for, get his notes on the interview with Darby logged in and head home. Maybe he'd make a steak and a baked potato, the hearty meal a way to relax and recharge.

And then he'd eat it alone.

That thought hit harder than all the others that had bombarded him throughout the day.

He'd been alone since his divorce and had believed himself okay with it. He'd had dates from time to time. Had even progressed to something more like a relationship a few years back with a sweet teacher down in Black Hills City. But, ultimately, things hadn't worked out. She'd had visions of the future and in the end he simply couldn't get his head on the same page.

So why was he now imagining enjoying his steak and potato with a companion?

One who looked suspiciously like Darby Gage.

The squad room was quiet. His cousin Brayden, another K-9 cop on the team, was tapping away at his keyboard. He was nodding his head to whatever music pumped through his ears—classic rock, if Finn knew his cousin—but he did holler a "yo" as Finn passed.

Finn briefly toyed with inviting Brayden to join him for dinner, but for some reason the thought of sharing a steak and a beer with his cousin—whom he liked quite a bit—didn't entice the same way as images of dining with Darby.

Since his latest set of notes wouldn't write itself, Finn opted to ignore thoughts of dinner altogether as he sat down. His desk held what he considered a comfortable amount of clutter: stacks of files, a handful of notes, and a series of sticky notes that littered the top of his desk and the edges of his computer monitor. Shifting a stack of folders farther to the edge, he knocked over a dark box, the square packaging making a heavy thud as it hit the floor.

Finn bent to pick it up, quite sure the box hadn't been on his desk the night before. There was a small square card taped to the top and he flipped it open.

"'Chocolates for a cop with a big heart.'" The note was signed "an appreciative citizen" and had small hearts dotting the *i*'s in "citizen."

He wanted to think it was sweet—this wasn't the

first anonymous gift he'd received over the past few weeks—but it was beginning to get out of hand. Red Ridge was a small town and he appreciated the proprietary way the citizens treated their local law enforcement. The holidays typically brought a steady stream of cookies and cakes for the staff and homemade treats for the canine members of the team. Summer often brought picnic baskets of fried chicken and endless vats of lemonade.

In all of those cases, the townsfolk enjoyed bringing in the gifts and thanking the staff in person. What Finn couldn't quite reconcile with the recent spate of gifts directed at him was why the giver felt the need to be anonymous.

Going with his gut, he dropped the chocolate into the trash can under his desk and went back to his report.

There really was no accounting for the wacky things people did. And since he had a killer to catch, he hardly had the time to worry about someone too shy to come in to the precinct to say hello.

Darby stared at her checkbook and tried desperately not to think about the debt that loomed once she got through the month of February.

"Welcome to Monday," she muttered to herself, well aware she'd have the same problem on a Tuesday, a Wednesday or any other day of the week. There simply wasn't any more money. And the vet's visit the day before—a courtesy visit he'd called it—

had proved conclusively she couldn't breed Penny again. The risk to Penny's health was too great to support another litter, especially coming on the heels of the litter she'd had the previous fall.

He'd mentioned a sweet German shepherd he'd taken care of in a nearby town—one ready for breeding and whose owner would sell for a fair price assuming she could keep one of the litter as part of the arrangement. But Darby knew it was hopeless. She barely had enough to take care of herself and Penny. There was no way she could afford a new dog right now.

The breeding program would have to wait until she got back on her feet. A few more months of her regular jobs—waitressing at the diner and helping out at the K-9 training center—and she'd reassess. That was assuming the taxes on Bo's property didn't put her underwater before she could earn what she needed.

On a hard sigh, she slammed the checkbook cover closed and shoved it, along with several open bills, across the kitchen table. She'd worry about it later. The problem wasn't going anywhere and she had one more room to clean before she'd finally feel like she'd officially moved in to her own home.

When had Bo become such a slob?

While she hadn't lied to Chief Colton the other day—that she was pleased to be out of her marriage—Bo hadn't been a terrible guy. They weren't compatible in the least and once she'd gotten past the fact that she'd fallen in love with an image instead of an actual person, it had become far easier for her to assess her marriage through objective eyes.

Even his roving nature—undoubtedly the worst aspect of their relationship—had an odd sense of immaturity wrapped up in it. If Bo wanted something, he went after it. Like a child unable to leave a sweet on the counter or Penny snatching something from the trash. The item was taken because it was there.

Bo was the same with women.

What he hadn't been, if memory served, was a piggish man with a dirty home. Granted, he'd been a bachelor before she'd moved in the first time, and had spent more time out of the house than in, but she hadn't remembered the dirt.

Or maybe she'd simply had the blind gaze of a newlywed, determined to create a new life.

She crossed to the counter and picked up her scrub brush, soap and a large container of bleach. She'd nearly gone through the entire thing over the past week, scrubbing down anything and everything she could find. The small second bathroom at the back of the house was her last hurdle to conquer. She could then at least take comfort that she laid her head down each evening in a clean home.

An hour later, with the last section of shower tile shining a gleaming white, a heavy pounding on the front door jarred Darby from her thoughts and the throbbing strains of pop music that played through her earbuds. The addition of Penny's barking had her peeling off her rubber gloves and dropping everything into the tub to go see who was at the door.

"Penny!" The dog had her nose pressed to the floor in front of the door, a low growl emanating from deep in her throat.

The pounding kicked up again and without the earbuds Darby had no trouble making out who was knocking. The high-pitched screech gave it away even before Darby pulled aside the small panel curtain that hid the glass beside the door.

Hayley Patton.

"Darby Gage, you let me in!"

Although it had been a few years since she'd lived with Bo and Penny, Darby hadn't forgotten her training skills or the way Bo had taught her to manage the dog. She used the required instructions to order Penny away from the door, satisfied when she took up her post a few feet back, blocking the small hallway entrance into the main living area of the house.

The uncontrolled barking was odd, but not unexpected. For all her skill with dogs as a trainer at the K-9 training center, Hayley had a worse relationship with Penny than Darby did. Whether there was something about the woman that disturbed Penny or just the pure knowledge that Hayley was a jerk, Darby didn't know. But nothing changed the fact that the two of them did not get along.

She didn't like another woman in her territory?

The conversation that had haunted her throughout the weekend popped up once more, the chief's question ringing in her ears. Did Penny resent Hayley's place in Bo's life? Was that the root of her upset? Or was it possible there was something more?

Hayley had been playing the grieving fiancée to the hilt and while it pained Darby to think otherwise, was it possible the woman was responsible for Bo's death? She knew it was beyond unkind—the woman had lost her fiancée the night before the wedding—but something about Hayley had always run false to her.

Yet thinking Hayley had a hand in Bo's death seemed far-fetched. Especially now that there had been a second murder—one that had nothing to do with Hayley.

Dismissing the thought, Darby opened the door. Arm raised, Hayley had clearly been preparing to emit another round of pounding. The motion was enough to have her stumbling through the door on one high-heeled boot. Darby caught her, along with a whiff of heavy perfume and the knowledge that Bo had moved on to something bigger and better in the high, tight breasts that even now pressed against Darby's chest.

"Let go of me!" Hayley twisted out of the hold and quickly regained her feet. Penny let out another low growl, only to be on the receiving end of a trademark Hayley Patton eye roll. "Enough already! You know me!"

Penny dropped her head on her paws, as if acknowledging the truth of Hayley's statement, but kept her gaze firmly on her nemesis.

"What do you want, Hayley?"

"Nice welcome, Darb. You've gotten awful bossy since moving in to Bo's house."

"It's my house now."

"One you don't deserve," Hayley snapped.

Since the house was old and shabby and, up until the thorough cleaning had been as much of a physical mess as its meager finances, Darby toyed briefly with snapping a leash on Penny, tossing Hayley the keys and breezing right on out the door. Since that fantasy was easier than the reality of just walking out, Darby opted to play along to see what the woman wanted.

"Then maybe you and Bo should have talked about something important leading up to your wedding, like wills and finances."

"How dare you bring up something so crass and cold? I loved my Bow-tie."

Darby avoided making her mental eye roll a real one at the childish nickname and tried to summon up her cool. "I'm not suggesting you didn't. But you obviously didn't discuss your future if you're mad at me."

"I loved him and I thought he loved me. How did I even know he had a will? What twenty-nine-year-old has a will?"

A smart one, Darby thought. She'd made hers the moment she'd turned twenty-one and kept it in a lockbox with her other personal papers. "Well, Bo did."

"It's like tempting fate." Hayley shivered before her big blue eyes widened so far it was practically comical. "Do you think that's why he's dead?"

"I doubt it."

"Why not?"

"Bo's dead because someone put a bullet in his heart. I don't think a will had anything to do with it."

The sneer Hayley had carried through the door faded at the harsh image Darby had painted. "I'm well aware of what happened to him."

"Are you also aware, then, that Michael Hayden was killed on Friday night?"

"The police have already been by to question me about it."

"They don't think you did it, do they?"

"Chief Colton says he's ruling out my involvement but I'm not so sure about that. He questioned me for a long time about Michael. Bo, too, on the night it happened."

Although Darby wanted to bite her tongue at the ready defense, it sprang to her lips all the same. "He's being thorough."

"Well, he should be looking at the real killer."

"You think you know who that is?" Darby didn't think anyone beside Demi Colton had been formally announced as a suspect, especially since the chief had visited on Saturday asking questions. She'd also been head down in trying to fix her life, so it was equally possible things had progressed and she was unaware.

"His cousin, of course. Demi Colton had a thing for my Bow-tie and I know she's the one who did it."

She'd heard the rumors about Demi Colton—that she'd been jilted by Bo for Hayley after only a one-week engagement, and had put her work as a bounty hunter to good use to go after the fickle man. But somehow Darby couldn't picture the woman as a murderess. Especially against Bo. She'd met Demi several times and the woman struck her as too smart, sharp and interesting to ever sacrifice her freedom over a man.

"I don't see it."

"Of course, you don't. You're too busy moving in to *my* house."

"Legal documents say otherwise."

"Which you're clearly milking to your advantage."

Patience at an end, Darby dropped the polite veneer. "What are you doing here?"

"I left a few things in Bow-tie's closet."

Darby had seen "Bow-tie's" closet and didn't recall anything that would have fit Hayley, but she gestured toward the bedroom. "Be my guest. I've packed up most of Bo's things to go to charity and I didn't see anything that looked overtly feminine, but have a go at it."

"You packed up his things?"

For the first time since the other woman's arrival Darby felt a shot of something. Not warmth, exactly, but something that smacked decidedly of compassion. "Well, sure. I'd rather see someone get use out of it."

The moment shifted and the screeching began before Darby could even process what was happening. "His things are mine! You can't have any of it!"

Finn heard the ruckus the moment he and Lotte got out of his police-issued SUV. The sound was a cross between a charging rhino and what he'd always imagined a "screaming banshee" actually sounded like. Since he already recognized Hayley Patton's cherry-red sports car in the small dirt driveway, Finn had some sense of what he was walking into.

And while he didn't anticipate violence, he did put his hand on his service weapon as he and Lotte approached the house.

When three heavy knocks and equally loud shouts for "Ms. Gage" went unaddressed, Finn opened the door and let himself inside. Penny sat at full alert, staring at the two women who currently faced off in the hallway leading to the living room.

"My Bow-tie!" Hayley kept wailing the words over and over, pointing toward the door and intermittently screaming about Darby's cold heart, her grubby, grabbing hands and her temptress ways.

It didn't take long to piece together the root of the battle, especially when Hayley thrust her hands into a large black garbage bag, pulled out men's clothing and tossed it all over the small space.

Darby was calmer, but she didn't take the screaming laying down, either. She'd begun picking up the clothes, hollering back that she had every right to clean her home and deal with her ex-husband's old clothes.

"Ladies!"

Finn ordered Lotte to stay and moved forward, his focus on keeping the women apart and further separating Hayley from the bag of clothes.

"Miss Patton!" He pushed every ounce of authority into his tone and saw the moment when he finally got through. Hayley's gaze flicked past his on another dive toward the bag and it was only when she was about to throw a pair of shorts that his presence seemed to register.

Finn took his chance, moving in and taking hold of the shorts to still her movements. "Miss Patton?"

On a gulp of air, she tugged once before seeming to give up on a hard exhale of breath. Her shoulders dropped and her hands fell to her sides before she rushed into his arms. "Chief Colton. I'm so glad you're here."

Her arms tightened around his waist and tears immediately wet his button-down shirt as Hayley basically wiped her cheeks over his chest. Hands now full of another man's shorts, Finn tried a small "come now" as he patted her back. "It'll be okay."

Hayley only tightened her hold, the racking sobs growing harder as she shuddered against his body.

"Oh, for heaven's sake," Darby said as she

marched toward the pile of clothes. In moments she had pieces bunched in her hands and was shoving them into the depleted garbage bag. "This is ridiculous."

Finn smiled at the muttered voice and had to agree. Hayley Patton had a reputation for making drama wherever she went. If the tableau playing out before his eyes was any indication, she'd brought a steaming-hot serving of drama to Darby Gage's new home.

"What seems to be the problem, Ms. Gage?" He congratulated himself on changing his salutation at the last moment, suspecting that calling Darby "Mrs. Gage" in front of Hayley would send the woman into another round of fits.

"She seems upset by my desire to give Bo's clothing to charity."

"It's so mean and cold," Hayley said against his chest before lifting her head, her eyes narrowing. "And why would an innocent person rush to throw away the clothes of a dead man? She planned this."

Finn's attention sharpened and he took a firm hold on Hayley's shoulders, pushing her an arm's length away. "Excuse me? Do you have relevant information in the death of Bo Gage or Michael Hayden?"

Hayley gulped, as if realizing she'd possibly overstepped. "I'm not talking about Michael Hayden."

"Then what are you talking about?"

"Her!" Hayley pointed to Darby, her expression

murderous. "She's getting rid of Bo's clothes. What else has she gotten rid of?"

Although he wasn't ready to rule out anything, the mix of heightened emotions and melodrama wasn't something he could realistically take at face value.

"Why don't we move this into the living room and everyone can calm down for a few moments."

Without waiting for either woman's agreement, Finn directed Hayley into the living room. He gave Darby a quick nod, as well. "If you'd join us, please."

Darby reluctantly followed and waited, arms folded, as he settled Hayley on the couch. Lotte and Penny had remained in their places, but he could have sworn there was some silent communication going on between the two animals.

It took several long minutes for him to get to the bottom of the situation. After more rounds of tears, accusations and a moment when he thought things might come to blows, he finally had the details. And every last one of them centered on Hayley Patton resenting the hell out of the fact that her near-husband had left his home and his business to his ex-wife.

What wasn't quite so easy to gather was why Darby seemed on the verge of saying something, only to clamp her jaws tight each and every time, holding back whatever she'd been tempted to say. It was suspicious. More than that, it smacked of a secret that he couldn't understand.

Did she know something?

And why did her pretty blue gaze keep skipping around the room, landing at various points before settling on the dog and then racing around the room again?

After another tense fifteen minutes with Hayley persisting in her belief that she had some right to Bo's belongings, Darby finally gave in.

"Would you just take the clothes already? I want them out of the house. Give them to charity when you're ready."

"I'll never be ready to give up my Bow-tie's things."

Darby had remained stoic throughout the mix of sobbing tears and hard-edged rants, but something softened in her eyes when Hayley reached for the bag. Something that smacked quite a bit of compassion for the younger woman and all she'd lost.

On a hard cough, he excused himself from the couch and walked to the large bag that had been at the center of their tussle. "I can carry this out to the car for you, Miss Patton."

Hayley got off the couch and followed him, her sobs fading away to be replaced with a surprising amount of venom. "You're cold and heartless, Darby Gage. You stole a dead man's home and now want to erase all trace of him. Bo was right to leave you."

Whatever calm Finn had managed to inject into the room vanished at Hayley's parting shot. The compassion now gone, Darby pointed to where he stood holding the large bag of clothes. Her voice carried the slightest quaver, but her hand was firm and steady.

"Take what you came for and get out of my house."

Chapter 4

Darby walked down the hallway to collect her things from the bathroom. The lingering scent of bleach hit her nose as she cleared the bathroom doorway and, while harsh, it effectively removed the cloying scent of Hayley Patton's perfume.

What it couldn't erase quite as easily were the spiteful, hateful words.

Cold and heartless.

She supposed there were worse things to be called, but when tallied on top of a stressful weekend and a bleak future, Darby was close to shattering.

She wasn't cold. And she was far from heartless. If she were, she'd already have lined up Penny's next breeding session. Or worse, she'd have put the house and the business up for sale, effectively breaking Bo's father's heart.

Gathering up her cleaning supplies, she marched back down the hall, her arms overflowing with scrub brushes, chemicals and the now nearly empty container of bleach dangling from her index finger. It was only when she got to the living room that she realized her tactical mistake. The chief had returned and was even now pacing the living room, his large German shepherd blocking a path to the door.

"You're still here."

"I wanted to make sure Miss Patton was on her way. Now that she is, I can discuss why I'm here."

"That's not why you came?"

"No."

Short and succinct. Was the man a robot? Every time she saw him he was straitlaced and to the point.

And, of course, he wasn't here about Hayley Patton. How would he have even known the woman would come over today of all days? But it still didn't explain why Finn Colton had returned to her home.

"Do you have a lead on Bo and that poor Michael Hayden?"

Although she'd kept close to home that weekend, a few friends had called her in continued concern. Her true friends—the ones who hadn't been seeking a gossip session—had called each week since Bo's death, wanting to make sure she was doing well. But even without any intended gossip, the strange connection between Bo's murder and Michael's the Friday past had churned up conversation.

Finn's gaze dipped to her supplies, his eyes narrowing on her hands before working their way back up to her face. It was strange, the way his gaze went cold and flat. *Cop's eyes*, she thought to herself, and finally understood what that term meant. A chill ran up her spine like someone walked over her grave.

Why did the man always look at her in a way that made her feel like she'd done something wrong?

She appreciated his position and his dedication to his job. She'd always been someone who valued determination and hard work. Yet the fact that he kept looking in her direction for a crime not only that she hadn't committed but that wouldn't have even crossed her mind on her worst day, didn't sit well.

"If you have something to say to me, please just say it. I'd like to get back to my day and avoid thinking about the fact that I've somehow become the money-grubbing town whore." She turned away from the chief, determined to keep the lingering threat of tears out of his line of sight. "You'd think I'd be having a bit more fun if that was my angle."

She continued on to the kitchen, reordering her cleaning supplies in the plastic container she kept under the sink. She'd nearly finished lining up each item when heavy footsteps sounded behind her.

Would the man never leave? What did he want, anyway? A front-row seat to her public humiliation and shame?

"Can I see that bleach?"

She'd nearly shut the cabinet door when the chief's question registered. "I'm sorry?"

"The bleach. May I see it?"

Confused about the ask, but more than willing to hand over a two-dollar container of cleaning supply, she pulled the bleach out from the cabinet. "Here."

He took the bottle, seeming to weigh the heft before lifting it in the air to look at the sides of the container. "How long have you had this?"

"The bleach?"

"Yes."

She wanted to laugh at the odd request but sensed there was something deeper underneath his questions. "A few days, I guess. I was out and needed it as part of my cleaning of the house."

"You've used a lot of it."

"Have you seen this house? It's shabby now but at least it's clean. When I moved in, it was shabby and filthy."

Since he seemed unconvinced, she pressed on. "What's this about, Chief Colton?"

"Nothing."

"Right. Because everyone's fascinated with cleaning products. I've got a really great glass cleaner I can share. And my steel wool is top-of-the-line. You want those, too?"

His expression never changed. If anything, it grew darker at her attempts at lightheartedness.

"Why are you asking me this?"

"It's police business. I would like to take this container."

"But why?" Darby pressed once more.

"I'll give you a receipt for it."

Something slick and oily settled like a large ball in the pit of her stomach. Hayley's visit had been unpleasant, but Darby had held her own. Yet something about the chief's visit—a person who should put her at ease instead of spiking her fight-or-flight response—had her in knots.

"Why are you really here? It obviously wasn't to intercept Hayley Patton. And I'm quite sure it's not to talk cleaning supplies."

"I wanted to see if you remember anything from Friday night."

"I told you the other day. I stayed in that night. Penny and I are still acclimating to each other and I had hopes a quiet night in would help cement our new relationship."

And, she added silently to herself, *I have no money to go out so it was easy to pick a dog over my social life.*

"Can anyone prove that?"

"I spoke with my friend Karen around eight. You're welcome to call her and confirm."

"I did."

"And?"

"And she said the two of you spoke. But you could have called her from anywhere."

Darby fought the urge to roll her eyes and pointed

in the direction of the living room toward the couch instead. "I was sitting right there all evening."

"Which can't be proven."

"It was about fifteen degrees on Friday night. I was bundled up in flannel pajamas, thick wool socks and that blanket right there."

Finn turned, his gaze settling on the area she'd pointed out. His deep voice grew husky, the tones low, as if he were talking to himself. "You could have snuck out. It would be easy enough to bundle up, drive across town, shoot Michael Hayden in the chest, then drive back here and fall right back into that cozy spot on the couch. It wasn't a big secret that he smoked. As a waitress in town, you'd know all about those secret habits Red Ridge's citizens engage in. It would be easy enough to wait him out. Wait for his next nicotine hit."

The image that he painted so casually—like he saw it all in his mind's eye—had that ball of fear rising from her stomach to crawl up her throat. "What are you talking about?"

"Michael Hayden. Your ex-husband, Bo. Bo, I understand. Killing him gave you all this." He stuck out a hand to gesture toward the room at large before whirling around to stare her down. "But what about Hayden? Did you enjoy your first kill so much you had to go back for more?"

Demi Colton reached for the small tube of travel toothpaste off the bathroom sink and coated her toothbrush, then added a second swipe for good measure. She scrubbed at the layer of fuzz on her teeth, desperate to remove the sour, sick taste that had been a part of nearly every morning for the past four months.

Four months.

She stared at herself in the mirror as she brushed, still barely able to believe the truth. She was going to be a mother.

To a tiny, helpless baby who was going to be born fatherless.

The panic that had accompanied her at the news she was unexpectedly pregnant with Bo Gage's child had changed to fierce protection when it became evident Bo wasn't fit to be a parent. Heck, the man was barely fit to be an adult. His ethics were beyond shaky—a fact she'd discovered a few days before she was going to tell him about the baby. Instead of sharing the joyful news, they'd had a wicked fight that had driven Bo into Hayley Patton's arms.

Or, at least, that's what the town thought.

If anyone had bothered to ask her—and no one had since they were all too busy thinking she'd gone and offed the jerk—they'd have known that Bo had already spent more than a few evenings in Hayley's bed. All while Demi had still blithely believed them to be a couple.

The lightest flutter rumbled in her belly and she pressed a hand there, amazed by the feeling.

Life.

Bo's child.

Her child.

This baby was hers and there wasn't anything she wouldn't do to protect him or her.

Which meant she had to stay on the run, continue to lie low and figure out how to get away from the roving eye of the law long enough to find out who really had it in for Bo. Because the roving eye of the law—one serious blue eye, in particular—certainly had it in for her.

Chief Finn Colton.

She'd always had a strained relationship with the various branches of her family. Her father, Rusty, wasn't particularly tight with his two cousins, Fenwick and Judson, but they'd all seen to it that the Colton family populated Red Ridge in prolific fashion. Their grudging acceptance of each other had further ensured that their children hadn't formed particularly close attachments to their cousins.

But even with that distance, it still hurt that Finn had zeroed in on her as one of his prime suspects.

Yes, the evidence looked bad. And, yes, she did have motive against Bo if you counted the jilted-lover routine. And she'd even accept that her experience as a bounty hunter gave her exposure to some of the more unsavory ways to live a life.

But, damn it, she didn't kill Bo. Only now it was up to her to determine who did.

And why.

Finn Colton wasn't a man who intimidated women. But in that moment, the color leeching from Darby

Gage's face as her blue eyes grew bigger and bigger, Finn knew he'd overstepped.

"You not only think I killed someone, but you think I enjoyed it? Enjoyed it so much I killed someone else?" Disbelief and a solid veneer of horror coated Darby's words, reinforcing what a bastard he was.

But what about that bleach? And the fact that she'd inherited Bo's home and business? She had no alibi he could verify for either murder and even less reason for inheriting the business.

None of which gave him the right to come into her home and intimidate her.

The near-empty container of bleach still hung from his fingers and he settled the bottle on a small end table at the edge of the couch. His gaze caught on Lotte's when he did and he could have sworn he saw serious disappointment in her eyes.

Which was ridiculous.

The last time he checked, all his knowledge of canine learning and understanding did not extend to castigating humans for unspoken thoughts.

He could manage that damn well all by himself.

"It's my job to consider all the angles."

"You call stomping in here and accusing me of unspeakable things angles?" Where he'd expected her to rant and rail, the stiff shoulders and steady voice suggested something else.

Darby Gage was a woman who could handle crisis. More, she'd obviously had to somewhere in her past. "Chief Colton, am I under suspicion for murder?"

"Do you want the truth?"

"Of course." Even though the color hadn't returned to her features, her voice was pure steel.

"You are a suspect in the murders of Bo Gage and Michael Hayden."

"Because I was in a will I had no clue I was a part of? And because I bought some cleaning supplies."

"You had motive."

"Not as far as I'm concerned. But even if I apply your logic to Bo, where do you get off accusing me of harming a man I never met?"

"There are any number of reasons."

"No, there aren't. Including the biggest, which is that I'm not a murderer."

"So you keep saying."

"If you think that, then I clearly need to get a lawyer."

"Suspicion isn't formal charges."

"Then why do you keep coming to my home?"

Once again, he had to give her credit. She held her own. She'd gone toe-to-toe with Hayley and was standing firm with him. Heck, she'd even settled in with the dog, determined to take care of Penny despite the animal's loyalty to Bo.

"I told you. I'm doing my job."

"Then go do your job. Get out on the streets of Red Ridge and find a killer."

Was he looking in the wrong place? Or was he so

anxious to have some lead on the case he was willing to look anywhere? His gaze shot to the bleach once more before flicking back to Darby. "Why are you here?"

"Excuse me?"

"Bo's house. His dog. You had a life and, by your own admission the other day, you moved on from your marriage. So why come here and pick up your ex-husband's business?"

"Because there's no one else to do it," she snapped.

His interview with her on Saturday had nagged at him throughout the weekend. There was something about Darby Gage he couldn't define, but couldn't get out of his head. She was a combination of innocence and knowledge, and had become a complete puzzle to him.

"Hayley presumably would like the job."

"Hayley wants the house. There's the difference."

"And you don't?"

"I want stability and a future. And as of right now I don't have either."

The color had returned to her cheeks throughout their exchange, but at her last comment a flush crept up her neck. Was she embarrassed about something?

"I'd think moving out of your apartment into a home while also becoming a business owner would offer a considerable amount of stability and security."

"It might have if Bo Gage had possessed a lick of sense."

Although he wasn't proud of his behavior, Finn

was pleased to see that he'd made a dent in her armor. "That wasn't a particularly big secret around town."

"I suppose not." She took a seat at the small drop-leaf table that sat up against the kitchen window overlooking the backyard. The stiff set of her shoulders loosened, like a balloon deflating, as her gaze drifted toward the yard. "Other than a love for his dogs and a roving eye, I'm not sure the man had much to show for his life."

"He seemed to think it was a good life. I'd only met Bo a few times but I work with his brother and sister. Bo came around to visit them a few times and he was always a jovial sort."

"He lived life to the hilt." Darby pulled her gaze from the window, a sad haze dulling that bright blue. "And took whoever and whatever he wanted along on that ride with him."

Finn took a seat opposite her, softening his voice. Since she hadn't responded to his blunt approach, perhaps he'd get further if he slowed down a bit and actually listened to her. "Not a glowing testament to his personality or his life."

"Sadly, no. But it doesn't mean he deserved to die for it." That gaze lifted to his, a blaze of fire igniting. "I didn't kill my ex-husband. You have to believe me on that. I thought I was done with Bo Gage and have been living my life perfectly happy with that fact. How would I have possibly known the man left me in his will?"

"You were married to him."

"And the day I filed for divorce, I changed my will to remove any trace of him. I'd have expected he'd do the same."

"Well, he didn't."

"No, he didn't. And instead of leaving me some sort of fabulous inheritance, he left me with bills, a dog unable to continue breeding and a business I have no interest in owning."

Bills?

"I thought Bo's business was strong and solvent. Our K-9 unit buys several of his dogs. I know he's got others throughout the county who are on a waiting list for Penny's puppies."

"Then Bo expanded his business beyond what he could reasonably make." She shrugged. "Another sign of the Bo Gage mystique. Make people think you're successful and you are."

Reluctantly, Finn saw the picture she painted, of a man with too much charm and too little sense. Regardless of the destruction he'd wrought, it was Finn's job to do right by a murdered man. But that picture did point to someone who might have had more than a few enemies.

None of which explained why Darby needed to be stuck with her ex's mistakes.

"So why keep the business?" Finn asked.

"Because I made a promise to Bo's father that I'd try. And because I also feel a debt to Penny. She's gone through an awful lot and she deserves as much care and attention as I can give her."

For the first time since he'd seen the bleach bottle dangling from her hands did something ease inside Finn, tilting the scales from suspicion to sympathy. He wasn't ready to let her off the hook—not by a long shot—but he also wasn't entirely sure the woman who sat before him was guilty of murder.

Or even capable of it.

Which was when another thought struck him with even more force. It was so simple.

So easy.

And it would allow him to keep an eye on her while doing the necessary work to draw out the Groom Killer.

"What have you heard around town? About the murders."

"Same as everyone else. The killer seems to have a strange fixation on men who are about to get married. Bo and Michael Hayden were both shot in the chest." She hesitated the briefest moment before continuing on. "And rumors have been running high that your cousin Demi is responsible. Though I find that hard to believe."

It was a curious observation, especially as he didn't think Darby and Demi were particularly well acquainted, if at all. "Why's that?"

"I know her to say hello. I've waited on her several times at the Red Ridge diner. She's…well, she's—" Darby broke off before offering up a lift of her shoulders. "She's just so capable. Her reputation as a bounty hunter is rock solid."

"Which means she knows her way around weapons."

"Maybe." Although her comment seemed to acknowledge the thought, skepticism rode her features, narrowing her gaze.

"Maybe?" Finn asked.

"It's just that she's so cool and confident. Demi Colton is not the sort of woman who murders a guy who can't appreciate her. Especially if that guy was dumb enough to dump her for Hayley."

"So you think it's someone else?"

"Yes, I do. And that someone isn't me," she added in a rush.

That tempting idea snaked through his mind once more, sly in its promise of a solution to his current dilemma.

Catch a killer and keep an eye on Darby Gage. It's not exactly a hardship to spend time with her.

"Maybe you can help me, then."

"Help you how? I thought you were convinced I'm the town murderess."

"I'm neither judge nor jury. It's my job to find evidence to put away a killer and that's what I'm looking to do."

"Then what do you want with me?" The skepticism that had painted her features was further telegraphed in her words. Finn heard the clear notes of disbelief, but underneath them he heard something else.

Curiosity.

"Fingers pointing at my cousin isn't all that's going around town. What began as whispers has gotten louder with Michael Hayden's murder."

"What are people saying?"

Finn weighed his stupid idea, quickly racing through a mental list of pros and cons. Since the list was pretty evenly matched, it was only his desperation to find a killer that tipped the scales toward the pro.

With that goal in mind—closing this case and catching a killer as quickly as possible—he opted to go for broke.

"Bo Gage was killed the night of his bachelor party. Michael Hayden was killed the night of his rehearsal dinner. One thing the victims had in common—they were grooms-to-be. And in a matter of weeks half the town has called off any and all plans to get married or host an engagement party."

"I still can't see what this has to do with me."

"If you're as innocent as you say you are, surely you'd be willing to help me."

"Help you do what?"

"Pretend to be my fiancée, Darby. Help me catch a killer."

Chapter 5

She was losing her mind. That was the only reason—*surely* it was the only reason—that Finn Colton stood in her living room proposing the most absurd thing she'd ever heard.

"Get engaged to you?"

"Pretend. Only pretend until we can lure out the killer."

"But you think I'm the killer," she pointed out.

The words chafed—more than she wanted to admit—but they needed to be said. Fifteen minutes ago he was looking at her like she belonged in the state penitentiary doing forty to life and now he was proposing they traipse around town like an engaged couple? Maybe he was the one out of his mind.

"I said you were a suspect."

"Careful, Chief. You might give me the warm fuzzies."

The problem was, the man did give her the warm fuzzies. Despite her better judgment—and she liked to think she had her fair share of it—Finn Colton did something to her. The man was too big, too in control, too…too everything.

And it bothered her more than she could say that the prospect of going on a date with him, even if it was fake from start to finish, warmed something way down deep inside her.

"Think of it as a win-win."

"How's that?"

"You can prove to me that you're innocent and I can catch myself a killer. Everyone ends up happy."

"You actually want to put yourself in the line of fire? The Groom Killer is actually killing the grooms."

"I'm a cop. I'll catch the killer before they can do any real harm."

She mentally added cocky to the attractive list. Bo had been cocky, too. It had been one of the things that had drawn her to him. That bright, shiny grin that smacked of sass and confidence. The swagger that went along with it.

She'd been hooked like a fish and let herself be reeled in by that smile, that confidence and a host of empty promises.

Even as she thought it, it felt wrong to lump Finn

in the same category as Bo. The two men weren't the same, even if her hormones were having a difficult time parsing the differences.

"You're pretty sure of yourself."

"I'm pretty sure that this person needs to be stopped. And I'm also sure I need help to do it. Red Ridge is small. No one will believe it if I suddenly begin dating one of my employees at the station. People will believe you and I are for real."

Once again, those sly fingers of need wove around her spine, gripping hard. "Why do you think that?"

"You're an attractive woman. Presumably unattached right now?"

She ignored the sting of the presumption and gave him a quietly muttered "Yes."

"I'm equally unattached. We've seen each other around town and decided we each liked what we saw. We got to talking and quietly began dating. I've been so wrapped in the case, I haven't had a chance to take you out good and proper. So, now that it's the month of love, I've resolved to change that."

The month of love?

Was it possible she'd been so head down for the past few months she hadn't even realized it was almost Valentine's Day?

Even as Darby asked herself the question she knew the answer was a resounding yes. Not only had she forgotten it was nearly Valentine's Day, but she'd long stopped looking for a valentine. Or even a man to enjoy an occasional date. When had she stopped trying?

Or worse, stopped expecting that she could be part of another relationship?

For the longest time she'd convinced herself that she was well rid of Bo Gage. And while it pained her that he was dead, on a very real level, she *was* better off since their divorce. But had she somehow closed her heart off to believing that she could love again?

Even before the reading of Bo's will and the revelation of her inheritance, she'd been busy working. She'd had the occasional date or two but when they hadn't turned into anything more, she hadn't worried about it. Instead she'd focused on keeping her head down and her meager bank account growing.

Funny how little she had to show for it.

Maybe it was that little spark of defiance. Or maybe it was simply the idea of going out for an evening with an attractive man, no matter the pretense. Whatever the cause, Darby found herself warming to the idea of fake dating Finn, even with the warning bells that jangled like sirens in her mind.

"You want to take me out?"

"Every night, and I want to be as public about it as possible. Dates in the front windows of all the restaurants on Main Street. Walks in Red Ridge park, snuggling with each other for warmth." He leaned in, his gaze direct. "We're going to make everyone in town think we're deeply in love and anxious to get married."

"No one's going to believe that."

"Why not?"

"Because—" Darby scrambled to find some answer but came up empty. "We're not in love. People can see the real thing."

"Bo certainly made people think the real thing. He had a string of girlfriends, an ex-wife and a soon-to-be wife, and everyone believed he was as deeply in love with the next woman as the one before."

"That's different."

"How?"

"Bo was… Bo. He was charming and a sweet talker. But none of it was real. There wasn't any substance beneath the veneer."

"Yet people believed it. Ate it up hook, line and sinker, best I can tell."

Finn made a convincing argument—people did see what they wanted to see—but could the two of them really pull it off? And while it was fine for him to brush off the danger of the situation, it *was* dangerous. He might be a big, bad cop, but he was also as vulnerable to a bullet as the next person.

"You really think this is a good idea?"

"I do."

"With me?" She pressed the point, unwilling to think too hard about the steady hum of desire that tightened her skin and tingled her nerve endings.

"Absolutely." That gaze never wavered, but Darby didn't miss the subtle calculation he couldn't fully bury. "But I'll do you one better."

His gaze shifted then, focusing on Penny before roaming over the kitchen. When he finally looked at her again, all hint of calculation was gone. "You help me with this and I'll pay off all your debts."

"You'll what?"

"Pay it off. All of them. I've got solid savings and I'm always open to an investment. You help me with this and I'll see to it that you're out from underneath whatever debt Bo Gage managed to run up in his twenty-nine years of living and then inconveniently deposited into your lap."

It wasn't possible. Whatever emotions had carried her to this moment, from anger to sadness to frustration, none of them compared to the sheer disbelief at his words.

"Why would you do that?"

"I consider it a fair exchange."

"But you can't pay for all of it. The house. The breeding business. I need a new dog because Penny can't breed another litter."

"Then I'll pay for a new dog. I'll pay for three of them if you want. Tell me what you need to get set up and I'll do it."

Three dogs? Not just fixing the business but an expansion, too? A real opportunity to go for it and make something of the business Bo had loved but clearly hadn't had a head for.

"But why?"

"Why not? It's my money. More, it's my town and I want to invest in it. You help me catch a killer and

I'll help ensure Bo's business continues on under your ownership and management."

"But—"

"Consider it an offer you can't refuse."

That cocky smile was back, along with something warm and endearing that made her think of naughty little boys who swiped extra chocolate-chip cookies then tried to hide the chocolate stains on their fingers.

Only, Finn Colton wasn't a little boy.

And the stakes were far higher than a possible tummy ache from overeating sweets.

"You want to catch a killer so badly you'll put yourself in their sights?"

"Yes."

"That's the only reason?"

The smile faded, all trace of humor gone. In its place was a sincerity that nearly took her breath away.

"There is another reason. If I'm as wrong about you as you say—" He held up a hand before she could even protest her innocence. "Give me a chance to finish."

She nodded, willing him to continue. It hurt to hear how little he still thought of her, but she was willing to give him his due. "Okay."

"If I am wrong about you, and I'm perfectly willing to accept that truth, I'd like to see you end up in a better place. I've come to understand Bo Gage a bit better since his murder. It's abundantly clear he made life easy for one person. Bo."

It seemed mean to speak that ill of the dead but Darby could hardly argue with Finn's assessment. Bo had lived life for himself, the rest of the world be damned.

"But the one other thing I've learned is that Bo loved his dogs more than anything else in his life. He loved Penny and he loved the litters he ultimately sold to the K-9 unit and beyond. More than once he'd head over to the training center, catching up on how a pup was doing and seeing that he or she performed to their utmost potential."

"He did love the business. And Penny was as important to him as anyone in his life."

"Maybe he saddled you with all this because he believed you'd take care of it. That you'd handle it and make something of it all."

Darby's gaze drifted to Penny. The dog had eventually lost interest in their conversation and had stretched out near Lotte, her head on her paws and her eyes closed.

"You have no reason to take care of her," Finn continued. "Yet you're caring for that dog as if she were your own."

The compliment—and the glowing kindness— had caught her off guard. Where she'd come to accept the grudging acknowledgment that Finn believed her guilty, it was something else for him to extend such a kindhearted thought.

"She is now."

"Can you honestly tell me Hayley Patton would have done the same?"

"I try hard not to compare myself to her."

"That's wise." Even though he kept a straight face, there were distinct notes of humor lilting his voice. "You also know I'm right."

"Maybe I do."

"So, what do you say? Are you in? Are you willing to help me catch a killer?"

Darby had long known that choices made in desperation usually came out poorly. She needed Finn Colton's help and she was hardly in a position to say no him.

She should feel trapped. Caged. And thoroughly out of options.

So why was it that she couldn't feel anything but a clamoring sense of excitement?

"I'm in."

Finn took his first deep breath in a month as he walked to his SUV, Lotte at his side. It had taken some convincing, but Darby had agreed with his ploy.

The idea had seemed so right at the time, but now that he considered his actions in the bright winter sunlight, they struck him as reckless and stupid. He'd always prided himself on being neither, so it was a bit of a head slap to realize he might have misstepped.

His conversation with Darby replayed in his mind.

He did his level best to recall when he'd suddenly veered off into the realm of stupid romantic comedy movies and TV shows that had been on for too many seasons.

A fake relationship and engagement.

Was he insane?

Putting aside his doubts about Darby—and the bleach bottle he'd just stuffed in the back of his SUV offered up a big one—he had no business dragging a civilian into a police investigation. Yes, the Groom Killer had targeted men so far, but who knew if the perp would add brides into the mix?

Was Finn putting Darby in danger, inadvertently making her a target?

Their county profiler had indicated the targets seemed deliberately male, with the method of death cold, impersonal and somehow masculine. But that didn't mean anything. Or it wouldn't mean anything if something happened to Darby under his watch…

Finn squelched the thought. Nothing was going to happen to her. He'd protect her and see to it that he caught a killer in the meantime.

The drive to the precinct was quick and he detoured through the lab with the bleach before heading toward his desk. The squad room was humming, his staff all in full swing with a busy start to their week. He was pleased to see Detective Gage at his desk, focused on his computer screen.

Carson had taken Bo's death hard. Despite the half brothers not being close, Carson had found Bo's body and was determined to see his killer behind bars. He'd worked so hard for the past month to uncover who was responsible. He was also on the way to becoming family, since he and Finn's younger half sister Serena, were a serious couple—on the down low.

He'd always enjoyed working with Carson, but their camaraderie was even stronger now and Finn wanted to update him on the latest. The work he'd managed over the weekend, his morning visit to Darby and the plan he'd hatched on the fly to bring out a killer. Shrugging out of his coat, he headed for his desk to drop it off when he saw the bouquet of roses laid over top of his piles.

A card, propped on the flowers, had his name written in bold scrawl on the envelope.

"You've been holding out on us, Chief!" another of Finn's cousins, Blake, ribbed him, his voice carrying across the sea of desks in the squad room. "Looks like you've got yourself a valentine."

An image of Darby filled his thoughts before he quickly brushed it off. She wasn't his valentine or anything else that suggested permanent girlfriend. She was a means to an end, nothing more.

Even as *more* tempted him with thoughts of heated kisses and even more heated moments wrapped up in each other.

He had no business thinking of her that way.

No business at all, Colton.

Which made it that much more unbelievable to

realize that somewhere in the back of his mind, he *had* been thinking of her in that way.

Finn shot back a good-natured and off-color remark in Blake's general direction before picking up the card. The scent of the roses—expensive ones for the middle of winter in South Dakota—filled his nose and he fought the rising sense of unease that crept up his spine.

The card offered less-than-helpful details about the sender, simply reading, "For a special cop, with love."

Unwilling to interrupt the laughter that still rumbled through the squad room at his exchange with Blake, Finn dropped the card into his top desk drawer and left the flowers where they lay. He needed to talk to Carson, anyway, and he didn't have time to deal with the mystery of who had suddenly developed a *tendresse* for the chief of police. He'd have Lorelei take them home if she really wanted them. Or, like the chocolates, he'd toss them.

The anonymous angle hadn't sat well the other day and he wasn't feeling any more comfortable with the increasing expense of the gifts. While he knew the flowers were pricey, he didn't feel honor bound to keep them if the sender couldn't be bothered to make a personal appearance.

Loping toward Carson's desk, Finn thought through his plan, the bouquet quickly forgotten. While it still nagged at him like a dull tooth ache that he might be putting Darby in danger, talking it all through with Carson should help to set his mind at ease. This was an op, nothing more. If they planned it well and put all the proper safety measures in place, including backup in shouting distance and advance recon of each of his proposed date sights, things would be fine.

She'd be safe.

"Who's the secret admirer, big guy?" Carson's grin was infectious as he stared up over the top of his computer monitor.

"Someone's just deeply grateful for the Red Ridge PD."

"Sure." Carson nodded. Finn didn't miss the clear skepticism in his gaze or the quirk of his lips, but it vanished without Carson saying anything. "What can I do for you?"

"I've got an idea cooking and I want to talk it through with you."

"What sort of idea?"

"We're going to smoke out a killer."

Carson's smile faded in full as he sat straighter. "You have a new lead?"

"Not much more than we've been going off of, but I have an idea and a plan I think might work."

He walked Carson through the specifics. How he was going to put himself in the line of fire, pretending to be Red Ridge's latest, most smitten suitor. A date every night, public displays of affection, even a showy romantic dinner for Valentine's Day.

"Who'd you convince here to go in on this with

you? You've got way too many cousins in this department not to make it seriously creepy, Colton."

While Carson spoke the truth—nearly half the department was a relative, including several of his female cousins—that was the exact reason he'd gone outside the precinct.

"Darby Gage has agreed to be my date for the month."

"Darby? My sister-in-law, Darby? You can't be serious."

Where Finn had expected support, or at least basic agreement, the immediate shuttering of Carson's gaze as he rose to his full height was a clear sign of his displeasure. It also had Finn forcing his point, unwilling to stand down. "Of course, I'm serious. And, last time I checked, she's your ex-sister-in-law."

"She's also one of the chief suspects in my brother's murder."

"Which makes this the perfect plan. She claims she's innocent, but I can keep a close watch on her. She can hardly act again if I'm glued to her side."

"This is insanity."

Carson wasn't convinced of the brilliance of Finn's plan and Finn was just stubborn enough to hold his ground on principle. He had a good relationship with all his cops and he had no interest in changing that, but he was also the boss and the weight of the department rested on his shoulders. He'd be damned if he'd sit around and let problems happen in his town when he could be out there doing something about it.

"Think of it as an undercover op."

"With one of the chief suspects on a damned short list."

An image of a nearly empty bottle of bleach flitted through his mind before Finn pushed it away. Carson was one of his lead detectives and he was good at his job, but the bleach was a line Finn was tugging on his own, nothing more. There was no need to poison the well against Darby any further in her former brother-in-law's mind, but the coincidence between her having a nearly empty bottle and the bleach that had been laid down to get him off the trail of Michael Hayden's killer was too timely for him to let it go.

But even if he chose to keep a few suspicions to himself, Finn wanted to better understand his detective's reservations. "What do you have against Darby?"

"Nothing until my brother's will said she got everything he had. That spells motive to me."

"What about Demi? Bo dumped her for Hayley and Demi's name was written in blood next to Bo's body. Bo pissed off a lot of people over the years."

At the mention of his cousin Demi and her connection to Bo, something flickered clearly in Carson's gaze. The words were nearly out of Finn's mouth to question the response when Carson pushed forward on his own. "You have other leads? Someone my brother pissed off?"

"Nothing concrete, but you know Bo wasn't a saint. I know he was your brother, and I'm not trying to speak ill of the dead, but we have to look at all the angles."

The comment about Bo—and it *was* speaking ill of the dead, no matter how Finn wanted to couch it—took the wind out of Carson's bluster. He dropped back into his seat, his dark eyes clouding with trouble. Finn had seen that look more than a few times over the past month and was glad that Carson now had a family to go home to.

Carson had made no secret of how unexpected his romance with Finn's half sister Serena had been. Her vulnerability—having had another man's child and navigating the waters of single parenthood—hadn't been easy, but they'd found their way. And now Carson had Serena and her daughter, Lora, to go home to.

The fact that Carson had found a way to chase those shadows with Finn's younger half sister and her baby girl had shifted the dynamic between the two men. He and his lead detective were still navigating all the nuances. Being on opposite sides of the issue when it came to Darby Gage looked like it was going to be one of those nuances.

"I know, Finn. Damn it, I do know. I've always cared for Darby. She's a good woman and I know my brother didn't do right by her. But I can't shake the fact that, of all the people in Bo's life, including a bright and shiny fiancée he was a day away from marrying, Darby is the one who ends up with my brother's life's work."

"For what it's worth, I think she's been wondering the same thing."

"She doesn't want the house or the business?" Carson asked, the conflicting anger over Bo's death that clouded his dark gaze fading, replaced by the hard, flinty edges that defined a cop.

Finn didn't miss the interest in the question, but kept his words carefully measured. "She's committed to the business and she's cleaned up that house like a whirling dervish. But I'm not sure it's the life she'd have chosen for herself."

He wasn't sure why he kept the issue of Bo's debt to himself but, like sharing the details on the bleach, something held him back. With the bleach it was respect for Darby as he waited for the lab to come back with some thoughts.

For the inheritance, it was respect for Carson.

The man had struggled enough knowing someone in Red Ridge had wanted his brother dead. The least he could do was allow Carson to hang on to one of the few illusions he might have possessed about his little brother.

Sometimes, Finn knew, illusions were all a person had.

The bouquet of bright red roses came through the front door of the police station first, visible for anyone who was looking. And she was looking.

And waiting.

She'd had them delivered earlier and had spent the afternoon waiting to see what Chief Colton would do with the gorgeous bouquet. She'd read up on the meaning of flowers and knew the blood-red blooms were the very definition of love, affection and desire.

The flowers came out first. Only, instead of seeing the object of that desire walking behind them, she saw the petite little secretary who manned the front desk like a pit bull.

A wave of fury filled her at the insult. How dare he? Those flowers were for Finn Colton. Why had he given them to the stupid little woman like they were some gift for her? Something white-hot began beating in her chest; a thick feeling that slammed blood through her veins even as she had an image of making Finn Colton pay for his unkindness.

She thought he was heroic. Perfect. Superior in every way.

More, she believed they shared something special and it would only take a few more gifts before he understood—no, before he *knew*—who was sending the gifts. Like a little game between them.

A lover's game.

That stupid little secretary carried the roses in her arms, juggling them as she dug for keys in her purse. Only, once she found them, she opened the back door and threw the roses onto the seat.

Threw them!

The white-hot anger that bubbled in her veins took

on a new form as, suddenly, it all became clear. Finn Colton hadn't disregarded the blooms. That stupid little woman had kept them for herself.

The bitch thought she was so crafty, stealing what wasn't hers.

But the woman would know soon enough.

As she watched, she toyed briefly with going after the secretary, following the little hatchback through town and running her off the road. There were patches of black ice all over Red Ridge this time of year and no one would think twice about an untimely skid.

The thought tempted—sorely tempted—but she'd hold off for now. If she acted too hastily, she might attract Finn's attention in ways that weren't welcome.

And she couldn't afford to upset him. Not now. Not yet.

She had big plans for herself and Finn Colton.

The thought had the anger fading in her mind to be replaced with the sweetest anticipation. There'd be other bouquets. Other gifts. There was the one in particular that she couldn't wait to give him.

It wouldn't do to be hasty.

Oh, no. She needed to focus on her plans. If she kept to her schedule, they'd be laughing with each other and dreaming with each other and planning a future with each other. It was all coming together.

It was only a matter of time now.

Chapter 6

Be ready at seven sharp.

That was all the man had said that morning when he'd left. What had seemed like a simple set of instructions had grown maddeningly empty of information as the day wore on and the minutes ticked closer and closer to seven.

Should she dress up? Go casual? Were they going to dinner or dancing? Or both? Should she bundle up in her thickest coat or try to outmaneuver a frigid South Dakota night with nothing more than a wrap to get her from the car to the door of wherever it was they were going.

Wherever it was they were going.

Why hadn't she asked these things when she'd had the chance?

"Because I was too busy trying to keep my tongue in my mouth at the instruction to be ready at seven sharp." The words came out in a disgusted rush to her partner in crime, Penny.

Although the dog hadn't warmed enough to allow even the most simple gesture of a pat on the head, she'd taken to following Darby around the house. Even now, she lay spread out on the bed, her eyes following as Darby paced a hole in the already-threadbare carpet.

"I don't even have anything to wear. Cinderella dressed better than I did and that was after her stepsisters got done with her." Darby muttered the words as she pawed through the meager line of clothes in the closet she used to share with Bo. Her work at the Red Ridge diner consisted of a uniform provided by the owner, and she would never dream of wearing anything dressier than jeans and a T-shirt or sweatshirt when working at the K-9 training center.

In the end, she opted for a black dress she'd bought for a wedding a million years ago and called it a day. It wasn't exactly dowdy but she wasn't going to set Red Ridge on fire this evening, either. But it did have a nice neckline and exposed enough cleavage that she might hope Finn Colton's eyes didn't stray to the unfashionable style as it wrapped around her hips and on down to her knees.

"Not that the man needs to be looking at my breasts."

Penny's eyebrows shot up but her gaze remained

steady. Darby had the rueful thought that the dog had had sex more recently than she had.

Since that train of thought left her feeling worse than she'd have expected, Darby slipped into a pair of heels that were as old as the dress and marched out of the room. The clock read four minutes before seven and she'd barely cleared the hallway when a heavy knock sounded on the front door.

"Right on time." She didn't attempt to play coy by making him wait, nor was she willing to spend one more moment primping, so she skipped the hallway mirror.

Which made the funny little jump in her heartbeat that much odder when she opened the door to see Chief Finn Colton standing on the other side. Although she'd seen him around town without his uniform on, something about the black slacks, untucked gray shirt and leather jacket still caught her by the throat.

Oh, my, did the man look good.

Too good.

Confusingly good.

She ignored the rush of something a younger, more foolish Darby might have called lust and gestured him inside. "Come on in. I'll just get my things and we can get going."

"Take your time. I'm early."

"Bo was always twenty minutes late. Far be it from me to argue with a man who arrives when he says he will."

Finn's smile never wavered but something she couldn't define registered in his steady gaze. Was it the mention of Bo? This might not be a real date, but few men wanted to be compared to another man, even if that comparison was in their favor.

"Still, feel free to take your time."

Finn's smile lit up his face when he caught sight of her roommate.

Penny had followed her out to the hallway and was even now allowing Finn to rub and scratch at her ears and face, seeming to bask in the glow of male attention. Not that Darby could blame Penny. She wouldn't mind basking in the glow of Finn Colton's attention, either.

The man thinks you're a murder suspect. You've got plenty of his attention.

The practical little voice inside tossed that bucket of ice water, as cold as the Red Ridge River in... well, February. And while Darby tried momentarily to cling to the truth of that jarring thought, her hormones unfortunately won the battle and succeeded in shutting up her whiny voice of indignation.

Finn did look good. And watching the man pet and love on her dog thawed something deep inside her.

"Let me just get my coat."

Since he wore only his leather jacket, she opted for a thinner wool coat instead of the large puffy one she favored in winter that wrapped her from the bottom of her chin to the top of her ankles. It was the height of ugly, the puffy material giving her the fashion equivalent of round tires from her shoulders to her feet, but it kept her warm.

Which had her roundly cursing herself a few minutes later when Finn walked her to his SUV. Cold crept up her dress, freezing her legs on contact, and a series of shivers settled deep into her bones before he'd barely helped her up into the passenger seat of his large SUV. Finn rounded the vehicle and hopped in, but even with the sudden blast of warmth from the heater, she couldn't warm up.

"Penny seems to be warming up."

The choice of words—and the chattering that set in despite her best efforts—had a small burst of laughter bubbling in her throat. "She likes y-you m-more th-than she li-likes me."

"Darby?"

"So—sorry." A wave of chattering hit her again and she tried to bite back her words.

"Are you okay?"

"Ju-just got a ch-chill."

Finn turned the heater on even higher, then pulled to the side of the road. In seconds, he had his seat belt off and then his jacket. "Here. Put this on."

"I'm f-fine."

"Right."

Before she could register his actions, that big body simply seemed to envelop her. He twisted in his seat, his focus on her as he settled his large coat over her, tucking the sides up against her body, and then rubbing her arms to warm her. "It's a cold night."

"An-and now you're wi-without a c-coat." The chattering had already gotten better and Darby felt her jaw calming from the incessant rattling. "Aren't you cold?"

"I'm a furnace. Which does me well in the middle of winter and ensures I hate summer with a passion."

"Who h-hates summer?" The question came out almost normal but Darby had to hold back the stammer as he kept his focus on her. His eyes never left hers, even as he continued to rub at her arms through the warmth of his coat.

Between the layers of his jacket, her inadequate wool coat and the long sleeves of her dress, his touch should have felt impersonal. Or difficult to even distinguish.

But, oh, how she felt him.

The solid strokes of his hands. The long, capable fingers. And that penetrating, sloe-eyed gaze that did as much to increase her temperature as the body-warmed coat and steady movements to circulate her blood.

His hands slowed but he didn't break contact. "Better?"

"Yes." She nodded but didn't say anything else. The chattering teeth had faded completely but she couldn't be too sure her voice wouldn't crack under the scrutiny.

Finn didn't break contact but it was only after

another long, tense moment that he seemed to catch himself. With a light pat on her shoulder, he repositioned himself in his seat and pulled on his seat belt. "South Dakota winters are nothing to mess with."

"No," she agreed, pleased when her voice came out steady. "They're not."

"Even when you do have a killer pair of legs."

The bright lights of the Red Ridge Trattoria beckoned them closer as Finn pulled up to the curb. The owner, Paolo, had worked in the competitive restaurant community of Los Angeles for nearly twenty years. He'd uprooted himself a decade ago, moved to Red Ridge and, in short order, had wooed—and won—the county beauty queen and opened up the Trattoria. Although Paolo had slowly adjusted to the slower pace of things in Red Ridge, he'd insisted on three things. Reservations. The highest quality meats flown in three times a week. And a valet that managed parking.

Finn handed over his keys to the young man who'd clearly drawn the short straw to get parking duty on a night below freezing and mentally calculated an increased tip for the service. He then came around the SUV to help Darby out of the passenger seat.

He hadn't been joking about the legs. She was already starting to shift out of the vehicle, struggling beneath the extra weight of his coat, when he took her hand and pulled her out. Her legs came first, followed by the rest of her and, once again, he was struck by the sexy path from knee to ankle on display.

She was a looker. One that caught a man by surprise. She was pretty, in a simple sense, until you looked closer. Then you realized that what seemed cute on first glance had more depth and nuance that deserved a second look.

And a third.

What he couldn't quite get a grip on was why he hadn't looked closer before.

Her dark hair curled slightly, the light catching the swoops of her curls and setting off vibrant red undertones. Her eyes were large and round, that fascinating blue edging toward violet, and sat in a face carved with high cheekbones, a pert nose and a lush lower lip that drew his attention with the same fervor as her legs.

Although he'd certainly looked her over the past few days, as well as in the years he'd seen her peripherally around town, it surprised him to realize just how truly pretty she was.

And how small.

Strong, yes, but a petite little thing. Even in her heels she barely cleared his shoulder. Although he usually went for taller women—his ex-wife had been a statuesque brunette who was nearly eye level to him—he couldn't deny the surge of protectiveness that coursed through him as he took in the small frame beside him.

A fresh burst of cold air helped clear his head

and he concentrated on walking her to the door. He hadn't been lying—he was warm-blooded—but the heat that suffused his limbs came from something else.

Something that struck him a lot like desire.

Once inside, Paolo himself greeted them, his proprietor's smile in place as he shook Finn's hand and fussed over Darby. Although he still took the reins in the kitchen from time to time, Paolo had firmly moved in to the role of restaurant owner and left most of the cooking to a young protégé from California who had figured out a lot sooner than Paolo had that he wanted a vibrant life away from the rat race.

Finn was still thinking about the kid as they were seated, a list of specials handed to him along with the wine list.

"That's an awfully enigmatic smile," Darby commented as she settled her napkin in her lap. "Care to let me in on the joke?"

Finn handed over the sheet of specials before opening his napkin. "Just thinking about the appeal of our small town."

"Oh?"

He tilted his head in the direction of the front door. "Paolo. The chef in the back that he hired from L.A. Both came here to change their lives and soak in the steady, easy pace we have here. Small-town life isn't all bad."

"Did someone say it was?"

"No. But there are times it can be, at the risk of sounding cliché, small."

She glanced out the window beside their table—the one front and center he'd specifically requested—her gaze roaming over Main Street. On a soft sigh she turned back to look at him. "I don't know. After the events of the past month, I sort of wish we could go back to small and quiet."

"We will. Soon."

"You seem awfully sure of that."

"Because I am."

The same searching glance she'd given the street transferred to him. "You can't know that."

"I know what I know. We're going to catch a killer. And we're going to figure out why they've done what they've done."

He just hoped he could do it before anyone else got hurt.

Or before the town's business owners went belly-up. It hadn't escaped his notice that there were few cars parked in the lot beside the restaurant when the valet had taken his car. Nor had he missed the number of empty tables. Even on a Monday, the Trattoria typically did more business than six scattered tables of diners.

Their waiter hurried over and reiterated the specials before asking for drink orders, gesturing to Darby to go first.

"I'll have a glass of your Chianti."

"And a club soda for me," Finn added.

"Oh. Well, then. I'll have an iced tea."

Finn reached over and laid a hand on hers. "Don't let me be the spoilsport, darling. Enjoy the glass of wine. It'll go well with whatever you order."

On immediate contact her hand stiffened beneath his, going positively rigid at the endearment before relaxing. "Okay, then. One glass."

She slipped her hand away once the waiter was out of view. "I don't need to drink."

"On the contrary. You should enjoy yourself. I can't drink because I'm technically on duty."

"Of course."

It was an op but Finn wasn't anxious to keep reminding Darby of that. He much preferred the wide eyes and small, supple body he'd wrapped up in his coat than the subtle defeat he saw in both now.

So act like it's a real date, Colton.

Although he couldn't afford to let his focus fade, it didn't mean he couldn't enjoy an evening with a beautiful woman. And while his dating skills were hardly legendary, he did know how to take a woman to dinner and give her an enjoyable evening.

Which took him right back to where they'd started the evening.

"I meant what I said in the car. Penny does seem to be warming up."

"I'm not sure. I mean, I see it in small ways. She's become my shadow, following me all over the house, but she still won't let me get near her."

"She'll come around. She knows you want to care for her and that'll win her over in the end."

"There's that Finn Colton confidence once more."

Before he could question the comment, the waiter arrived with their drinks and took their orders. Finn was pleased to see she'd ordered a hearty lasagna; he'd requested a Bolognese that was a particular favorite.

Picking up where they'd left off, he pressed his point. "Dogs have amazing empathy. She knows you care for her. She's just working on building up her trust with you."

"Did you go through it with Lotte?"

"Not in the same way. I've worked with her since she was a puppy, so the trust has been different between us. But it did take us a while to get her on a service path."

"How do you mean?"

Their food arrived and after requested refills on their drinks, Finn took his mind back once again to his earliest days with Lotte. He hadn't thought of them in a long time, so it was funny to realize how much of that time he did remember.

"She showed a lot of promise as a puppy, picking up all the basic training exercises and obedience drills."

Darby nodded as she cut a piece of her lasagna. "Most of the work I do at the training center is centered on cleaning, but I also help out with the obedience trials since I have experience training puppies.

Managing them around food and ensuring they can sit or move on command. The really little ones always break my heart. They're so wiggly and squirmy, I just want to pick them up and cuddle them."

"It gets harder for them after that, once they start learning how to track scents. Lotte made it through the early training really well but once we got together she wasn't able to keep her focus on tracking. I'd gotten so attached to her and had a rough month convinced she wasn't going to make it through the program."

"What was the breakthrough?"

"I had a really bad day at work. A domestic abuse case gone bad. I knew I shouldn't have gone to training but went anyway, and just couldn't keep my focus. We were using an old blanket soaked in something unmentionable here as we eat dinner and either I shoved it too hard in her face or I was just frustrated enough she wanted my attention."

He'd always judged himself for that moment, his selfish behavior toward Lotte an experience he was hardly proud of. So it was humbling when Darby's reaction was not only encouraging but innately kind, as well.

"She knew you needed something."

"I guess she did. I've always been sorry it took a bad moment to make the connection, but the pure empathy and her ability to read my emotions is something I've never forgotten. I knew I wanted K-9, but after that day I realized I wanted K-9 with Lotte."

"And she found the prize?"

"Then and every time since."

"Maybe it was a breakthrough for both of you."

In many ways it had been and he'd remembered the lesson in the ensuing years. "It's certainly made me a gentler handler and a better handler. When I finally understood how much she was taking in around her, I realized that all my actions had an impact on her."

"So Penny's just taking in what's around her?"

"She absolutely is. Her world has been upended and she's just trying to right herself again. She'll settle. And when she does, I predict you're going to have a beautiful friendship."

"I'll hang in there, then. I know she's worth it. And she's wonderful company." A mischievous light filled Darby's eyes as she laid her fork and knife on her plate. "She also functions incredibly well as a silent yet supportive girlfriend when nothing in the closet seems quite right for dinner."

"I'd say she did her job well, then. You look great."

A pretty blush filled her cheeks but she held his gaze. "I wasn't asking for a compliment, but maybe next time you can give me a clue where we're going."

"That takes all the fun out of it."

"Maybe yes, maybe no. Since I've proven I can't dress for winter weather to save my life, perhaps you can give me a clue."

While he wasn't crazy about her covering up those pretty legs, he had already planned out the week and the next night was straight-up-the-line casual. "Okay. Tomorrow night, jeans and a sweatshirt."

"We're staying in?"

"Hardly. You're joining me for bowling night."

All hints of mischief fled as she leaned forward over the table. "I'm horrible at bowling."

"Then you'll be an improvement over me."

"No, I'm really horrible. I throw gutter balls at least four frames per game."

"And I throw 'em at least five. Seriously, you can't imagine how much I stink at bowling. I believe my cousin Brayden calls it the height of suck-a-tude."

"Why do you play, then?"

"It's a league and it's the one place I can shame myself in front of my men and women and still hold my head high in the squad room. The RRPD fields three teams, along with one each from the fire department, the K-9 training center and the EMS squad, and two from the teachers at the high school."

"And you want me to come play?"

"We've been down a player since Carson has been dating my sister Serena. Between a newborn and a budding romance, he hasn't been all that interested in bowling."

Finn knew it was also an opportunity for his team to review Darby and to get a sense of her for the investigation. His head was growing increasingly cloudy as he found it harder and harder to see the woman as a killer. It would do him good to have her reviewed by other seasoned professionals.

Having Carson distracted also gave him a chance to solicit an opinion from someone who *wasn't* Darby's ex-brother-in-law.

"I haven't been Carson's favorite person. Not since the reading of the will."

"He'll come around."

"First Penny. Now Carson. Is that how you deal with everyone who doesn't agree with you?"

"Most things reveal themselves in time. It just takes patience and a willingness to wait them out."

"Like a killer?"

Whatever tentative truce they'd built over the evening faded at the clear reminder in her words. He and Darby weren't out on a date. Nor were they building a relationship between the two of them.

They were hunting a killer.

He'd always had a legendary focus and commitment to his job. With a murderer on the loose, it was a damn poor time to suddenly lose his concentration.

Chapter 7

Darby ignored the cloudy skies and the threat of snow that had hovered since she'd woken that morning and worked her way through downtown Red Ridge, checking off her list of errands. The evening before hadn't been far from her thoughts, but the errands kept her busy and focused on more than Finn Colton's sky blue eyes, which reminded her of a pretty June day, or his broad shoulders, which were strong and oh, so capable.

They were a mirage. An oasis in the desert and she'd do well to remember that. Spending time with him was a job and nothing more.

The check in her hand that she was about to deposit at the Red Ridge Savings and Loan was tangible proof of that fact.

A job. That's all you are. And since it pays well and it's the path to get you off the suspect list and out of debt, you'd do well to remember that.

She kept up the mental pep talk as she walked into the bank, only to find a line of people gaping at a bellowing Fenwick Colton.

Red Ridge was a small town and everyone knew the owner of Colton Energy. Not only did the man employ half the town, but he was legendary for prancing through the streets like a proud peacock on display. Even his head bobbed in time to his own mental beat, Darby thought as she watched his small frame pace up and down in front of one of the desks used for conducting business.

Private business, she'd always thought.

"Half my investments in this town are sucking wind because of this damned Groom Killer!"

Darby tried not to listen, taking a place in line to wait her turn. But Fenwick's loud rant made that impossible.

"My daughter's supposed to get married at the end of the year. How's that going to happen if every wedding company in a fifty-mile radius is out of business?" Fenwick's voice echoed off the high marble walls.

"Mr. Colton." The bank manager did his best to calm him, but even those efforts were loud enough for everyone to hear. "If you'd like to take this to my office, I'm sure we can discuss this calmly and—"

"Don't you patronize me, Tommy Sanders. I remember when you were just a teller here." A loud thwap as Fenwick slapped a hand on the marble counter echoed off the ceiling before the distinct rustling of newspaper added to the din. "And we can just as easily discuss things here in front of the damn town. We're all reading the same garbage each and every day in the *Red Ridge Gazette*."

"Yes, Mr. Colton, but if you'd—"

Again, Fenwick interrupted the poor, beleaguered Tommy, his voice straining as he read the headline Darby had already passed in a glass-fronted box out on the street. "Groom Killer Waiting to Make Next Kill. That's considered news?"

"Well, it's a big deal," Tommy said, his voice placating.

"It's salacious garbage and it's ruining this town day by day!"

While she didn't agree with his public display, Darby had to admit Fenwick had a point. The killings were awful enough and already had the entire town whispering, scared for its safety. Daily updates in the local paper, the front page screaming out all sorts of salacious innuendo, was hardly a way to keep everyone calm.

It also gave the killer what he or she wanted. If you were going to behave in such an awful way, wouldn't you want credit for it?

She wasn't a thrill seeker—she never had been—but she'd overheard enough conversations in the diner to know that when people did something out of the ordinary, they wanted credit for it.

Wouldn't killing someone be the height of that?

It was enough to bring a chill back to her bones, only, unlike the wind the night before, this chill went far deeper, settling into her soul.

Was it really possible they had someone walking the streets of Red Ridge who not only had killed her ex-husband and another man, but who was waiting to kill again? Someone who cared so little for another's life they felt it was theirs for the taking?

For the first time since learning of Bo's death, Darby felt something other than confusion or sadness or surprise. Something small flickered to life, burning away that veneer of cold.

Something a lot like anger.

She'd been so focused on her own problems the past few weeks she hadn't truly given thought to what was going on in her town. A remorseless killer, determined to snuff out a life as if it was no more than a fly to be swatted or an animal to be put down.

But it was more than that. People's lives were at stake. And, with sudden clarity, she realized that while the one who'd lost a life paid the highest price, those who loved them were paying a terrible toll, as well.

"Next!"

The call from the teller pulled Darby from her

musings and she headed for the window. The trans-
action moved quickly, the money going into her account so quickly it was nearly anticlimactic. The
hours and days of worry vanished as if they'd never
been, Finn Colton's generosity now lining her bank
account and her future along with it.

Which meant she had a choice. She could take
what he offered and rebuild her life. Or she could
fight back against the nameless, faceless injustice
and help him catch a killer.

As Darby walked back out onto the street a few
moments later, several large flakes dropped from the
sky, coating her hair and coat immediately.

Instead of feeling the cold, all she felt was a fire
in her belly that emanated outward, setting her entire being into motion.

Finn ran Lotte through a familiar series of drills
at the training center, pleased for the chance to get
outside and move a bit. Although he spent a fair
amount of time away from his desk, his work taking him into town more often than not, the threat
of snow had indicated a day that was likely to keep
him in more than out. When the thought of sitting
inside the precinct all day had left him with a stifling sense of claustrophobia, he'd opted for a trip
to the training center.

The cold did a lot to clear his head as Lotte did
a series of agility drills before they switched gears
and worked on tracking some new scents. He'd read

up recently on a dog who'd actually discovered electronics data and he was anxious to see what Lotte could do with scents that weren't innately natural in origin. So far she hadn't been nearly as successful as one of their other K-9 members—a large, lumbering basset hound named Goose—but he remained hopeful she'd get the hang of things.

In the meantime, they'd practice and he'd keep his focus on helping her learn.

By the time they'd finished an hour later, Lotte's tongue was lolling a bit and even Finn's warm blood had finally worn thin in the cold air. He took them both inside to warm up and came face-to-face with Hayley Patton.

"Chief." She had a puppy on a leash and was gently pulling him down the hallway toward the kennels.

"Miss Patton." Finn nodded, curious to watch her retreat down the hall. The quiet moment gave him a chance to consider her and he was surprised to see how gentle and patient Hayley was with the puppy after the fireworks she'd put on at Darby's.

It had been more than obvious Penny didn't like the woman and Finn had always trusted a dog's sense about people as an important barometer. While not foolproof, there had been several occasions when Lotte had detected someone who was just "off." It was never the people who were afraid of dogs, but the ones who had a disdain that went beyond basic dislike or legitimate fear.

So what was up with Hayley Patton?

Was she the grieving bride-to-be she'd been play-ing around town? The raging shrew who expected everyone to bow and scrape now that she was practi-cally widowed? Or was she really a gentle, misguided woman who channeled her energy and affection into dogs instead of the world around her? More ques-tions without answers.

"Chief!"

He tucked away thoughts of Hayley and focused on the voice squawking through the portable radio clipped to his shirt. Answering the summons, he moved into a small conference room off the main hallway. "What's up, Lorelei?"

"Trouble brewing at the bank."

He'd known Lorelei long enough to take her state-ment as more gossip than danger, but held back the sigh at the unhelpful level of detail. "What kind of trouble?"

"Your uncle Fenwick was in there making a ruckus about the Groom Killer."

"What was he on about now?"

Lorelei clearly warmed to her story, her voice echoing from his radio with all the authority of a newscaster. He'd already gotten the gist of Fenwick's antics within in a few statements but let Lorelei keep on as he poured himself a cup of coffee from the steady supply kept on the conference room's ban-quette.

"He's claiming his daughter Layla's wedding is in jeopardy because of the Groom Killer, the headlines the paper keeps running and your ineptitude to find a killer."

Finn put his cup down, a streak of annoyance lighting up his limbs.

He tolerated his uncle on most days, but when the man insinuated he wasn't able to do his job, they had a problem. "I'll go see him now."

"Figured you'd want to know."

"You figured right."

As he disconnected with Lorelei, Finn drained the last of his coffee, fortifying himself for the conversation to come. Fenwick Colton saw himself as the king of Red Ridge and, normally, Finn was willing to let him have the crown.

But when the king started talking trash about Finn's hard work and the hard work of his department, he wasn't above taking action. It was mighty comfortable sitting on a throne, watching the world go by.

It was another matter entirely to take up a sword and battle the real monsters that lived in it.

Finn put little stock in legends and stories, especially when they gave people an excuse for bad behavior. The century-long feud between the Coltons and the Gages was one of those stories and he'd spent his life fighting the expectation that somehow his birth and his last name predisposed him to a set of choices.

He liked who he wanted to like. Disliked for the

same reasons. And refused to believe that someone was bad simply because they'd been born into a family who lived across town.

Fortunately, his generation seemed to be the first in a hundred years that might truly trample the battleground that perpetually stretched between the Colton family homes on one end of town and the Gage family homes on the opposite end.

Carson and Serena had certainly trampled up everything in their path, finding each other despite the specter of a family feud. He'd also caught wind of another romance brewing between the youngest member of each family, his sister Valeria and the youngest Gage, Vincent. Word around town was that the smitten lovers had been caught kissing more than once and their parents were both determined to break them up. A position that had only grown stronger since fear had spread over the antilove-based motives of the Groom Killer.

He'd purposely stayed out of the teen love drama, even though his stepmother, Joanelle, had been haranguing him for a month to do something about the pair. Since he figured the kids had a right to their feelings, he'd left them alone, but had instructed his team to keep a watch on them. Fools might rush in but a well-trained police force should be able to keep an eye on two swoony teens.

No matter how easygoing Finn wanted to be about the teens, he had been forced to manage the Colton-Gage situation a bit tighter with his cousin Demi.

Nothing could change the fact that one of the lead suspects in the investigation into Bo Gage's death was a Colton. And that hadn't sat well with any member of the Gage family.

He and Carson had questioned his cousin, insisting she stay in Red Ridge until the whole situation quieted down, but she'd up and run at the first opportunity. Finn still wasn't sure if he'd want to throttle her or to hug her when they finally found her, but in the meantime Demi wasn't doing herself any favors in the "raising suspicions" department.

Which made Darby's assessment the day before that much more interesting. If Darby *was* the killer, wouldn't she grasp at any opportunity to deflect interest her way? And if she wasn't—and her assessment of Demi was right on—then maybe they were all looking in the wrong place.

It's just that she's so cool and confident. Demi Colton is not the sort of woman who murders a guy who can't appreciate her. Especially if that guy was dumb enough to dump her for Hayley.

With his thoughts racing through all the implications, Finn pulled off Bay Boulevard and into his uncle Fenwick's driveway. The large house sat on the very edge of Red Ridge, not far from one of the mountain passes that led up into the Black Hills. Fenwick's land was the farthest you could get from a Gage and still say you lived in Red Ridge, and Fenwick paid dearly to keep the mansion in pristine condition.

He also reveled in living on the edge of town along with the town's ritziest citizens, including the Larson twins. Evan and Noel had made quite a name for themselves in the past few years, their various investments including quite a few in tech, putting them on several lists of South Dakota's mavens under thirty.

Finn glanced down the street at the large, garish mansion the twins called home as he jumped out and rounded his SUV, not entirely convinced all their money was on the up-and-up. He'd put considerable focus on them before the Groom Killer situation had blown up but had very little to show for it.

Yet every time he saw either of the twins, something set off his radar. They were attractive and charming and played the "bright, shining citizen" roll to the hilt. Only, none of it could hide the fact that something mean seemed to live behind their eyes.

Finn sighed, again aware that the assessments he made of people didn't mean they were guilty of anything more than breathing air. The role of chief weighed heavy on his shoulders, but it didn't do to go looking for trouble where there wasn't any.

Even so, the Larsons bothered him.

Shrugging off the disdain, Finn climbed the steps to Fenwick's mansion, bracing himself for battle. He wasn't disappointed when his uncle greeted him with a sharp grunt a few minutes later after the butler led him to Fenwick's home office. The grunt was quickly followed up with Fenwick's play for the conversational upper hand. "Heard you had dinner last night with that Gage woman."

"Word travels fast."

"It does when my nephew is parading around town with a murder suspect."

"What would you know of my suspects?"

"I keep my ear to the ground."

The words carried quite a bit less bluster and Finn used the moment of quiet to press his advantage. "You messing around in my investigation?"

"Don't sass me, boy."

"Are you?"

Fenwick held Finn's stare, his lifelong success in business ensuring he wasn't going to back down. But the bluster didn't return to his tone, either, when he finally spoke. "I'm an interested citizen. Nothing more."

"Then why are you making things worse by carrying on at the Red Ridge Savings and Loan?"

Small and skinny, Fenwick Colton had spent his life with a chip on his shoulder. He'd used it to make something of himself, which Finn gave him considerable credit for, even if his methods were unorthodox and often annoying. The man ran his mouth, pushing his ornery attitude on anyone who would listen. He wasn't above engaging in a verbal battle of wills and he'd often reminded Finn of a Chihuahua.

Which was likely an insult to Chihuahuas.

But he'd be damned if he wanted his uncle mucking around in a murder investigation.

"Like I said, I'm an interested citizen."

"You're deliberately causing trouble and making a spectacle of yourself in front of the town."

The accusation was enough to have Fenwick dropping into his chair. "I'm trying to make a point, only no one's listening."

"What point would that be?"

"This killer out on the loose is ruining the town. Business is dropping. Half the couples getting married have ended their engagements. I'm a month away from Layla marrying Hamlin Harrington and the old coward's threatening to call it all off on account of this Groom Killer on the loose."

Finn feigned compassion, but was pleased he'd finally gotten to the bottom of Fenwick's real problem. Although he avoided family drama as much as possible, his avoidance didn't fully shield him from the goings-on of the Coltons. Just like his stepmother's insistence he interfere in Valeria's life, he was well aware of the sacrifices his cousin Layla was about to make on the altar of business by marrying the considerably older Harrington. Finn kept himself out of the gossip, but it wasn't a stretch to realize that the marriage of his cousin, a top VP at Colton Energy, to Hamlin Harrington, the long-time CEO of green energy company, Harrington Inc., was a front for a business merger.

Hamlin and Fenwick had a long-standing rivalry that would come to a lucrative end if the two entities united. A marriage of convenience between the

Colton heir apparent and the old man would obviously see that through and create the largest combined energy company in the entire northwest.

Finn mentally shook his head and held in a sigh, unwilling to show even a moment's weakness in front of his uncle. But he couldn't deny this was the reason he liked dogs. They were far less complicated. And they sure as hell didn't marry their daughters off to smarmy old men to garner a big payday.

"I've told you before, the department is working as fast as it can to find out who's responsible."

"Well, work faster. Maybe if you quit roaming around town on dates, you'd make a bit more progress."

His patience at an end, Finn moved up to the edge of Fenwick's desk, more than willing to use his size to his advantage. "I suggest you focus on your own problems and off me."

"And what if I don't? I can't lose this deal, Finn."

"What does Layla say about all this?"

"She knows her role."

Finn had never been close with his cousin, but even he had a hard time seeing how she would want to bind her life to Hamlin Harrington.

Since he wasn't going to get an answer to that question any more than he was going to get his uncle to stand down and quit bullying everyone in town, Finn opted for retreat. But not before he got in his closing salvo.

"I'd suggest you understand your role, too. And stop making trouble in my town."

Pins clanged, the scent of beer permeated the air and a steady hum of conversation filled the bowling alley as the Tuesday night competition got under way. As Finn had promised, eight teams had showed up for the night's matchups, dominating the four lanes at the far end of the twenty-lane alley.

Finn's team—Large and In Charge—was up against Bad Teachers, and Darby was mentally reviewing everyone's name as she bent to tie her genuinely ugly green-and-gold bowling shoes.

"Be careful. They might see you in Montana," Finn teased her as he eased into the seat next to her.

"I was thinking eastern Washington, so Montana is a definite improvement." Darby lifted a foot, tilting right then left as she admired the truly heinous shoe.

Finn patted a hand on her thigh before pointing to his cousin two lanes over. "At least they're better than Blake's. We can only be thankful these shoes have no support and get no traction on the ground outside. He's threatened to wear those out in public."

Darby tried to ignore the warm outline of his palm that still imprinted her thigh as she looked down the lanes. True to Finn's word, the purple-and-orange monstrosities on Blake's feet were a sight to behold.

"Where did he get those?"

"Somewhere online that should be shut down for deliberately trying to blind people."

"Colton! You're up!" someone hollered from the direction of the ball machine.

"Which Colton?" a woman Darby recognized as Patience Colton from the K-9 training center hollered from her seat.

"Chief's up!"

Finn stood, his little-boy grin firmly in place. "This won't take long. I'll be back shortly."

"Convinced you'll strike out? That's not very forward thinking of you, Chief Colton."

Finn stilled, seeming to think about it. "You're right. Maybe a kiss for good luck will help me out."

Before she could register his words or the movements that matched them, Finn leaned in, caging her between his arms, his mouth on an unerring course for hers. *I should stop him* was the last coherent thought to enter her head before those gorgeous lips landed on hers, eradicating her ability to think.

All she could do was feel.

The hum of the bowling alley faded away, replaced by nothing but the slamming, insistent beat of her heart. Just like the night before in the SUV when he'd wrapped his jacket around her, the man seemed to envelop her. He effectively shut out the world around them and she quickly caught up to the kiss, unwilling to be a passive participant.

He gently coaxed her mouth open, his tongue seeking entrance, and she welcomed him in, glorying in the way he made her feel. Light and airy, even as a heavy weight suffused her limbs. Was it need? Want?

No, a quiet voice whispered in her mind. *Desire*.

This was what desire felt like, pure and simple. Only it wasn't simple at all.

And while her feelings might be pure, reality quickly diluted them with the fact that this was a game of pretend. An act. A pretense to draw out a murderer.

A piercing whistle pulled them both fully out of the moment and Finn ended the kiss, lifting his head and smiling down at her. The little-boy grin was gone, replaced with something more adult. Something that spoke of the knowledge of darkened bedrooms and heated sheets.

A smile that held promises if she was only brave enough to reach out and take them.

"You're up, Chief."

The smile faded and he held her gaze a moment longer before standing to his full height. "Looks like I am."

She watched him walk to the ball machine and pick up the large green ball he'd selected earlier. Unlike some of other players, he'd claimed that he was so bad at bowling he refused to invest in one of his own. Hefting the ball, he walked up to the lane and lined up his shot.

And threw a perfect strike.

Darby let out a cheer before she could stop herself, pleased to see his initial attempt produce a significantly better outcome than a gutter ball. She was still clapping when he walked back over to take the seat next to her.

"That was pretty lucky."

Finn shrugged. "Must have been the kiss."

"I don't know. I—" She broke off, awareness dawning like a sudden dousing. "You're good at this!"

"You give me too much credit."

She leaped up at that, whirling on him. "The whole gutter ball thing was just a big lie to get me to come. That's why you said you'd be quick. You're *really* good at this!"

"Look out, Chief." One of the men on the other team hollered the words before adding an eyebrow wiggle for effect. "Looks like you've been discovered."

"I'm not that good," Finn said.

Darby slammed her hands on her hips, staring him down. "When was the last time you threw a gutter ball?"

"I don't remember." He mumbled—actually mumbled—the words.

Darby turned to his teammates. "When was his last one?" She didn't even bother qualifying the question because she knew they'd all been listening.

"Oh, about never," Bo's sister, Elle, added.

Darby shot her former sister-in-law a grateful smile. "Finally. One truthful person on this team."

One of the other players smiled before adding,

"He just wanted to land a good one on ya. Come on, show him what you're made of. It's your turn."

She harrumphed before marching over to the machine and picking up the lavender ball she'd selected earlier. She inserted her fingers in the holes, testing the weight before marching up to the lane.

She'd show him. Finn Colton and his hot lips and crooked grin and *lying* ways.

Positioning herself a few steps from the small dots lining the floor, Darby pushed herself into motion, allowing the ball to fly from the end of her hand. It made a heavy thud as it hit the lane, but to her utter surprise, ran true down the center of the glossy wood. The thick sound of tumbling pins echoed back toward her and, while it wasn't a strike like her lying, fake date's, she managed to knock out six pins.

They were split straight down the middle, but at least it was points on the board.

She managed to get two more on her second roll before taking her seat once more. Finn, having obviously decided he was better off making himself scarce, was at the counter a few lanes down, ordering food.

"I'm glad you came out with us tonight." Elle took the seat next to her. Although they'd been friendly when she and Bo were married, Darby had lost regular touch with her former sister-in-law since the divorce.

"I'm glad I came, too."

"He's smitten."

"Excuse me?"

"The chief. The man doesn't bring dates to bowling. Heck, he doesn't bring dates anywhere."

Darby wanted to correct Elle but fought back the words. This wasn't a date. Nor was it the start of a major relationship for either of them. It was playacting, plain and simple. No one was smitten and her scrambled brain would do well to remember that.

Even as that thought struck a chord of sadness, Darby realized there was a silver lining. She'd conceded to herself that working with Finn was a chance to help keep Red Ridge safe. It was also a chance to do whatever she could to avenge Bo's death as well as Michael Hayden's. If she was doing a good enough job to fool a cop, then she had to take some solace in that.

Deftly ignoring Elle's words about Finn's dating history, she focused on the noisy alley. "I haven't been bowling in years."

"What have you been waiting for?"

Darby grinned. "I'm not sure."

"Well, I'm glad you're here." Elle jumped up to take her turn and Darby watched her go. Bo's sister was three years younger than her and there was a time when that had felt like an eternity. Now it just seemed like she'd missed the chance to make—and keep—a true friend.

How odd to realize now that she'd lost so many years by not keeping up with the other relationships in her life.

"Still mad at me?"

Finn took the seat next to her once more, his voice low as he leaned in to bump his shoulder against hers.

"I still think you're a liar, if that's what you're asking."

"You can't blame a man for trying."

"For trying what?"

"To kiss you."

The comment was so unexpected—and so at odds with their fake situation—that Darby's mouth dropped open. "I don't need to be lied to in order to kiss a man."

Was that really her voice?

When had she turned into her mother? The prim-and-prissy attitude had been a staple of her mother's personality. Darby had believed herself free of the curse. Had she been operating under a delusion? Or had she simply grown old before her time?

"Then maybe I should try the honest way."

Once more, Finn Colton had the advantage as his hands tightened over her shoulders, pulling her close. His mouth clamped onto hers and, where the first kiss had been playful and exploratory, this one was all hot, lusty need. His lips traveled a familiar if more urgent path over hers and she opened as his tongue slipped inside.

The move was bold—the kiss even more so—and she lifted her hands to cling to his forearms as she kissed him back. A small moan caught in the back of her throat and she could only be glad the noise of the alley hid that verbal evidence of her need.

What she couldn't hide quite so easily was the warmth that filled her face or the sheer enjoyment she'd taken from the simple joining of their lips.

As Darby watched Finn get up to take his next roll—a second strike—she was forced to admit something to herself. Their situation might be fake, but that kiss had been 100 percent real.

The watcher had intended to enjoy an evening out at the bowling alley, nursing a few drinks at the bar while taking in the supreme moves of her most favorite cop. She looked forward to Tuesday nights and had been pleased when the long wait for bowling season to start up again after the holiday break had finally ended.

A month was too long to go without her Tuesday night watch party.

Only he'd brought *her*.

She had no idea who the woman was, but she'd been readily accepted by the other bowlers even though she played horribly. The first game had been unbearable to sit through. By the second, when the woman had kissed *her* cop yet again, the watcher had paid her bill and fled into the night.

Even now she sat in her car at the edge of the parking lot. Out of sight and far away from the powerful overhead lights, she watched the various league members head to their cars.

How oblivious they all were. Going about their days unaware of how boring and dull and *routine* their lives really were. It made her smile, a small giggle bubbling in her throat. They were all so boring and uninteresting and they didn't even know it.

Only Finn was different.

Only Finn understood her and would understand what life could be like between them.

Only Finn would take away this desperate clawing and craving that filled her chest, desperate to get out.

So she sat there in her car, waiting for Finn Colton to come out. As people filed out of the bowling alley, alone or in pairs, she knew none of them saw the woman watching them.

Chapter 8

Thick russet-colored fur bunched in Darby's hands as she smoothed her palms over the German shepherd her vet had recommended to her last Saturday. Doc Cooper had vouched for the dog and had helped set up Darby's meeting with the family selling her. Patience Colton, the vet at the K-9 center, had kindly offered them a backdrop for the meeting and had been more than willing to give a second opinion while also reinforcing the reputation of Darby's business.

Satisfied, Patience got up off the floor from where she'd sat, performing her checkup. "I'm pleased to say this girl looks amazing."

The owner, Mavis Whitley, smiled fondly as she

looked down on the dog they called Lucy. "She's been such a sweet girl. We just want her to go to a loving home and I'd love for her to be part of such a good program. Dr. Cooper spoke highly of your business, Ms. Gage."

"I can promise you she'll be treated like a queen," Darby said.

"We're very impressed that you've decided not to breed your other dog. Care for her health is obviously your priority and it makes us feel that Lucy will be in good hands."

"Thank you." Darby appreciated the kindness, but she'd never questioned the rightness of her decision. Her first priority was Penny—the business had to be second. She could only be grateful Finn had ensured she'd still have a business. Bringing home Lucy was the next step in that process. Of course, taking that step was predicated on a match with Penny.

Darby had brought Penny along, as well, and gestured toward a windowed play area. "I would like to introduce her to my dog, if you don't mind?"

The Whitleys didn't mind. In moments they had Penny and Lucy meeting each other in supervised play. Darby let out her first easy breath of the morning when the dogs cautiously sniffed each other before raising their paws and swatting happily in play.

"I think they're on a path to being BFFs." Patience took a spot next to her, her arms crossed, a satisfied smile playing about her lips. They'd known one another for a while, Darby's work at the training center ensuring she'd spent time with nearly everyone there. Patience was one of her favorites, though.

"I'm just grateful we have a match. Lucy's so sweet, and I'm not sure what I'd have done if she and Penny didn't get along."

"You'd try again until you found the right one." Patience waved at the happily playing dogs, her love of animals clear in her smitten gaze. "You're strong and determined that way"

As compliments went, it was one of the nicest she'd ever received. "I'm not quite sure I agree, but thank you."

Patience laid a hand on Darby's arm, effectively pulling her attention from Penny and Lucy. "Don't underestimate yourself. I know you've had a rough go for the past few years, but you're strong and you're solid and you've got a big heart. The universe loves those traits and loves rewarding them."

The added compliment caught her so off guard, Darby could only goggle at the vet. Tall and pretty, Patience had an easy grace about her that was more boho than Red Ridge chic, despite being born with Fenwick Colton's silver spoon lodged firmly in her mouth.

It was the warmth in her dark brown eyes that was the real clincher.

"Thank you."

"You're welcome. Now—" Patience turned to

watch the dogs at play but Darby couldn't help feeling the woman's attention hadn't wavered. "Tell me about these hot date nights you've been having with my cousin Finn."

Finn swung by the lab on his way into the precinct, the text he'd received earlier suggesting there was something that required his attention. The week had produced little news or evidence in the battle to find the Groom Killer. The fact that it was Friday—an entire week since Michael Hayden's death—and they had next to nothing to go on, had only ratcheted up the pressure on finding the killer.

Finn had kept up his dates with Darby, taking her to another showy dinner on Wednesday night and a movie Thursday, but so far they'd been unsuccessful in attracting any unsavory attention. Which was a major departure from everyone else in town who had suddenly become fixated on the chief of police's new love interest.

He'd gotten teasing comments from nearly every member of his family as well as several Gages. With the exception of Elle, his K-9 rookie, everyone in the Gage family had remained stubbornly skeptical, Carson's suspicion over Darby ensuring no one in Bo's family had mentally let her off the hook.

But adding on the general interest in town had become a bit much. That morning, in fact, he'd gotten questioned by Mae Larson while he'd waited for his coffee at Java Station. He'd always seen her as a sweet older member of the community, but her grandmotherly ways were surprisingly randy if the eyebrow wiggles she'd given him were any indication.

Did people really have nothing better to do?

Of course, their focus on his love life had helped some of the conversation die down over the Groom Killer. Even the *Gazette* had seemed to run out of headlines, taking a break and focusing on an impending snowstorm heading their way and threatening to dump over a foot and a half of snow.

While the snow was expected this time of year, it was only going to further ruin the crime scenes he and his team had run over and over throughout the week. The Groom Killer had chosen well, using the forests and thick covered ground that made up the edges of the town to an advantage.

The chase he and Lotte had given the week before over the terrain behind the Circle T Steakhouse had resulted in no discernible leads and they'd finally given the restaurant leave to reopen for business.

To further prove his commitment, Finn had booked a reservation for him and Darby that very night and the owner had agreed to give them the center table.

He was excited to see her again, the charade they'd kept up all week growing more and more intimate by the day. He knew he needed to keep his emotions in check, but he couldn't deny how much he enjoyed spending time with her. And while he hardly needed the public interest the two of them seemed to generate, he couldn't find too much fault since big and showy had been his intention from the start.

He wasn't so sure she felt the same.

It was subtle, but it was there. She'd yet to initiate anything intimate. That had been all him. And while he'd told himself the hand holding and the endearments and the kissing were all for show, in his quiet moments, he had to ask himself if that was the truth.

Mae Larson's eyebrow wiggles aside, he couldn't deny he enjoyed kissing Darby Gage.

A lot.

Brushing off the matter of Darby's kisses, Finn took the long hallway that led to the lab, willing himself to focus on the matter at hand. He did have a killer in his midst and no amount of time spent with a pretty woman with gorgeous legs and enticing lips was going to change that.

More, if he was going to keep his head and his focus, he had to remind himself that dating Darby was all for show. The dates and the kisses were meant to draw out a killer, not allow him to forget he was hunting one.

He pushed through the heavy metal doors of the crime lab and found their resident lab geek, Charlie, outfitted head to toe in scrubs. Other than the four-inch heels she persistently wore, Dr. Charlotte "Charlie" Wallace looked like she was ready to march into a hazmat area.

"Doc."

"Finn." She turned from the microscope she peered into to face him. Dark eyes twinkled above a face mask and he looked down over his clothes before meeting her gaze once more. "I think I'm underdressed."

"Not at all. I swung out here because I knew you were coming. I'm dressed like this for some work in the other room." She pointed toward a door marked Do Not Enter and Finn wondered, not for the first time, what lived in the depths of Charlie's lab.

"Everything okay?"

"Of course. Just some necrotic tissue I want to handle with care."

Finn nodded. "As one does."

"Your gallows humor is noted. And appreciated." Charlie waved to a point about halfway down the long counter that ran the length of her lab. "Come on over here."

He followed her, admiring her tall, capable form. What caught him off guard was the quick leap he made to imagining Darby's smaller, more petite curves in his mind. Instantly he recalled the feel of her beneath his palms and the fierce need that settled in his bones each time he kissed her.

"Finn?"

Charlie's question pulled him from his musings. "Hmm?"

"You okay? You look about a million miles away."

"Sure. Yeah, I'm good."

Charlie pointed to a setup on the counter. "Here's

the bleach you brought me the other day and then the samples that were collected in the forest."

"You've kept this under wraps?"

"Of course." She tugged a pair of rubber gloves out of a box before handing the box to him to do the same. "I know how to manage an investigation and I've sent my notes to you only, as you requested. I'm not sure why Carson isn't updated on these developments, though, as one of the lead investigators."

"I want an unbiased opinion."

Charlie's dark eyes clouded. "You think he's biased in some way?"

"I think investigating the murder of his brother is a sensitive topic. Where I can take some of the load off or tug a few leads that may be inconsequential, I want to do that."

Her dark gaze remained sharp, but she finally nodded. "I'll defer to your wishes, but don't underestimate Gage. He's a good man and he wants justice."

"And I don't?"

Finn knew the question was steeped in his unusual secretive approach to the bleach, which was all the more reason he needed to recognize it was possible he was losing his objectivity, as well.

"That's not what I meant," Charlie said.

Finn slapped the gloves against his thigh. "I know it's not. And I know I'm not being fair."

Charlie hesitated for the briefest moment, as if weighing something, before pushing forward.

"Would this have anything to do with your recent attentions toward Darby Gage?"

Finn understood the hesitation—and waited a few beats himself before ultimately opting for the truth. He'd had tough cases in his past and the duties of chief often meant he had to make hard choices, even between the members of his department. He did want Carson to assess the situation with the Groom Killer through a clear pair of eyes but he held himself to the same set of expectations.

None of it was a reason to keep the truth from Charlie.

"Yes, it does. Carson refuses to take her off his suspect list. Truth of the matter is, she's not fully off mine yet, either."

"And the bleach?"

"You've been analyzing the bleach found at the crime scene. The bottle I gave you was in Ms. Gage's possession as she cleaned Bo Gage's home. Which she inherited upon his death."

"I see."

Did she?

"I know it's a basic chemical compound, so I don't know if you can tell any differences, but the connection seemed suspicious."

"Did Ms. Gage act strange when you wanted the bottle?"

"She seemed confused that I wanted it, but otherwise didn't seem bothered by the request."

"What I can tell you is that the bleach you removed from her home isn't the same as what was laid down at the crime scene. The scene was highly compromised but the base chemicals and strength were different."

"You could tell that? From what I gave you?"

"What was at the crime scene was most likely a consumer brand. The strength level was high and had been liberally dumped on the ground. Even with the dilution of the snow cover, there was enough base product that I'd say the killer used at least two bottles, maybe a third."

"Wow."

"What Ms. Gage has is a generic brand. It's still potent, but the concentration was lower and likely cost her less. You're looking for someone who bought several bottles at once." She pointed to the setup on the counter. "Want to take a look?"

"Sure." Finn followed Charlie to the counter, taking her lead as she walked him through the various tests she'd run to assess the differences between samples.

As he left the lab fifteen minutes later, Finn took solace in the irrefutable proof that Darby hadn't doused the crime scene.

And struggled with the way he was going to tell Carson what he'd kept to himself since Monday.

Darby inhaled the savory aroma of her steak and breathed in deep. The filet was cooked perfectly, in just the way she preferred. Medium, with a side of mashed potatoes and creamed corn that would make the angels weep.

She'd only ever been to the Circle T once. She and Bo had come to the restaurant for their first anniversary. He'd wined and dined her, lavishing her with compliments. Three days later she'd discovered his cheating—and the fact that the woman he'd cheated with was the fourth since they'd married—and had moved out.

Aside from the matter that she couldn't afford it, she'd diligently avoided the Circle T and the role the restaurant played in the last good memory from her marriage.

"Is something wrong with your steak?"

Darby glanced up at Finn, his frown of concern a sweet rebuke against those memories. "It's fine. Better than fine, as a matter of fact."

"You sure?"

"Absolutely. In fact, I'm warning you now, I'm clearing my plate. No leftovers for me."

"Penny will be disappointed."

"Penny will survive." She cut into her steak, pleased when another delicious scent wafted up toward her. "And there's no way I'm feeding a dog a thirty-eight-dollar steak, no matter how much I care for her."

"There are many in this town who don't feel the same."

For all the time they'd spent together this week, she'd rarely heard Finn speak ill of anyone. Yet his comment—and the dry tone—had her considering that maybe the man did have enemies.

Or at least a few people who rubbed him the wrong way.

"You thinking of anyone in particular?"

"My uncle Fenwick, for starters. He's always enjoyed his role as the richest in the family. He'd think nothing of an expensive meal, or feeding it to the dogs."

Darby thought about the funny little man who'd bellowed his way around the bank on Tuesday. "I saw him. Tuesday morning, when I was depositing the check for the business. This word's highly inadequate, but he seemed to be in quite a snit."

The answering smile she received made her think it might be the perfect word. "I saw him shortly after that. I'd gotten a call that he was doing his level best to act like the town jerk, and headed over to see what was wrong."

"You find out?"

"He's upset about the Groom Killer. Claims it's ruining the wedding plans for his daughter. My cousin Layla," Finn added.

"Did something happen to her plans?"

"Her groom's crying off. Or threatening to. Claims he's at risk of getting killed if he goes through with it."

"That's an awful reason."

Darby understood what she and Finn were doing. The very real risks they were taking to draw out a killer. Even with that understanding, she hadn't given much thought to the fact that people who were actually in love would call off their plans.

"I'd say it makes Layla lucky," Finn said.

"What?"

"She's marrying Hamlin Harrington. The man's twice her age and it's basically a business merger. I'd think she had better things to do with her future than marry an old man."

Once again, Finn surprised her. He'd been so casual about them pretending to date each other, she'd internalized that to mean he had little interest in finding love himself. Yet to hear him talk about his cousin and his disgust at her marriage gave Darby an opportunity to probe a bit.

"I didn't realize you were so close to your extended family."

"I'm not."

"Yet you're upset that she's choosing to enter this marriage?"

Finn sawed at his T-bone, his movements deliberate and precise, as he removed the steak from the bone. "I don't understand people who don't get married for love. Marriage is hard enough. Why add that pressure on top?"

"People get married for a lot of reasons. Love isn't always at the top of the list. Or on the list at all."

His movements stopped abruptly. "Why did you get married?"

Images of that anniversary dinner flitted through

her mind once again, followed quickly by the memory of the bunched-up panties she'd found three days later in Bo's car. "I was in love. Or thought I was."

"Would you do it again?"

"I don't know." In an abstract way, Darby had believed she would get married again, but in reality she hadn't been all that quick to go looking for it. "Would you?"

"I haven't given it much thought."

"What about your marriage, then? Were you in love?"

"Yes." His shoulders had grown more and more stiff as they spoke of their pasts, but it was like something broke. He laid down his fork and knife and looked at her. "But I might have been the same as you. I went into it with the best of intentions but somewhere along the way realized I wasn't really in love. And then, after a while, I began to question if I'd ever been in love at all."

"It's easy to armchair quarterback at the end. After all the bad things have been said, it's hard to remember there were ever good things."

"I suppose."

"It doesn't mean there wasn't anything good about the time you spent together. Which is why I need to thank you."

"Thank me? For what?"

"For this week. For however long this charade lasts. I've been existing these past few years but I haven't really been living. You've reminded me that I'm still young and still have something to give."

Finn stared at her, that firm jaw and penetrating gaze that had increasingly been occupying more and more of her thoughts holding her captive. In such a short time, he'd reminded her that she had a future. One she should work a bit harder for.

"Whoever is lucky enough to receive all you have to give, Darby Gage, will be a lucky man."

The sweet words hovered between them, as delicate as cotton candy at the state fair. She debated saying something, but hesitated to break the moment. And then the choice was taken out of her hands by the arrival of the Larson twins, with two equally vapid women on their arms.

"Look at this little party." Evan Larson spoke first. Or who she thought was Evan, but maybe it was his twin, Noel. She'd always had some trouble figuring out who was who. They were handsome men, but Darby had always steered clear of both of them. She'd waited on them from time to time at the diner, but in recent years when they'd lined their coffers with even more money from whatever interests they had going—real estate was the latest, she'd heard—they'd believed themselves above diner fare.

"Heard you're running Bo's business now." The one she believed was Noel spoke up, his eyes hazed with what she assumed was liquor.

"Yes, I inherited Bo's business."

"I want one of your puppies. Two, as a matter of

fact." The woman at his side cooed when she heard the mention of puppies and he squeezed her waist in response.

"I don't know when my next litter will be ready."

The jovial smile on the man's face dropped. "Why the hell not? Bo said he was getting ready to breed his bitch."

"Penny's not ready to have more puppies." Darby held her ground but chaffed at the arrogance. And while she understood the technical term for Penny was *bitch*, somehow Noel's use of the word was more slur than descriptor.

"Well, get her ready. She's a damned dog."

The other Larson stepped up, laying a hand on his brother's free shoulder. "You'll have to excuse my brother's excitement. He's been looking forward to adding to his team of guard dogs. The training takes a while and he'd hoped to include some young blood into his team."

Finn stood then, his movements slow as he came to his full height. Although neither of the twins was a small man, Finn's tall form and broad shoulders had them backing up. "I'm sure Ms. Gage will be happy to let you know when she's ready for buyers."

Again, the one Darby she believed was Evan spoke up. "I'm sure she will."

He tightened his grip on his date and shot a smile to his brother that smacked of warning. "We'll let you get back to your dinner, then. Enjoy your evening."

The foursome walked to a private table in the back. Noel's tumble into his chair reinforced her belief he was drunk, though it didn't negate the dark look he shot her from across the room.

Finn took his seat after shooting a few dark looks of his own in the direction of the brothers.

"I guess your investment's already paying off." Darby tried to keep her attitude light and breezy, but the image of giving one of her puppies to Evan or Noel Larson stuck in her stomach and spoiled her appetite.

"What investment?"

"The money you've put into the business. I've already got buyers. Not the Larson brothers, of course. I'd never do business with them."

"That money's yours. I don't expect any of it back."

Although the past week hadn't been anything like she'd expected, Darby distinctly remembered their conversation when he'd offered to pay off her debts. "But you said the money was an investment."

"In you. In getting your help, yes. But I don't expect anything back from you."

"Why would you do that?"

"Because you needed help. And since I needed help, too, this was the quickest way to solve both our problems." Finn reached across the table and took her hand in his. Unlike the purposeful attempts at public displays of affection over the past week, there was something impulsive in the gesture. Like he meant it and wasn't trying to show off for anyone who might be watching.

"Thank you for the help, then." She turned her hand over beneath his, allowing his palm to rest against hers, and took solace in the simple gesture of affection.

Chapter 9

"Bring it to me! Come on, girl!" Finn hollered the words as he watched Darby's newest addition race toward the back fence surrounding the backyard. The property was larger than the fenced area, but the cordoned space provided lots of room to play and roam yet still kept the dogs near the house.

Lucy had picked up the game quickly, her transition to Darby's home seeming to go smoothly as he took her through several games and drills. Lotte and Penny were enjoying themselves, as well, racing around the backyard, chasing each other and generally roughhousing on the snow-covered ground.

"Do they ever get tired?"

Darby, bundled up in a thick coat, carried two

travel mugs of coffee in her hands. She hip bumped the back door closed before crossing to him and extending one of the mugs. Finn took the offering and laughed as Lucy bounded back over the snow, racing close enough to kick up some powder as she skidded to a stop at his feet.

"Once again, the Finn Colton charm is taking down another one. What is your secret with my dogs?"

"I think they know I'm as big a kid as they are."

Darby cocked her head, the bold morning sun catching the red highlights in her hair. "The big, bad chief has a childish side?"

"One I pull out on rare occasions. Dogs are a safe space to do that."

"Have you had times in your life where you didn't feel you could be a kid? Where you needed a safe space?"

Finn heard the interest and knew he was the one who'd put the idea out there. What surprised him was how comfortable he felt continuing the conversation.

"It's a trait that started young and I guess I've kept it." He tossed the ball again, sending Lucy off on a race to catch it, her delighted barks filling the air.

"You're the oldest?" she asked.

"The oldest. And the only from my father's marriage to my mother. My half siblings are from my father's second marriage."

"I can see where that would be hard."

"It might have been easier with a different woman, but Joanelle is a tough woman on a good day."

"And on a bad one?" Darby asked, going to the heart of the matter.

"She made it perfectly clear she'd be perfectly happy if I hadn't been a part of her life most days. Fortunately my siblings aren't the same. But I spent as much time out of the house as I could."

"You couldn't have been that old. I've met your sister Serena. She's not that much younger than you."

"Five years."

"So you could hardly run through town by yourself. Where did you go when you went out of the house?"

"The stables, mostly. I made friends with the ranch hands and they were good to me, but they kept their distance, too. Owner's kid and all that. The dogs, on the other hand—they were always good for long hours together."

He saw the concern in her eyes—saw the way the sympathy came over her like a wool blanket—and was positively suffocated by it. "It was no big deal. I survived. And I have a good relationship with Anders and Serena and Valeria. Joanelle couldn't mess that up, no matter how much she tried to poison the well."

Darby didn't say anything. Instead she turned and set her coffee down on a small table, then reached for his and did the same. The dog had bounded back during their conversation and before he could send her running again, Darby picked up the ball at his feet and tossed it, sending Lucy off like a shot in its wake.

She focused on him once more, the warmth in

her gaze changing as he stared at her in the fresh morning air. Where Finn believed he'd seen sympathy only moments before, the light in her eyes had changed, reflecting something that looked a lot like want.

Then she proved him 100 percent correct by lifting up on her tiptoes and pressing her lips to his.

Finn caught her around the waist, boosting her up and crushing her to his chest at the same time. The tentative press of her lips on his picked up steam as she got into the moment with him, her tongue darting out to mate with his. In moments the kiss went from sweet and heated to wanton and erotic, a feast for the senses. He was beyond pleased she'd initiated the kiss—everything up to now had been all him—but he couldn't deny the need to touch her was overwhelming.

His hands roamed over her back, pulling her close and seeking the shape of her through the thick, heavy winter material. For the first time in his life, he wished for summer.

And wasn't that a kick?

A heavy paw swatted at his thigh before the distinct outline of a ball pressed into the same spot. He broke the kiss to stare down at Lucy, her eyes big and unrepentant as she stared up at him.

"She doesn't care she's interrupted something." The husky register of Darby's voice grabbed at him, a fist closing over the base of his spine as he kept one hand firmly wrapped around her. With the other, he took the ball and flung it as hard and as far as he could, not surprised when he heard a heavy thud where it met the fence line.

"That was some throw."

"That's because I want more time." Finn bent his head to hers once more, their breaths shooting puffs of steam into the cold morning air. He ignored all of it as he took her mouth, anxious to devour as much of her as he could.

Where had this come from?

A week ago he'd accused her of murder. When had he veered from thinking of her as a suspect to thinking of her as a lover?

Lucy's barks interrupted them once more and he sighed against Darby's lips.

"It's like a race against the clock," Darby said before a giggle spilled out.

"It's not funny."

"Yeah." She giggled again. "It sort of is. I've got one who won't let me pet her and one that won't let me kiss you. Maybe I should sell the business. I'm not sure I'm going to be very successful at it anyway."

Finn considered her in that moment—the big smile, the infectious laughter, and the clear love and commitment for the dogs—and knew it was time to tell her she was no longer a suspect. The bleach had provided proof, but the longer he spent with her, the less proof he needed.

She was a good woman. And she'd done right by

Bo Gage's family and his business and his beloved dog. A killer would have run long before, but Darby had stuck around.

Their conversation about his childhood struck him once more. He'd pushed aside that time in his life, refusing to dwell too long on what it had meant to be an outsider in his own family. Yet she'd understood.

More, she'd taken an interest and asked.

Yes, it was definitely time to tell her she wasn't a suspect any longer. And it was time to give her a choice. He appreciated her help more than he could say, but she deserved a chance to get out of hunting a killer.

"There's something I need to tell you."

"About what?"

"Let's go inside. I'd like to update you on the case."

The watcher lifted the glass heart out of its velvet bed, turning the piece over and over in her hands. It was so delicate. Fragile.

Like the bonds she had with Finn Colton.

How was it he didn't see that?

She'd been to the precinct before. They'd spoken, for heaven's sake. *Connected.* How could he not know?

How could he not see how she felt about him?

But he obviously didn't. Not if the spectacle he'd made of himself this week was any indication. Dinner dates. Movies. The bowling Tuesday night. All week long she'd been forced to watch him squire around that woman. The murderer.

Oh, she knew what the town whispered about. And they'd been whispering long and low about Darby Gage, the Groom Killer. It wasn't a leap. She'd been married to the first victim. She was probably bitter and upset that he'd moved on. And then it had made her so mad, she'd killed another groom. Another man seeking his eternal happiness.

She traced her finger over the fragile heart, the glass so fine she could imagine it beating in her hand.

Like Finn Colton's heart. She'd have it someday, all to herself.

Soon, he'd be hers.

In the meantime, maybe she needed to help him out. Help make sure that woman, the murderer, wasn't able to kill again.

Darby set down refreshed water in three large bowls and heard the lapping before she'd even cleared the kitchen into the living room. With any luck the intense play session outside had tired out her charges. Of course, it wouldn't do Finn much good if his partner fell asleep on the job, but with it being Saturday, hopefully they wouldn't be called off to too much. In the relatively short time they'd spent together, she'd come to realize how dedicated he was to his job and his team. Even when he was technically off duty, he was always available to them.

Finn had poured fresh mugs of coffee for the two of them while she'd taken care of the dogs and had settled hers on the small coffee table in the living room.

He stood at the window that overlooked the back-yard, his back to her when she walked into the room. The quiet moment gave her a chance to look him over and it struck her once again how big and strong he was.

Capable.

And very male.

It was funny, she'd never been a particular fan of big men. Bo had been physically well built but he'd been of average height. Most people didn't notice it because his personality had been so oversize, but he hadn't come anywhere near to clearing six feet. The few men she'd dated before getting married had all been average size, as well.

She'd liked it that way. While she'd never been afraid of men, growing up with a single mother, her life had revolved around being careful and being a good girl. Dating a large, overbearing man had always seemed like the antithesis of that.

Sunlight framed Finn's body, backlighting him and showing off the gold in his thick dark blond hair. Once again, she could see traces of the little boy she imagined in her mind every time he smiled. Only, now she had a different picture. One he'd painted of lonely days with only the farm animals for company.

It explained his innate sense and easy comfort

with the dogs. It also explained his unconditional love for them. While having a pet was a responsibility—running a business with them even more so—there was also an ease there. They genuinely craved care and affection and, if given, gave back far more than asked for.

It was that belief that had her hanging in there with Penny, persistent and steady as she worked to build a trusting relationship between them. And it was that same belief that had her so excited Lucy was now a part of their lives.

Finn turned from the window, catching her staring. She knew she should be embarrassed—it wasn't like she'd acted shy that morning, either—yet she couldn't see her way to even a blush. She enjoyed his company. And while things were confusing between them, especially with Bo's death still unsolved, it wasn't like he'd pushed her away.

Was it possible he considered things between them, as well?

The thought warmed her until a second followed on its heels. He'd said more than once that he'd wanted to keep their romance front and center to catch a killer. And he'd told her that he'd had a development in the case.

Had she only imagined a relationship building in her mind? She hadn't dated in quite a while. And she had reveled in the affection he'd lavished on her over the past week. Maybe she'd fantasized this all out of control and turned it into something it wasn't.

Something ugly and sick began to swirl in her veins, clouding her vision with memories of that morning when she'd thrown herself at him.

"Darby? You okay?"

"Sure. Fine. Of course." She crossed the small space to the oversize chair that sat at the corner of the couch. "I know you have something you wanted to discuss. I'm sure I've taken up way too much of your time this morning and here I am lollygagging."

"You're not—"

She patted the arm of the couch, a gesture to call him over. "What was it you wanted to discuss?"

A strange expression passed over his face and he looked about to say something, but opted not to at the last minute and took the seat she'd suggested. He stared at her for a few more moments before taking a sip of his coffee.

"What is it, Finn?"

That intense gaze didn't let up and the sinking feeling that had carried her to her seat grew more intense. *Oh, no, you really did misread the situation. Smooth move, Darbs.*

"I need to update you on the investigation."

"You're allowed to do that?"

"I'd say so, since I've pulled you into it. I also need to talk to Carson and I thought you might like to go with me."

Whatever she'd been expecting him to say, inviting her to a meeting with her ex-brother-in-law wasn't it. "On official police business?"

"Yes and no. Technically you've been helping out on official police business, so I'm not quite sure I should get uppity about it all of a sudden."

"Oo-kay." She nearly smiled at the image of Finn getting uppity about anything, but his serious expression had her reconsidering. Something had him bothered and he was making her crazy as she waited to hear what it was. "Why don't you tell me what's going on?"

"You're no longer a suspect."

A weight she hadn't even realized she'd carried lifted off her. Like the deal he'd struck the past week, releasing her from the bonds of debt Bo had left her in, yet different at the same time. That had simply been money. While difficult, it was something she knew she would find her way past.

This was her life.

And she had no idea how she'd worried that her freedom and her choices would be taken away.

"What changed your mind?" she asked.

"Several things. But the bleach was a big one."

Bleach? What was he talking about? "I'm afraid you've lost me."

"The bleach last Monday. The bottle I took from you."

"Right." She nodded, puzzling through the odd change in conversation. "I figured you needed to clean something up."

"That's all you thought?"

"Yeah, sure." She shrugged, trying to recall the

situation. He'd seemed fixated on the bottle when he'd seen it in her hand. When he'd finally asked for it, she'd handed it over. "You do have a dog in your car. I can't say I gave it much thought."

"I needed to take it to the lab."

"And you've lost me again."

The jangling of dog tags pulled her attention from Finn as Penny, Lucy and Lotte all trotted into the living room in single file, Penny in front. They lined themselves up on the floor and Darby was fascinated to watch how they positioned themselves with Lotte closest to Finn and Penny nearest to Darby. Lucy had taken the middle, as if she understood where she fit in the pecking order.

Simple. Understood.

Unlike the conversation she was having with Finn. "Why don't you take this one apart for me? I really don't understand what you're talking about or what it has to do with deciding I'm no longer a suspect."

"That's what I'm trying to tell you. I was doing my job."

"What did you think I was doing with the bleach besides cleaning?"

"There was bleach discovered as part of the Hayden crime scene. I thought maybe you'd put it there."

That strange, inscrutable expression on his face when he'd stared at her cleaning supplies suddenly made sense. She had noticed it then, even if she hadn't understood why. "That's why you looked at the bottle like it was a coiled snake?"

"Yes."

"And you thought I used bleach to commit a murder?" She quickly cycled through the headlines she'd read over the past month on the town paper. "But the killer has used a gun. Bo and the other man were shot and killed. What does bleach have to do with it?"

"Why don't you come with me to see Carson? I'll explain everything."

Finn turned into the entrance of the Double C Ranch, his childhood home. He visited as little as possible, taking part in only the basic requirements of family life. Since his stepmother liked it that way, preferring to ignore the fact that her husband had a family before they'd met, it was a mutually agreeable situation.

Despite the active avoidance, he'd been here several times in the past few months. His sister Serena had just had a baby and Lora was the apple of everyone's eye, including her uncle Finn's.

Serena had also been at the heart of the mystery surrounding Bo's death and their cousin Demi's possible involvement. Although Serena had defended Demi, claiming she couldn't possibly be involved in Bo's murder, she hadn't been able to give any good reason why Demi's necklace had been found at the murder scene. Nor could she explain why Bo Gage, with his last breath, would have written "Demi C" in his own blood.

It had been one of the most grisly things Finn had ever witnessed. While he wanted to believe his sister, he simply couldn't remove their cousin off the suspects list because Serena thought she was being framed. The fact Demi had jumped town hadn't helped her case one bit.

"We're not going in the front door?" Darby asked after they parked at the side of the house.

"I'd prefer to avoid my stepmother. Serena has a private entrance and it's just easier."

"Of course."

She seemed to take his comments in stride, but surprised him when she took his hand as they walked toward the entrance to Serena's wing of the ranch.

He surprised himself even more by how good it felt to have her support. He squeezed her fingers before dropping her hand to knock on the door.

As expected, Carson was there with his fiancée and soon-to-be adopted daughter and was the one to answer the door. His normally impassive gaze—known for giving away nothing—widened when he saw Darby. "Finn. Darb. What can I do for you?"

"Can we come in? I have news."

Carson backed up immediately. "You have a breakthrough on the case?"

Finn laid a hand on Carson's shoulder, stilling him. "No breakthroughs, but an update you should know about."

His top detective seemed to consider things for a moment before nodding. "Since Darby is here, I presume Serena can hear the details?"

"Of course." Finn nodded.

"Let's go get Serena, then, and we'll sit down."

Since he'd been there a few weeks before, Finn was surprised by the additional changes that had taken place in such a short time. Although there had been blankets and bottles scattered around, on the walk from the door through the living area, he passed a cradle, a stack of toys there was no way Lora was big enough to play with and a large colorful mat that had what looked like a bridge arcing above it.

"It sure does look different in here."

Carson grinned, the weight of the investigation fading in his excitement. "We're baby central around here. Lora's so close to rolling over, it's going to be any day."

Finn had no idea why that was important but began to nod at the news when Darby spoke up. "Already? She's still so young. She must be a fast learner."

"She's a champ," Carson agreed, gesturing them to the kitchen table before excusing himself to go find Serena.

Finn waited until Carson was out of earshot to question Darby. "What just happened?"

"What just happened?"

"Since Bo's death, he's been convinced you're a

hardened criminal and now you make one comment about Lora and he's ready to be your best friend?"

"For starters, I don't think Carson really thinks I'm guilty. I think he wants to think I'm guilty so he can catch his brother's killer. Second, every parent wants to talk about their child's achievements and milestones."

"But he's not—" Finn broke off, realization dawning. He'd certainly not minded when his sister had hooked up with Carson. The detective was not only one of his best members of the force, he was a good man with a good head on his shoulders. But to realize that he loved Lora as much as he loved Serena...

"He's her father in every way that counts," Darby said, her voice gentle.

Finn was prevented from saying anything as his sister walked into the kitchen, Carson trailing behind her. Unable to stop himself, Finn gathered her up for a huge hug, lifting her off her feet and spinning her around.

"Finn! What's going on with you?"

"I'm happy to see you. And I assume she's sleeping, but I expect to see Lora before I leave, too."

"We can make that happen. And since my daughter has decided to eat with the timing and precision of a train conductor, she should be up in about—" Serena glanced at the clock over the stove "—thirty minutes."

Carson got them all settled at the table with coffee.

Recognizing they were under a ticking clock before his niece woke up, Finn started in with his story.

Carson and Serena listened to his overview of the chase he and Lotte had given the night of Michael Hayden's death, the bleach finish line that had stopped them and the bottle he'd discovered at Darby's house. They nodded throughout, seeming to understand the implications, of both the killer's craftiness and the possible connection to Darby. When Finn explained his initial thoughts about the bottle Darby had used to clean her home, Serena had reached over and laid a comforting hand on Darby's arm.

But it was when he'd explained the results of the lab tests that Carson got up and went around the table, pulling Darby to her feet.

"I'm sorry. I'm so sorry I doubted you."

Finn had known relief when Charlie had cleared Darby's involvement via the bleach lab testing. But as he watched Darby cling to Carson, for the first time since Bo Gage's body had been discovered, Finn had hope they'd all come out the other side of this.

They'd stop the Groom Killer and allow the residents of Red Ridge to sleep safe at night once again.

Chapter 10

Darby brushed away tears, shocked at how deeply she felt Carson's forgiveness. They'd always gotten along and from the first time they met she'd enjoyed and cared for Bo's oldest brother. She'd often thought that Carson was the type of brother she'd have loved to have if she'd had any siblings. Strong, sure of himself and deeply committed to his family.

While she'd understood on a visceral level how much it hurt to lose that approval, it was only now that she had it back that she understood how much his doubt had truly pained her.

And though she'd meant what she'd told Finn—on some level she had believed that Carson had found her to be an easy scapegoat for Bo's murder—it was freeing to move past all of it.

Carson and Serena held hands, their simple joining evidence of their support for one another. Carson directed his attention to Finn, yet it was clear he had remained focused on Serena, especially when he squeezed her hand. "I'd like to be mad at you, Colton, for not telling me about the bleach and the lab work, but I've got something I've been holding on to, as well."

"Me, too," Serena added.

"Serena?"

His sister nodded, before seeming to take strength in a subtle head nod from Carson. "You know Demi and I got close over the past year. Since I got pregnant with Lora. I was alone and scared, and Mom hasn't exactly been a pillar of support."

Darby registered the comment about Finn's stepmother and, when added to the story he'd told of his own childhood loneliness, she couldn't quite hold back her judgment of Joanelle Colton.

Had the woman really abandoned her daughter—even if only emotionally—when she'd gotten pregnant? She vaguely knew the circumstances of Serena's pregnancy—a one-night stand gone wrong—but even if they hadn't been ideal, the joy and celebration of a baby was something to treasure. Thankfully Carson had seen the beauty and the joy and was clearly smitten with both Serena *and* her daughter.

It was unfair and unkind to judge, but Joanelle's treatment of her children was unfeeling and cold, and Darby fully understood why Finn had favored the side entrance to the house. Although her thoughts were uncharitable and judgmental, Finn said nothing against Joanelle, and instead pressed his sister to continue.

"Demi has been a good friend to me. The best friend. Which is why I've not wanted to share this."

"It's okay, Serena," Carson coaxed. "Tell them."

Serena gathered herself, coming to some sort of conclusion in her mind. "Demi took a pregnancy test the same week Bo was murdered. She believed she was pregnant with his child."

Demi Colton pregnant? With Bo's baby?

Everything stilled inside Darby, seeming to slow as she sat at the table with the others. Bo was going to be a father?

Somewhere inside, Darby figured she should be upset. She had never been lucky enough to start a family with Bo. Yet even as she thought it, she could only find relief that a child had never resulted from their union.

Bo had been careless with others' emotions and if Demi was that recently pregnant and Bo was still planning to marry Hayley, the situation only reinforced his negligence. He jumped from woman to woman, with little thought to feelings or, obviously, consequences.

"Is Demi pregnant?" Darby asked.

"I think so." Serena nodded. "But I don't know for sure. I know she bought the pregnancy test but I don't know the results."

"Even with that news, you don't think she killed Bo in a crime of passion, do you?" Finn spoke up, but his question to his sister had a gentleness that touched Darby's heart.

Whatever the situation—and certainly it was increasingly convoluted—Serena's certainty was evident. "Demi's a tough woman and she doesn't take lip from anyone. Bo was a charming man and I know she had a time when they first began dating that she was smitten with him. But she's also not one to pine for someone who couldn't be committed to her. Nor would she kill a man just because her feelings were hurt."

Darby was surprised by how much Serena's assessment matched her own impressions of Demi Colton. She was well aware people could act in any number of unexpected ways, but Finn's cousin didn't come off like a woman who'd give a man who scorned her the time of day, let alone put her personal freedom at risk. If she did carry Bo's baby, those risks would be even higher.

But if Demi wasn't the killer, what was Bo trying to say with the words he'd written in blood? Did he know his killer? Or had someone tried to frame Demi? So far, there was nothing to connect Demi to the murder of Michael Hayden. But Demi Colton was their only real suspect in Bo's murder—and the MO for both crimes was the same.

Grooms-to-be shot in the heart of the night of wedding festivities, a black cummerbund stuffed in their mouths.

So were they back to square one?

No suspects and an unnamed, unsuspected murderer still on the loose in Red Ridge. If they had no idea who the killer could be, then they were all at risk with no idea when he or she might strike again.

The distinct cry of a hungry baby filled the air, breaking the tension at the table and acting as an odd punctuation to the discussion of pregnancy tests.

"Someone's hungry." Serena smiled, her immediate concern for her child taking priority. She got up and quickly left the kitchen.

Darby watched her go and was surprised to again find herself thinking of children. What if she and Bo had found themselves pregnant? Her child would be a toddler by now, running around, likely chasing after Penny and adding a dimension to her life Darby had never really imagined.

She'd always wanted children, but in a sort of abstract way. A "someday" thought instead of something that was concrete and defined in her mind. Just like her love life, since her divorce she'd allowed the idea of children to remain an unformed thought instead of an active need. Was it self-preservation? A way of keeping her heart safe from wanting something she wasn't in a position to have?

Or was it another example of living her life in a haze, grinding through day by day instead of really living?

Carson and Finn continued their discussion of the case, talking through angles, lab results and strategy. Their discussion—and topics she didn't fully understand—gave Darby a new insight into what Finn did every day. She wasn't a big fan of crime shows and had never given much thought to police work. It was fascinating to realize how complex it was, as well as how scientific much of it had become. From the lab results on the bleach to their continued discussion of scientific reports on everything from the bullets that had killed the two men to the forensics details secured at each crime scene, Darby was amazed to realize how detailed Finn's job was.

And how small details were so key to police work.

She'd just gotten up to fix herself a fresh cup of coffee when Serena came out of the bedroom, Lora in her arms. Darby put down her mug, her attention immediately drawn by the baby. "She's beautiful."

A crop of dark hair covered her head like a cap and vivid brown eyes stared out of a sweet little face, alert and taking in her surroundings. Darby had never understood the term "cherubic" but one look at those cheeks and she had a good idea.

"Would you like to hold her?"

Serena was already handing over the baby before Darby could say otherwise and she suddenly had that sweet little bundle in her arms.

My, how long had it been since she'd held a baby? She'd babysat steadily throughout high school but since then she wasn't sure she could name a single time. She and Bo had never had children, nor had there been any babies born in his family during their marriage. Her own family was basically nonexistent, being an only child of an only child.

Which meant it had been over a decade since she'd felt that sweet heaviness in her arms or smelled that lovely scent that bespoke baby powder and innocence.

A shot of longing filled her and Darby couldn't quite hold back the streak of melancholy that had her thinking of her own empty future. When everything with the Groom Killer was over—and it needed to be over, she knew and believed that—she would go back to her home and her new business and her quiet life and all this would vanish. The companionship of others. The connectedness of spending time with others.

And Finn.

When this was all over, they'd each go back to their lives, like boxers returning to their separate corners.

Even with the beauty of new life in her arms, Darby couldn't deny just how bleak her future appeared.

Finn spent the remainder of the day actively avoiding the image of Darby Gage with a baby in her arms. He'd been excited to see his niece again,

Lora's arrival bringing a sense of familial bond he'd never fully known. He loved his siblings, but he had no idea what fierce protective instincts would be— or even could be—generated by the arrival of his sister's child.

One look at the baby and it was easy to understand why. She was so small and helpless, the natural urge was to protect. The fact she was family made that need infinitely stronger.

Yet the sight of Darby holding her had been off the charts. It made no sense, but he couldn't shake the image of the protective cradle of her arms securing Lora or the sweet cooing noises she made to his niece as she'd held her.

Which only made him imagine her with a baby of her own in her arms.

His baby.

The thought was so jarring he must have tensed up because Lotte barked beside him, the slightest whine edging her communication. She nudged his hand where he still held her favorite ball, her eyes full of question. He brushed her cheek with his crooked finger before tossing it once more.

The light touch and toss of her favorite rubber ball sent her off, barking all the way, down a long stretch of cleared path in the park by his apartment. The Red Ridge parks department had cleared the walking paths after the snowfall earlier that week and since the park was relatively empty he didn't mind using the areas for Lotte's exercise. The snow piles on either side of the path didn't deter her enthusiasm and she skittered toward the ball, tumbling over her quarry and landing with half her body in the snowbank.

Leaping up, she shook it off and raced back toward him, her tail wagging all the way.

This, he understood. Quiet moments with his dog, the one entity in the entire world he trusted more than himself. He didn't even trust Darby. Heck, up until the day before, he'd been half convinced she was a murderess.

But what about the other half?

All along he'd questioned if it was even possible she'd murdered anyone. His half-cocked plan to roust out a killer by pretending to be a couple was putting himself directly in the line of fire if she had been guilty. Yet it had never crossed his mind that Darby would hurt him or that he was in any sort of danger from her at all.

He tossed the ball again, watching it bounce down the path, with Lotte racing after it, and wondered when things had become so unexpected. Wondered even more when he had he begun thinking of Darby on such personal terms.

And where had that strange thought of children come from?

He'd accepted a long time ago that the family life that worked for so many wasn't meant for him. He'd gone into his marriage with good intentions and had realized fairly quickly that it wasn't for him. The commitment part he valued—even loved—but he'd never expected that the same level of fidelity extended to sharing his work or the requirements on his time that came with it.

Mary had quickly tired of the demands on his time and he'd tired of her frustration. He couldn't account for a bad day at work or the need to deal with a criminal problem over the weekend. And she was hardly at fault for wanting her husband around for family events or uninterrupted hours together. It had been the biggest revelation of his marriage. His calling to police work—one of the things that had attracted her to him—had been the same thing that had broken them apart.

He'd been divorced for five years and he still wasn't sure who he resented more for that fact.

As the thought lingered, Finn suddenly realized Lotte hadn't bounded back. He started down the path, surprised at how far the last toss had gone that he managed to send her around the bend in the path, only to stumble upon his sister Valeria.

And the boy she'd become inseparable from.

"Finn!" Valeria stared up from where she crouched, petting Lotte into a state of ecstasy.

"What are you doing here?" he asked before shifting his gaze to her companion. "Vincent."

"Sir."

Finn had to give Vincent credit. The youngest Gage held his ground, his hand already extended to say hello.

He shook the kid's hand, the grip firm. He was a solid young man, which made his stepmother's upset he was dating her youngest even more ridiculous. The kids were a couple. A seriously besotted one, if the looks the two passed each other—hot enough to melt an acre of snow—were any indication.

"What are you two doing here?" Finn asked. "Park's pretty deserted."

"Same as you. Getting a bit of fresh air." Valeria held his gaze, her stare direct, before her eyes dropped. "You're not gonna tell Mom, are you?"

"I'm not telling Joanelle anything." He owed his stepmother nothing and he wasn't going to be a hypocrite about that fact.

But he did love his baby sister. And he was determined to keep her safe, even if she wasn't thinking straight in the midst of her grand love affair.

"She's convinced something will happen to us because of this Groom Killer thing. As if." Valeria rolled her eyes.

"You don't think there's anything to worry about?" Finn shot a dark look at his sister before turning it on Vincent. "Because I have two dead bodies that say otherwise."

The eyes so like his own widened as Valeria reached for Vincent's hand. "You really think there's something to this? Something to worry about? Mom's such a drama queen about everything, I figured she was making it up."

Finn's assessment of Joanelle was less charitable, but the underlying message was the same. His father's second wife excelled at creating drama and seemed to enjoy living in a state of over-the-top panic about everything. She'd done it for so long, no one took her seriously when it truly counted.

"Valeria. Two men have been killed. Both were shot the night before their wedding. I'm not trying to start a full-on panic in Red Ridge, but I'm not going to sit here and blow smoke at you that nothing's wrong."

"We've been keeping a low profile. That's why we're here," Vincent said.

"If by 'low profile' you mean you don't know it's going around that you're planning a Christmas wedding?"

Once again, his sister's eyes grew round and Finn had the grim satisfaction that he still had his ear on the pulse of things in his town. The fact those "things" involved fear of a killer and raining on his baby sister's parade sucked.

Vincent spoke up and, once again, Finn had to give credit where it was due. The kid was respectful, but there was a distinct note of defiance in his words. "We are being careful, Chief Colton. But we're not going to live in fear, either."

"I don't want you to do that. But I do want you to be careful. Avoid making a splash of things. Stay closer to home. There are plenty of places to hide out on the ranch." Finn knew better than most, since he'd spent so much of his childhood hiding away.

"Mom's got all the ranch hands looking out for us."

"Come on, Val. Put all your sweetness and charm to good use. The hands love you way more than Joanelle. They'll go to bat for you."

"Cal is always winking at me and knows I always save the biggest pieces of cornbread for him on the days we make chili."

"There ya go." Finn pulled his sister close for a hug. "Just be careful."

She squeezed him back and it struck Finn that somewhere along the way his baby sister had grown up. She was still young—nineteen fell clearly in the innocent column—but she wasn't a child any longer.

And if she had her way, she'd be married before the year was out.

One sister had a baby. Another was getting married.

How was it that the people in his life had moved on and all he seemed to do was stand still?

His visits with his sisters still weighed heavy on Finn's mind when he climbed the front steps of Darby's house. He'd planned an elaborate evening out—something flashy and showy for anyone watching—and he tried to keep his focus on his plans instead of the weird thoughts that kept intruding. Yet, try as he might, he hadn't shaken the dark cloud that had accompanied him all day.

He should be happy for his sisters. Serena was a new mother and soon-to-be-wife, happy and as serene as her name implied. Valeria, while headstrong and a bit foolish with it, was in love with Vincent. After their meeting in the park, he'd dropped Lotte back at his condo and taken the lovebirds to lunch, pleased to see how innately kind and genuine they were to each other. From Vincent's quiet request to their waitress for a refill on Valeria's iced tea to his sister's excitement over Vincent's recent accomplishment in one of his college courses, they loved each other. More than that, they had a mutual care for each other that was tangible and the compatibility to make a real go of marriage.

The porch light on Darby's front door had been replaced and he stood in its warm glow as he knocked. She opened the door, gesturing him in out of the cold.

"Hurry up, get in here. It's freezing." She waved him in, a thick set of curlers covering her head. She had a blanket wrapped around her shoulders and he could see a silky robe peeking out from underneath. That flash of red silk had his body going on high alert, but it was the match of fuzzy shark slippers capping off those gorgeous legs that sent him over the edge.

Oblivious to his anguish, she shook her head as she closed the door. "What am I saying? It's South Dakota in February. Of course it's freezing. But it's extra cold tonight. Which is why I'm running so late. I couldn't get Penny and Lucy out of the backyard as they romped their way through the snow."

Alert to their names, Penny and Lucy raced over

to greet him. Their tails wagged in unison as he lavished praise on them, their pleasure in seeing him going a long way toward assuaging the roiling thoughts that had accompanied him to Darby's.

"I'm almost done. Promise!"

Finn watched Darby race off down the hall before refocusing on Penny and Lucy. And didn't miss the speculative look in Penny's eyes as she stared up at him.

"Don't go getting any ideas."

Penny just wagged her tail and kept up that close scrutiny. He was tempted to argue with her but recognized his sanity was on the line. So he maintained the steady combing of his fingers through her fur and ignored the thought that even the dog had a better sense of how he needed to live his life than he did.

Rather than stand in the entryway, Finn led the dogs over to the couch. With one eye on them and another on the room, he could see the progress Darby had made. The furniture and carpet were still threadbare, but she'd strategically placed a few blankets over the worst parts of the furniture and had added some colorful throw pillows to fool the eye. She'd spruced up the place and she'd done it with light and color.

Maybe it was that thought, still so vivid in his mind, that had him turning at the sound of her heels on the hallway floor. Or maybe it was the strange melancholy that had accompanied him all day. Or maybe it was simply being in the presence of a beautiful woman.

Finn didn't know and as he caught sight of Darby, clad in a colorful sheath that draped her body like a second skin, he didn't care. He wanted her. And in that moment, she was all he could see.

Before he could even process the move as rational thought, he was off the couch and headed for her, pulling her close and into his arms, his mouth on a determined path to hers. He caught the slightest sense of surprise in the widened O of her mouth and the light squeak of her voice as she said his name.

And then there were no words.

Or questions.

Or nagging thoughts that seemed to have no place to land.

There was only Darby. Sweet and sexy Darby. The woman did things to his good sense and he was fast losing his ability to keep his head around her.

But as her lips met his, her arms wrapping around his neck in warm welcome and acceptance, Finn didn't care. He was lost to her and the kiss.

Chapter 11

Hot. Liquid. Needy.

A run of abstract thoughts crisscrossed Darby's mind as she fought to keep up with Finn. Or fought to keep up with his mouth, which was more accurate at the moment.

Want—elemental and desperate—coursed through her body, tightening her nerve endings and making her skin feel as if it were on fire. Everywhere he touched seemed to explode with feeling. Every place his fingers settled lit from within.

She wasn't sure what had happened. One moment she was still fussing over a twisted curl that wouldn't lay straight and the next she was wrapped up in Finn's arms, being positively devoured. Thoughts of that errant curl fled as she got into the moment. After all, how often did a gal get devoured by a big, handsome man in her own living room?

And, oh, it was glorious.

Large hands covered her hips, pulling her flush against the hard planes of his body while his mouth maintained a steady pressure on hers, dragging sensation after sensation from somewhere inside her she hadn't even realized existed. Some deep well of feeling and emotion and need she'd never known—or even comprehended—was there.

Yet Finn knew. And he'd unerringly found it, with his kind eyes and his sexy lips and his determination to give his town peace and calm once more.

She'd bought the brightly colored dress on sale earlier in the week and even at a steep discount, she'd berated herself a bit for the extravagance. Now, feeling his hands over the thin fabric, Darby knew it had been the right call.

His mouth slanted over hers once more, greedily, and she amended her thought.

The *exact* right call.

"Finn?" His name bubbled to her lips, her questions in all she didn't say.

"Darby." He pressed his forehead to hers, a smile forming on his lips. "Did I mention you look beautiful tonight?"

"I'm pretty good at reading between the lines."

"So you don't have to, let me say it again. You look beautiful."

"Thank you." She nipped his lips for one more kiss before stepping back. Before stepping away from a man who could not only make her lose all rational thought but, if he only asked her, could likely convince her to stay in all evening. When the image of making love with him accompanied the mental invitation, she took another step back, putting solid distance between them.

"Let me just put down food for Penny and Lucy, and we can get going." She puttered nervously into the kitchen, her heels tapping against the linoleum as she crossed back and forth from the sink to the pantry for their water and food.

What had she been thinking?

More, what had he been thinking?

This was platonic. They'd had their moments, of course. Those fleeting kisses meant to fool anyone watching them from afar.

But this? In her house? It was so fierce. So *needy*.

Darby fought the small shudder that raced down her spine and finished preparing dinner for the dogs.

With that small moment of distraction over, there was no reason to remain in the kitchen. As she tap-tap-tapped her way toward the living room, she prayed for strength.

Strength to resist the most amazing man she'd ever met.

Finn pulled Darby's chair out and fought the urge to tug at one of the loose curls that covered her head.

They'd kept up a veneer of vague conversation in the car—their earlier visit with baby Lora had provided an excellent subject to distract them both— and he'd grasped at the conversational lifeline like a drowning man.

The chatter had kept them both from discussing what had happened in her living room.

What *had* happened in her living room? And when had he lost his focus?

He was running a murder investigation—the worst that had ever hit Red Ridge. He had no business stealing kisses from a woman who was only helping him do his job. More than that, he had no business wanting kisses from her.

"Smile, Finn."

"Hmm?" He still stood beside Darby's chair and it was only her pointed gaze and the lift of her hand to his cheek that had him refocusing.

"Smile, darling. We're the focus of the entire restaurant. It would hardly do to make people think I was dating a grizzly bear."

The grizzly bear comment was a funny one and he suddenly had the image of sprouting hair all over his body and roaring down Main Street. With a smile, he lifted her hand and pressed his lips to her palm. Whether it was the indulgent smile she gave him or the heat from earlier he couldn't quite shake, Finn wasn't sure, but he used his position to run his tongue lightly along the seam of her palm.

Indulgence shifted to desire in a heartbeat as her eyes went a smoky gray.

"Finn?" Her voice was as smoky as her eyes and as equally powerful.

Again, she used only his name. And again, that same impulse that pushed him earlier had him in its thrall once more, rushing through his body and forcing his ardor higher and higher.

Satisfied he'd made his point—and well aware he'd tempted himself equally—he squeezed her hand before gently settling it back on the table and taking his seat.

Their waiter, who'd hovered a discreet distance away, rushed over, menus in hand. The restaurant specialized in seafood, crafting dishes each night that could be inspired from anywhere. From the Pacific Rim to West Coast cuisine to the Mediterranean, the chef was whimsical and eclectic and had created a place with good buzz and consistently satisfied patrons.

Although he saw relatively few young couples—the lifeblood of a hip, happening place—Finn was pleased to see the restaurant was full. Maybe this was one place people still felt comfortable coming out for the night.

"Welcome to Pesce this evening," their waiter gushed. "We're so glad to have you."

The specials were duly noted and drink orders taken—wine for Darby and another one of the endless club sodas for Finn—before their waiter disappeared once more.

"I've heard good things about this place but haven't been here. Red Ridge has certainly improved its restaurant game in the past few years."

As conversation topics went, it was an easy one, empty of land mines. But Finn realized it gave him an opening he'd been curious about.

"Red Ridge is small, but between Colton Energy and Harrington Incorporated, there's enough business to keep things hopping in town. And enough people on their payroll who can afford to eat like this all the time."

"I suppose." She nodded and sipped the wine the waiter had set down. "It's progress and it's good to see. But it does make me think of what it was like when I was a kid. I couldn't have imagined a place like this, let alone expected to dine in one."

"You didn't go out much?"

"I had a single mother on a limited income. A place like this was so far out of our reach it was laughable."

Darby's gaze was distracted by the large mosaic mural of a mermaid hovering over undersea treasure. He waited until she returned her attention from the wall to him. "You don't say much about her."

"My mother?" When he only nodded, she continued. "There's not much to say. My father ran out when I was young and she blamed him and me until the day she died."

"When was that?"

"About five years ago. She worked two jobs until the very end and was found crumpled up against the Dumpster behind the diner."

Darby's words formed an image and Finn realized he remembered that day.

Vividly.

The small, slender woman found victim of a heart attack out behind the diner. She'd taken a large bag of trash outside and hadn't come back. It had only been when another waitress had gone out for a coffee break that she'd found Darby's mother.

"I'm sorry."

Darby's blue gaze remained direct and devoid of tears. "I am, too. I'm sorry she saw the world through such disillusioned eyes. And I'm sorry that her life ended as miserably as the rest of it. But I'm not sorry she's gone."

"That's understandable."

"Is it? She was my mother."

"Is it fair I can barely think of my stepmother without adding a mental string of curses to go with it?" Finn knew their situations weren't the same but also knew they weren't entirely different, either. Joanelle's behavior—and her inability to love a small boy—belonged solely to her.

On some level, he'd always known that. But after seeing how Carson had bonded with his niece, Lora—a child he would adopt through marriage—

Finn knew Joanelle's rejection had been that of a bitter and cold woman.

Carson had accepted Lora as his own and would never treat her as less than because she wasn't biologically his. It was a gift they'd both share—and a love that would grow through the years.

"She's earned every one of those curses, Finn. She emotionally mistreated a little boy. That's terrible."

Darby's ready defense touched him, but it also reinforced the point he was making to her. "And what your mother did was any better?"

"No." She shook her head. "I suppose not."

He reached out and ran the tip of his finger over her cheek, catching a lone tear that had finally surfaced. "I'm sorry to make you cry."

"It's okay. I've had a long time to come to grips with how I feel. Most of the time I'm okay with it. Every now and again, I'm not."

"I feel the same. Most days I don't give Joanelle Colton a second thought. For some reason, she's been front and center in my thoughts lately."

The waiter came back and took their orders, the small reprieve enough to give Finn an opportunity to collect his thoughts. Once they'd ordered, he picked up where they'd left off. "I saw my younger sister Valeria today."

He filled Darby in on the impromptu visit with Valeria and Vincent and their naive dismissal of the danger in town from the Groom Killer.

Darby's already pale skin grew even more so in

the muted lighting of the restaurant. "You don't think someone would hurt them? They're just children."

"I don't know what to think. And since we can't seem to get a handle on motive or anyone who might be a suspect aside from my cousin Demi, I told them to be careful."

"Do you think they'll listen?"

Finn thought about the subtle defiance in both of them to be together, but was also reminded of how innately kind they were to each other. There was something genuine and loving between them. He had to hope that underlying concern would override any youthful impulses to tempt fate.

"I think so. I'll keep an eye on them. The staff will watch out for them, too."

"Youth." She smiled before shrugging her shoulders. "I know it's been a decade since I was that age, but it feels like a lifetime ago."

"Would you go back if you could?"

"Never." A warm smile filled her face and, once again, he was caught. Captured by whatever it was that lit her up from the inside. "You?"

"Go back to being that young and dumb? No way."

She reached over and took his hand, lifting her glass with the other. "To adulting. Some days it stinks but at other times it's not so bad."

"Like now?" he asked, daring to hope she agreed.

"Like right now."

He clinked his club soda against her wineglass, the light tinkle rising between them. "To adulting."

* * *

The muted lights of the restaurant didn't hide a clear picture of the diners inside. Table after table filled with people having a good time and enjoying their expensive meals.

Expensive and wasteful.

Who spent that kind of money on something you could pull out of the river yourself? It was indulgent. And greedy.

And hurtful.

Once again, the chief was parading around town with that woman. She pranced beside him, a colorful whore in the dress that wrapped tight around her body and the hair teased out to draw a man's eye.

She'd believed the chief above such trickery.

Yet here he was, kissing the woman's hand and holding the chair for her and staring at her as if she'd walked out of a movie set. Actresses were whores, too, which only reinforced the point.

It was illusion.

Yet the chief's adoration looked very, very real.

Oh, how it burned.

She'd watched and waited…and for what? To be ignored and discarded in favor of some scantily dressed woman who lured him to her bed? Did the chief not understand? Had he not received her gifts?

An image of the fragile glass still nestled in its box in her closet drifted through her thoughts. She'd meant to save it for Valentine's Day. That was less than a week away. Could she wait? Or did she need to send it sooner?

Thoughts drifting as she sat in her car and stared into the restaurant, she imagined that glass heart beating in its box. Beating with love for her.

Beating the way her own heart pulsed and throbbed for Chief Colton.

If he only knew.

They had a connection. And once he understood that, the rest would fade away. The whore in the colorful dress meant nothing. Would mean nothing.

She'd make sure of it.

Darby snuggled deeper into her coat as she and Finn walked to the SUV. The air was cold and clear, the stars shining above them like glittering diamonds. It was cliché, but as she watched them shine from afar, she knew it was the only description that fit.

Red Ridge *had* grown since she was a child. It had prosperous businesses and a population of busy, industrious people. But it was still small enough to feel isolated and free, somehow. The Black Hills National Forest provided the perfect backdrop—wilderness for miles on end—and the Spearfish River added another natural border.

She'd not traveled much in her life, but she'd been to Seattle and Portland and had liked both. Had even enjoyed her time away. But neither had felt like home. The steady stream of strangers who had passed her on the street had seemed foreign and, while not threatening, just *separate* from her. The thought of trying to make a life in that throng of humanity hadn't appealed and she'd welcomed the flights home with open arms.

Maybe she wasn't so different from her mother, but she liked to think she'd channeled her needs and wants a bit differently. She stayed in Red Ridge because she chose to, not because she lacked options.

Which might have been laughable when she'd stared down a mountain of debt and an uncertain future. Yet even then, she'd been focused on doing right. By Bo. By Penny. And by the business that had meant so much to her ex-husband.

Never once had she felt trapped.

Without warning, the thought shifted and strangled, her adrenaline spiking as her gaze shifted toward the dark night that surrounded the parking lot. She reached for Finn's hand, so close to her own, and came to a tottering halt on her heels.

"What is it?"

"Someone's out there."

She kept her voice low, turning into his body to keep up the charade of closeness and to shroud her voice in the clear night air. Rising on her tiptoes, she pressed her lips to his ear. "Out there. I can feel it. Someone's watching us."

Finn's demeanor shifted immediately, his arm tightening around her waist as he held her in place. "Do you see anyone?"

"No. I feel them, but that's the best I can tell you."

He wrapped himself around her, shielding the majority of her body with his own. "I want you to get in the car and call for backup."

"Where are you going?"

"To check it out."

"What?" The screech edged out the whisper in her voice as she tried to slow his steady march toward the SUV. "You can't go out there by yourself."

"I have a gun."

"Maybe they do, too."

"It might be nothing."

"And it might be something." She tried standing still, pressing the back of her forearm against his flat, muscled stomach, but he continued to move them forward.

"In the car, Darby. Now."

Arguing with him was impossible and she almost wished she hadn't said anything when the throb of an engine roared to life.

"In the car. Now!" Finn had the door open and was shoving her inside, before slamming the door after her. She saw the glint of his gun reflected in the overhead lights of the parking lot and watched him race off.

What had she done?

Scrambling for her cell phone, she called in the situation, speaking as calmly as possible with her heart throbbing in her throat. She gave their location and the details as best as she could, stressing over and over that the chief needed backup.

"Where are you, ma'am?" The disembodied voice echoed through the phone, the urgency there suddenly penetrating her fear for Finn.

"I'm in the chief's car."

"Is a dangerous threat nearby?"

Threat?

Darby had ignored the parking lot, so focused on Finn's retreating back and on calling for help. Now she looked around. The parking lot was well lit, but the dark night beyond seemed to close in around that light, leaving lurking shadows at the edges.

"Ma'am?"

"Yes."

"Is there an immediate danger to you?"

"I don't think so," she said, her voice sounding foreign to her own ears.

"I've dispatched backup but I need you to stay on the line with me."

"Okay."

"My name is Frank. Frank Lanelli. I need you to stay where you are and lock your doors."

Darby fumbled the lock switch, the snick a small comfort in the creeping quiet.

"Did you do that?"

Frank's voice was kind yet firm and she found herself nodding, even if he couldn't see her. "Yes."

"Our chief's a fine man. I've got backup on the way. You can probably hear the sirens already."

At Frank's words, the distinct notes that screamed emergency came in muted through the SUV's windows. "Yes, I hear them."

"Now, who am I talking to?"

"Darby, sir. Darby Gage."

"Why, Ms. Gage, I had a feeling it was you." Frank's kind voice calmed her and she listened to him rattle on, securing information as he went.

"I heard you and the chief were headed out for the evening. Small towns and all. Took you to Pesce, did he?"

"Yes."

"Our chief is a sucker for a good meal and a pretty lady."

Darby smiled in spite of herself and the situation. "Frank, are you flirting with me?"

"Only to stay young. I'm a happily married man with five children of my own."

"Your wife is a lucky woman."

"She's the love of my life, Ms. Darby. Don't think there's a day that goes by that I don't know I'm the lucky one."

As she sat there huddled in the SUV, the flash of red and blue growing clearer through the front window, Darby figured Mrs. Lanelli was one lucky woman. And she was deeply grateful to her for sharing her husband for the evening to calm a frightened woman shivering inside an empty SUV.

One who waited for confirmation that the man who protected her would come back safe.

Chapter 12

Finn raced over the edge of the parking lot, heading as far into the woods as he dared before retreating and retracing his steps. He missed Lotte's keen nose and ears desperately, but did his best to keep watch for any telltale signs.

Footprints. Creaking branches as someone stepped. Any hint at all of movement.

Over and over again, he entered the shadows, then retreated, seeking some sense of who was there. Or who had been there. When nothing materialized, he backtracked to the parking lot, the flash of red and blue lights warring with the fluorescent overheads.

He'd hated leaving Darby but couldn't risk losing his potential quarry by waiting in the SUV. The order to lock the doors and call for backup had seemed like a good idea at the time, but as he thought about it now, he felt as if he'd let her down somehow, leaving her to fend for herself.

Without warning, Mary's voice came back to him, one of their last great fights drifting through his mind.

You leave me day in and day out, that damned job of yours more important than our marriage. More important than me!

You knew what I did when we got married. I have a responsibility. A duty.

You have a duty to me. To us.

Anger had filled her words, yet unlike their prior fights, he'd heard something hollow and empty echo beneath.

I know what my duties are. Devotion to my job doesn't make me a bad husband.

No. She'd shaken her head. *But my resentment of it all makes me a bad wife. Which is why I want out.*

Out?

He'd wanted to rant and rail at her in that moment. On some level he'd wanted to beg her to stay. To fight for their marriage. To fight for him.

That's what a good husband would have done.

But he'd only nodded and said okay. Agreed that he wanted out, too.

The life they'd built had dissolved quickly, their divorce making it well and truly final six months later. He should have been upset about that. Even now, five years later, he wondered at the lack of anger that had accompanied the dissolution of his marriage. Had he given up?

Or had he simply accepted that he wasn't fit for marriage? For the requirements of being devoted and committed to another person.

Two cruisers were parked next to his vehicle and he could see Darby in the front seat of the SUV, her door slightly open as she spoke with Elle Gage. Elle's bulldog partner, Merlin, stood by her side, sniffing around the SUV as his rookie officer kept Darby company. Merlin always looked a bit funny next to the larger dogs of the K-9 squad, but his smushed-up face hid a warrior. Finn had seen the dog sniff out any number of objects, beating the rest of the K-9 squad in nearly any trial involving retrieval by scent alone. His persistence had even turned up a small fragment of cloth six months ago that had led them to a robbery suspect.

He loped over to the vehicles, his cousin Brayden already out of his cruiser and scanning the parking lot.

Brayden started in the moment Finn was within earshot. "You always take off unaccompanied by backup, Chief?"

"I had a chance and I took it."

"You went in blind and you know it. Why didn't you wait?"

"There wasn't any time to wait. Darby sensed she was being watched."

Brayden shook his head but refrained from saying anything else. Finn knew he was right. He knew even better that haring off alone was the fast track to unexpected injury or even death. Every cop entered their job knowing they put their life on the line, but following protocol upped the odds of personal safety.

He'd disregarded all of it to chase after a faceless nemesis Darby hadn't even seen.

But, damn it, she'd felt something. He didn't take that sort of certainty—or sheer gut instinct—lightly.

Brayden handed him one of the heavy lined jackets they all kept in their SUVs and Finn pulled it on over his coat. The chase had heated him up but the frosty air was quickly clawing at the line of sweat at the back of his neck. Darby was already bundled in one from Elle's cruiser, her gaze on him even as she remained by his vehicle.

"Not a stellar way to end a hot date," Brayden teased him. "But sure is a way to get some attention."

Several diners at Pesce had paused at their cars to watch the proceedings. He could also see several members of the staff hanging around the back entrance, presumably on break, their attention laser focused on the parking lot.

Since attention was the very thing he was going for, Finn decided to use it to his advantage. If it also assuaged the trembling in his limbs and the raw, edgy fear that coated his stomach, then so be it. He crossed the remaining distance to Darby, pulled her from the SUV and into his arms. He pressed his lips to hers in a move meant to offer comfort and reassurance.

But as her sweet lips met his, warm, open and welcoming, Finn knew the truth.

She provided the comfort. He was simply using the opportunity to bask in the warmth.

"Take us through it again, if you don't mind?" Carson asked the question, but from the grim look on Finn's face, she could tell he was as eager for the answer as his top detective.

Darby sighed and wrapped her hands around the mug of tea Serena had pressed on her shortly after she and Finn had arrived at the ranch. "We were walking out of the restaurant and talking casually. Without warning, all I could feel were eyes on me."

As silly as it sounded, even now Darby could feel the way her blood had run cold. Her heart had leaped, her pulse ringing in her ears, and the only rational thought in her head had been to run for safety.

Only, Finn had done the running.

Straight into danger.

"You're staying here tonight." Serena walked into the kitchen with a heap of pillows and blankets in her arms. "I don't want any arguing."

The order had Darby leaping up. "Thank you. Really, thank you, but I can't leave the dogs all night. Penny and Lucy are good but they can't go that long."

Finn laid a hand on her arm. "I'll go get them. I'll get Lotte, too."

"I'll go with you." Carson was already up and out of his chair. "No time like the present."

She'd barely blinked and both men were gone. Which left her and Finn's sister all alone in the kitchen, the muted lighting and quiet calm in direct opposition to her roiling thoughts about Finn Colton.

"My brother is a force of nature." Serena smiled before crossing to the stove to make her own cup of tea.

"He certainly is sure of himself."

"Always."

While she had no interest in spying on him, this glimpse into the life of Finn Colton was too juicy to resist. "He's always been like this?"

"As long as I can remember. He's calm and capable, logical, and slow to anger. It drives my mother crazy."

"Your mother is Joanelle?"

"The one and only." Serena rolled her eyes. "She's a difficult woman on the best of days. On the worst… well, let's just say Finn got more than his fair share of those."

"It's a shame."

Serena nodded. "More than I can say."

Silence descended between them. While she had her definite opinions of Finn's stepmother, the woman was also Serena's mother. She, of all people, knew how complicated mother-daughter relationships could be and figured silence was best.

"You care for my brother."

"I—" Darby broke off, not sure what to say.

Serena was a kind woman but Darby hardly felt comfortable enough to spill her guts about her feelings toward Finn.

Did she actually have feelings about Finn?

Even as the question drifted through her thoughts, Darby knew the truth. Despite her best intentions—and every rational thought she possessed—she had come to care for him.

She was attracted to him, but attraction was the easy part. He was good-looking and competent, with a finely tuned moral compass and a need to protect the town. What wasn't there to be attracted to?

But to care for him? That was a different level of commitment entirely. That suggested sticking around and spending time with each other after the Groom Killer was caught. It was something she wanted, but did Finn?

Whether he did or not, it hardly changed her feelings. On a soft exhale, she looked Serena in the eye. "I guess I do."

"He cares for you, too."

"I don't think—"

Serena cut her off this time, laying a soft hand over hers. "Don't think. That's usually where we end up going wrong. I know I did with Carson and that was nearly the end of our relationship. Fortunately he had enough faith for the both of us."

Darby latched on to the lifeline and hung on for

all she was worth. "You and Carson had a tough go of it?"

"He's a Gage and I'm a Colton. That's usually more than enough to cause problems. But as someone who married into the family, I'm sure you already knew that."

Although Darby knew of the Colton-Gage feud—most people who'd spent any time in Red Ridge knew of the history between the two families—Bo had seemed somewhat oblivious to it. On the few occasions he'd mentioned it, it was usually laced with humor at how old-fashioned and "Wild Wild West" his family loved to act about their century-long feud with the family across town.

"Is this family feud really that big an issue?"

"For the older generation it is. That includes my difficult mother," Serena added. "And since my father follows along with anything she says, it was a problem for him when Carson and I got together."

"What else caused problems?"

"I'd just had a baby. That was quite a hurdle."

It was Darby's turn to offer comfort and she laid her free hand over Serena's. "It looks like Carson has more than embraced his role as father."

"That he has." Whatever shadows clouded Serena's gaze lifted immediately. "He really has. He's a wonderful father. Lora and I are so lucky."

"I think Carson's pretty lucky, too."

Serena smiled at that, her dark brown eyes warm and inviting. "I suppose he is."

Their conversation shifted and Darby was grateful that Serena didn't push again on the subject of her feelings for Finn. They were enough of a surprise to her as it was. Instead they seemed to find an endless series of topics from the baby to Darby's K-9 business until they finally ventured back around to the Groom Killer.

"It's a scary time in Red Ridge. I know we have crime now and again. People seem to find ways to do bad things no matter where they're put. But a killer?" Serena shivered. "It's hard to imagine."

Darby was prevented from saying anything when headlights reflected through the window and slamming car doors echoed from outside.

Something settled inside her when Carson came in the door, a trail of dogs in his wake, followed by Finn in the rear. The events of the night had unsettled her more than she'd realized and it was humbling to realize how good it was to see Finn back, safe and sound.

He carried a small gym bag she recognized from her bedroom closet as well as her pillow. "I wasn't sure if you were one of those people who preferred their own pillow so I grabbed it along with your toothbrush and the PJs on the edge of the bed."

"Thank you."

"It's the least I could do." He set the bag near the couch and put her pillow down, as well. "I'm sorry you're stuck with me tonight."

"It's okay." Carson had disappeared with Serena

and it was just her and Finn and their combined pack, who'd positioned themselves in an arc around the front door. "More than okay, actually. I can't say I'm anxious to spend the night by myself."

"Then it's good we're here. The Colton Ranch is pretty well fortified, but we'll batten down the hatches, anyway. Nothing wrong with settling in for the night."

"Thank you."

He pulled her close, wrapping her in his arms before his chin pressed down on the top of her head.

On a hard exhale she hadn't even realized she was holding in, all the fear she'd bottled up since the parking lot came tumbling out. "I was so afraid. So scared that you'd run into the killer. Or worse, that they were waiting for you."

"It's okay."

"No, it's not. What's out there, lurking and waiting? Who is so determined to kill and to ruin the lives of others?"

"I wish I knew."

"It's sick and twisted. And evil." Another shudder ripped through her and Darby fought the creeping sense of hopelessness that threatened to swamp her.

"We're going to figure this out. I know we are."

She wanted to believe him. With all her heart she wanted to believe Finn could hunt down a killer and put him away.

But what happened if he couldn't?

That question still haunted her twenty minutes

later as she settled into the couch. Serena had apologized profusely that there wasn't a spare room in her wing of the mansion now that Lora was here, but both Darby and Finn had brushed it off. He'd had no desire to move in to the main house and she could easily live with sleeping on the oversize sectional for the night.

Finn was still huddled with Carson at the kitchen table, their voices low as they worked through various scenarios over coffee.

She listened to the murmur of their voices and took solace in their presence even as she drifted toward sleep. Images filled her twilight moments, thoughts of a killer invading her mind. Bo, a hole in the center of his chest, reaching out to her from a shallow grave in the backyard, his arms stretching toward her. Penny racing around the hole, barking. But when Darby finally walked over, all she saw was Finn in the shallow grave, a gunshot wound spreading blood over his chest.

She came wide-awake on a harsh breath, narrowly holding back the scream that crawled up her throat.

Dropping back against the pillow, Darby fought to catch her breath. The image of Finn, his chest bloody, refused to leave her mind, lingering like a dark stain in her thoughts. A small whine echoed from beneath her and she turned onto her side to find Penny beside the couch, her gaze focused on hers.

"Hey, sweet girl. It's okay." She nearly reached

out but held back, aware the dog wasn't keen on her ministrations.

Penny whined once more before coming to a fully seated position and resting her head beside Darby on the couch. She reached out and pressed a hand to Penny's head, her fingers sinking into the thick fur. Penny edged forward a few steps, coming closer for Darby's touch, before burying her nose against her side.

The fear that had pulled her from sleep faded slowly, the soft, soothing strokes on Penny's head going a long way toward calming her. But it was Penny's light sigh several long minutes later that fully pushed the toxic images from Darby's mind. Seemingly satisfied she'd done her job, Penny jumped up onto the couch and curled up at her feet.

With the steady weight of her dog settled in against her, Darby allowed herself to drift off once more. Only this time, there were no dreams waiting for her.

Just the soft, gentle weight of Penny's body pressed against hers.

Finn rolled over on the thick air mattress to find a large, furry body sprawled next to him. The sprawl was accompanied by a steady snore and he fought the urge to poke Lotte until she cleared the mattress. He didn't allow her into his bed, having trained her to use the large, fluffy dog bed in the corner of his room, but the unusual setting and the presence of

Penny and Lucy had clearly tossed all his good training out the window.

He scanned the living room, his suspicions confirmed when he saw Penny curled up at Darby's feet and Lucy a few feet beyond, also curled up on his sister's well-stuffed and oversize sectional.

"I think this place has gone to the dogs," Darby whispered before punctuating the comment with a throaty giggle.

"My sister is going to kill me."

"I'll vacuum once we're all up. No one will know we were here."

Finn couldn't resist teasing her. "The Queen of Clean rides to the rescue once again."

"I told you my mother thought cleanliness was next to godliness. When I'm done with the couch and the carpet, you'll never know there was a dog in here, let alone three."

"I won't stand in your way."

"In the meantime, since we're here, the least we can do is be good houseguests. I'll put the coffee on."

Finn glanced at his wrist, his watch flashing back the time. "It's 6:00 a.m."

"Which means it's time to get up."

She was already off the couch, navigating the small space between it and his air mattress. She'd nearly cleared the space when inspiration hit and he reached for her ankle, tugging her close. The move was enough to unbalance her and he used her tumble to his advantage, pulling her neatly into his arms.

Semineatly, he had to admit as he underestimated the landing. He'd kept her from falling onto Lotte but caught the full weight of her body. She was small, but falling as a dead weight still hit him square in the stomach.

"Finn!" She breathed his name and struggled out of his arms. "What are you doing?"

"Kissing you good morning."

"It's—"

He cut her off, making his point more than clear as their lips met. She might have gotten off the couch with a distinct goal, but he was pleased to see she could be swayed to a new activity. Her body was still warm with sleep and he pulled her close, nestling her body against his. The desire that had been touched off the night before in her living room when he'd picked her up flared to life once again.

Had it ever really died?

As his hands roamed over her body, Finn knew it hadn't. And based on the light, eager moans that emanated from the back of her throat, he knew it hadn't for Darby, either.

His fingers drifted over her stomach, finding flesh where her pajama top rode up over her yoga pants. He teased the tip of his finger over the seam of her pants and was rewarded by a light shiver.

"Cold?" he whispered against her lips.

"Not at all."

As if to prove it—or, knowing Darby, not to be outdone—her hands drifted over his hips before moving up to mold to the lines of his chest. He normally slept naked, but in deference to a house full of people, he'd left a T-shirt on with a pair of K-9 team sweatpants that had grown threadbare from so many washes. The heat of her palms warmed him through the cotton T-shirt, but it was the slim body pressed against his that had his eyes crossing.

His erection strained against the thin material of his sweatpants, pressing into the slim vee of her thighs, and Finn suddenly wasn't sure of his own sanity. What had possessed him to start something with Darby this morning?

And when had he begun channeling his inner fifteen-year-old, convinced he'd die if they stopped?

Cosmic proof that he was wrong came in the form of his baby niece's early morning cries, breaking the thin threads that had woven around them both this morning.

"That's a baby crying," Darby said before pressing one last kiss to his lips. "Which means the house will be up shortly."

He reached for her, desperate for one more kiss, but she'd already backed away, stumbling over the edge of the air mattress before righting herself as she padded out of the living room. He was fool enough to enjoy watching her go, the sweet curve of her butt shown to perfection in the black yoga pants that sculpted her curves.

Lotte eyed him from the edge of the mattress where she'd moved at some point during his morn-

ing romp with Darby and even now wore a speculative gaze.

"I suppose you want to go out?"

Her eyebrows shot up, but her gaze remained
steady.

"Do I take that to mean you're irritated we woke
you? You were sleeping like the dead."

When Lucy trotted over, followed by Penny, seat-
ing themselves beside the mattress, he took in their
steady attention. "I'll be. I guess there were a few
more in this house watching the show this morning."

Since his witnesses would never tell, he figured he
and Darby could continue to fly under the radar. That
was assuming his niece kept his sister busy enough
for him to get the dogs out and to take a quick—and
cold—shower.

Satisfied his witnesses were well occupied outside, romping through the light coating of snow that
had come overnight, Finn headed off to the bathroom. He made his escape without anyone seeing
him and was in the shower in moments. But try as
he might, even standing underneath a shower as cold
as the snow outside, he couldn't quite get his body
to calm.

Nor could he shake the heated images of what
might have happened if his family hadn't been
twenty feet down the hall.

More than a few days had begun with the vague
thought that coffee was the elixir of life, but Darby

had to admit to herself that the almighty coffee bean had nothing on the glorious, mind-blowing powers of Finn Colton.

Oh, the man was fine. And waking up to slow kisses and lazy caresses over her body was something she could definitely get used to.

Since she needed to battle such fanciful thoughts, Darby threw herself into playing the perfect houseguest and had coffee on and muffins baking when Serena, Carson and Lora came into the kitchen a half hour later. The baby's sweet smile reached out and wrapped around her heart and Darby couldn't resist smiling in return.

Only to get an even bigger smile and a giggle to sweeten the deal.

"She loves the morning." Serena stopped by the stove and peeked in the front glass at the muffins even now rising with the heat. "You made breakfast."

"It's just muffins."

Serena turned to her, tears shining in her eyes. "You baked something."

Carson reached around Serena, easily plucking the baby from her grip and cuddling Lora into one elbow while comforting Serena with his free arm. "I promise you we'll get past eating all our meals as takeout soon. Lora needs your attention much more now than I need a home-cooked meal. And since my cooking is the equivalent of eating rocks, you really want me keeping up my dialing skills."

"But I don't cook anymore." Serena sniffed. "I had no idea it would upset me so badly."

Darby bent to take the muffins out. She briefly toyed with apologizing but decided that new-mom hormones had way more to do with Serena's reaction than any real upset over breakfast. Her faith was rewarded a few minutes later as they all sat around the table, digging in to the muffins.

"I'm so sorry." Serena waved the freshly buttered half of her muffin. "I'm not sure why I reacted like I did. These are amazing and I'm happy you made them."

"You're welcome." Darby finished slathering butter on her muffin top and broke off a piece. She was pleased with the outcome and slowly munched her breakfast when a vague thought struck her. "If Demi is pregnant, how is she eating?"

Finn paused, his muffin partway to his mouth. "How's she what?"

"Demi. If she really is pregnant, how is she getting by? She'd need food under any circumstances, but if she's an expectant mother she needs to take care of herself. How's she doing that in hiding?"

Carson looked up from where he helped soothe Lora with a pacifier. "Do you think that would pull her out of hiding?"

"It might. Or it might mean she's gone even farther to ground," Darby said.

"Why would it make her go into hiding?" Finn

had stopped eating his muffin, his attention fully focused on her.

"Well, it wouldn't be too hard to stock up at one of those big stores that sells in bulk. She'd need perishables like milk and eggs on an ongoing basis but she could get by for a while if she stocked up on food and maybe protein drinks?"

"All this is predicated on assuming she's pregnant," Finn added, voicing his thoughts out loud.

"Even if she isn't, she needs food."

Finn turned to Serena. "How sure are you that she's pregnant?"

"I don't really know. But—" Serena considered "—it's not like Demi to make things up, either. If she thought she was pregnant, she likely had a good reason."

"I don't know why I didn't think about this when you brought up the pregnancy." Finn was already on his feet. He headed for the stove, snagging two more muffins and wrapping them in a napkin.

"Where are you going?" Serena demanded.

"I need to get Lotte and go over Demi's apartment. See what we might find."

"You'll need a warrant," Carson pointed out.

The rational, reasonable note didn't deter Finn in the least. In fact, as she watched him stride around the kitchen, Darby wondered where the man who'd pressed sexy morning kisses on her had gone.

Hot, sexy Finn was nowhere in sight.

Cold, focused Chief Colton had taken his place.

As she watched him rally his resources, calling in orders to his team at the precinct and then putting in a call to the D.A.'s office to request a warrant, she had to give him credit. The man she'd made out with an hour before may have vanished, but the sharp-eyed, focused cop who'd taken his place looked more than capable of catching a killer.

Chapter 13

Finn made his pitch to the D.A.'s office and, in a matter of hours, a warrant was making its way through the system to allow him to enter his cousin's home.

While he'd waited, he'd run Lotte through several pieces of Demi's clothing and had also purchased a few pregnancy tests on the way on the off chance Lotte could process the plastic scent and chemicals in the test strip to make a match somewhere in the apartment.

It was a long shot, but since he'd been sitting on this damn case for nearly a month without a lead, he'd take what he could get.

Carson was with him. Darby and Serena had

wanted to join, as well. He'd ultimately won the battle, arguing they couldn't enter a suspect's house, but
it was a close thing. His sister had clearly had some
half-cocked idea that insulting him might change
his mind. Since "close-minded stick-in-the-mud"
hurt less than a paper cut, he'd won the round and
left them with the baby, the remaining muffins, and
a solemn promise that he and Carson would come
back and tell them everything.

"Serena pressed me again before we left, trying
to convince me Demi is innocent," Carson said to
break the silence. "Evidence is evidence, but my gut
says she's innocent."

"I hope she is." Finn wanted that, he realized,
more than he'd understood. He *wanted* his cousin to
be innocent. Wanted there to be an answer to why
she was on the run and hiding from them and the
help they could provide. But he couldn't run from
the facts, either.

That knowledge was sobering, but it kept him focused on their problem. "Look, we can't keep going
on instinct with this. We need proof. There's a killer
on the loose, and if Demi is carrying Bo Gage's
child, she had some degree of motive."

"I know," Carson said. "Damn it, I know."

"So what has you hesitant all of a sudden?"

Carson was probably his best detective, so the
fact that the man seemed so at odds with the investigation was a surprise. He couldn't dismiss the fact
that it was Carson's brother who'd been murdered.

Yet, somehow, it seemed bigger than that. And ran deeper, too.

"It's just that I can't think of a pregnant woman without thinking of Serena and Lora. It's messing with my head."

And there it was.

Finn considered and then tried to play devil's advocate. "Not every pregnant woman is as gloriously happy as my sister."

"No, but rarely, if ever, are pregnant women driven to murder."

Finn couldn't fully fault Carson's logic. Hormones might be at play—and he knew from his sister's behavior the past few months that they could be intense at times—but the leap to murder was a big one. Even if Demi was a tough woman, her ability to handle herself as a bounty hunter didn't mean she'd suddenly turned to murder to take care of men who pissed her off.

"That's pretty amazing how Darby came up with the food angle." Even though he couldn't see it for driving, it was hard to miss Carson's smile as it imprinted in his words. "The woman can cook some seriously delicious muffins and she's a pretty solid detective. She's a keeper, Chief."

Since his own thoughts hadn't been too far off the mark, Finn could hardly argue with Carson's assessment. So he ignored it, pulling into the small parking lot fronting Demi's apartment complex. "Let's get to work."

Finn retrieved the key from the super before circling back to the SUV to pick up Lotte and Carson.

They headed straight to Demi's apartment and let themselves in, the stale air proof no one had been there in a few weeks.

"She's pretty neat," Carson said, pulling on a pair of rubber gloves from his pocket as he walked the perimeter of the apartment. "I hate to say it, but for that reason alone I can't see her putting up with my brother."

Since Finn had seen Bo's clutter firsthand—and Darby's compulsive need to clean up after him— he had to agree with the assessment. He headed for the apartment's single bedroom, pulling on a pair of gloves of his own before riffling through Demi's closet. Several hangers were empty, giving more credence to the fact that she'd run. Opting for something with an even stronger scent, Finn went to the bed and pulled off several pillows.

He called Lotte to him, using the pillow to instruct her on what he was looking for. He then opened one of the pregnancy test kits, holding the small stick and walking her through his instructions once more.

Pillow. Test. Pillow. Test.

He gave her a few minutes to adjust to his intentions and, before he could instruct her further, she was off. She retraced Carson's walk around the perimeter of the living room before working her way into the center of the apartment in slowly narrowing circles. It took a little less than two minutes before she found her spot. On a deep bark, she sat, her tail thumping on the hardwood floor.

"Damn," Carson muttered. "That was fast. She'd give Merlin a run for his money."

"She *does* give Merlin a run for his money." Finn shot him a grin, exceedingly proud of his girl. "And she's a heck of a lot cuter."

"Don't let Elle hear you say that. She loves that bulldog more than life itself."

"Our secret," Finn muttered as he dropped beside Lotte and began feeling around the wooden planks of the floorboards. He ran his fingers over the smooth wood, satisfied when he felt the slightest give beneath his fingertips. He pulled a small knife out of his all-purpose kit and used it to pry at the board.

"You find something?"

"Looks like." The board came loose with minimal tugging and, in moments, Finn was staring down into a hidey-hole.

One that contained a pregnancy test that read positive, a stack of letters, and a photo of Demi and Bo during better times. There was a large red X over Bo's face and the word *liar* was scrawled across the photo.

Carson dropped to his knees beside Finn and let out a long, low whistle. "Wow. This does not look good."

"You can say that again."

Unwilling to simply sit and stare at the incriminating evidence, Finn began the careful work of removing Demi's belongings.

And another layer of proof that she had a vendetta against Bo Gage.

Darby bundled up against the cold in the oversize puffy coat Serena had lent her and gave Penny and Lucy a chance to stretch their legs. They'd stared longingly when Lotte had gone out earlier with Finn and Carson, and she'd finally taken pity on the two of them and taken them out for some exercise. The morning air was brisk but gave her a chance to clear her head as the dogs went off to sniff around on uncharted territory.

She'd made out with Finn this morning. It had caught her off guard at just how good it had felt to have a man's body pressed to hers after so long. Even now, she could still feel the imprint of his solid form against her skin. Which shouldn't have been a surprise, but was a reminder of just how much had been missing from her life.

Of course, none of it changed the fact that they were in a tense situation and it was natural to seek comfort where available. It didn't mean there was truly something there. They could enjoy each other's company—could even move things forward and satisfy the physical—but that wouldn't guarantee something long-term.

When had she begun thinking of him in that way?

A week ago he was her enemy, his suspicions that

she could be a murderess a massive gaping hole between them. And now here she was thinking about having a relationship with the man. Was she mad?

Or had she come to see him in a new light?

He was a good cop. She'd seen his dedication firsthand, including his willingness to put himself in the line of fire as they hunted a killer. She'd also seen him with his niece, making funny faces and sticking out his tongue to get a smile as he'd held her safely in the crook of his arm.

And then there was Lotte. His dedication and devotion to the dog indicated respect and affection as well as a dedication to the animal's well-being. There was a kinship there and absolute trust.

Was it really so silly to look at each of those things and tally them in the good column?

"What is with all that racket?"

The imperial voice interrupted her thoughts, seeming to float out of the ether behind her.

Darby whirled and came face to face with Joanelle Colton. "Mrs. Colton."

"Do I know you?"

"I'm Darby Gage. I'm a friend of Serena's."

"A Gage?"

Darby could have sworn the woman actually stared down her nose at Darby's introduction but she held her ground. "Yes. By marriage."

"One of Carson's people, then?"

"I should have been clear. My former marriage. I kept the name Gage."

Something lit in Joanelle's gaze, dark and calculating. "You're the ex-wife. The one who inherited the dead man's possessions."

Other than Penny, there'd been minimal possessions to possess but Darby chose not to point that out. "I used to be married to Bo Gage, yes. I'm sorry for his death and for Carson's loss."

She could have sworn the woman muttered something about one less Gage in the world but couldn't be entirely sure. Joanelle's reputation preceded her, but was she truly that cold?

"What are you doing here, Ms. Gage? And why are you letting those dogs roam over my property?"

"They're getting some morning exercise. And I know how to clean up after my pets."

"Mama!" Serena slipped from the house, a large blanket wrapped around her shoulders as she quickly crossed the yard. "What are you doing out in the cold?"

"I saw this woman on our property and I came to investigate."

"Darby is my friend. And last evening she was my houseguest. Surely you could be a bit more welcoming."

Joanelle let out a small huff before plastering on a smile. "What brings you out to the ranch, Darby?"

"She stayed here with Finn last night. It wasn't safe to go back to her home."

Joanelle's eyes grew round and her already stiff

frame seemed to go positively brittle. "Why ever not?"

"They were out for the evening and had an issue. Someone lurking in the shadows. Finn felt it best to stay here."

"He's the chief of police. While he may have trouble catching a killer, surely he can manage to keep one woman's home safe from harm?" Joanelle pressed on. "And whatever possessed you to allow them to stay here? You have an infant in the house and you're welcoming in a woman who's drawn the attention of our town's criminal element after everything that happened here last month? I must go speak to your father about this."

Joanelle huffed off without a backward glance and Darby wasn't sure if she should be grateful or prepare to suit up for round two.

"And that would be my mother." Serena waved a hand in the general direction of Joanelle's departure. "The very definition of hospitality."

"I don't know. She may have a point." Although the delivery was designed to belittle and demean, Darby couldn't argue with Joanelle's underlying meaning. "You do have a baby. You don't need the sort of trouble that's been hovering around me in your home."

Serena closed the short distance between them and wrapped Darby in a tight hug. "It's fine. And the ranch is now one of the safest places in Red Ridge.

You don't need to give it another thought. Nor do you need to worry about being here."

"But what about Lora?"

"No buts." Serena silenced her before she could protest further. "Come on. Let's go inside. It's cold and I've got hot coffee and a cute baby to distract us from my mother's unpleasant welcome."

Darby followed Serena into the house but couldn't shake the melancholy Joanelle had managed to impart in their short meeting. Nor could she fully shake the sadness that lingered when she thought of Finn growing up under the cold and unfeeling presence of Joanelle Colton.

"You okay?" Finn glanced over at Darby, seated in his passenger seat, when he pulled to a stop a few streets away from the police station. He and Carson had already been there to secure the evidence, then had headed back to the ranch to provide the promised updates on what they found to Serena and Darby.

After an elaborate game Finn had mentally dubbed "you'll stay with me no I won't" had finally ended to his satisfaction, he and Darby had run Penny and Lucy back to her house and were now on their way to the precinct.

"I'm fine," Darby said.

"You're mad at me, but that's okay. I know you'd rather have your day back and time to yourself, but I'm not comfortable having you stay at home alone just yet."

"What is possibly going to happen to me? And while I have absolute faith in you that you will catch the Groom Killer, do you expect to babysit me until he or she is caught?"

"Any number of things could happen to you."

"In my own home? With two German shepherds to protect me?"

"Could you humor me for a few hours? Something has had me itchy since last night and I'd rather know you're okay."

She didn't agree but, for the first time since leaving Serena's, she didn't argue, either, so he figured that was progress.

The precinct was quiet for a Sunday but busier than usual. The Groom Killer murders had everyone on high alert and every member of his staff was pulling extra time to try to stop the killer from striking again. The evidence he'd discovered at Demi's had been logged in and the team had been eager to begin a review of the forensics.

Although the evidence was heavily weighted to the circumstantial, coupled with Bo's bloody handwriting at the scene of his murder, it didn't paint a good picture of Demi's involvement.

Darby stared at the items in the evidence bags spread out on a table in the conference room, but didn't touch anything. "These are the items you and Carson found at Demi's apartment?"

"Yes."

"Where'd you find them?"

"Lotte sniffed them out in the floorboards."

Darby leaned closer, but still didn't make any attempt to touch anything before standing to question him. "She found a pregnancy test?"

"She's sensitive to a lot of scents."

"Including plastic?"

Finn considered all the tests they'd run on the various members of the K-9 team. "The dogs can find natural scents the easiest, but you'd be amazed what they can detect. Most recently we've been running trials on electronics equipment."

"Lotte can smell metal and plastic?"

"Yep. So can the other K-9 squad. Merlin's shown some of the strongest aptitude on that front, but I'm hopeful we can work on all the dogs over time."

"That's amazing. I wonder if we can breed them for that." Lost in her thoughts, she bent back over the table, focused on the items.

Finn watched her, that mix of curiosity and keen interest keeping her attention off him and on the evidence items as she worked her way down the table. Her hair fell in soft waves along the curve of her jaw and he could see reddish tones shining in the light that came in through the conference room's high overhead windows. The same fierce need that had gripped him that morning was back, only this time it was layered with an ice-cold veneer of raw-boned fear.

What if something happened to her?

He'd spent this op convinced he could make himself the target, but what if he'd miscalculated?

"Finn?"

He was so lost in his thoughts she neatly turned the tables, her attention now fully focused on him. And in that moment he had an overwhelming sense of remorse mixed in with the bone-numbing fear.

"I'm sorry. I'm so sorry."

"For what?"

"For dragging you into this. For coming up with this stupid scheme in the first place."

"But you needed help and—"

He reached for her hands, effectively cutting her off. "I had no right to drag you into this or to ask you to put your life on the line for this dumb idea."

"But I agreed."

"Only after I held your personal situation over your head."

"That's not true. You offered me a way out."

If only.

Something dark and bitter coated his throat as he thought about what he'd really done. He'd used a sweet, kind, generous woman to meet his own ends. Even worse, he used her financial situation against her, putting her in a position where she could hardly say no. "I used you to meet my own ends and it's wrong."

"But I want to help. I may have fallen out of love a long time ago with Bo Gage, but I was married to him. I also loved him once. I want justice for him and for the other poor soul who was gunned down so horrifically. No one deserves that and they certainly don't deserve it on the eve of one of the happiest days of their life."

"But I didn't give you a choice."

"Of course you did."

"That's not true and you know it. The one thing you needed was money and that's what I dangled in front of you to do what I wanted."

The sweet, quiet woman who'd snuggled in his arms that morning was nowhere in evidence as she shoved at a chair. The thick metal made a heavy clanging sound as it hit the floor as she whirled on him, her voice rising with each syllable.

"You may have steamrolled over me to get me out of my house today but you're not going to steamroll me on this, Finn Colton. I had a choice! I could have easily let go of it all except for Penny. I could have kept her and gone back to my life."

"You would have done that?"

"Of course, I'd have done it. I was going to do my very best by Bo, but if I couldn't handle it or couldn't find a way out of the financial situation, I'd have explained all that to Bo's dad, sold off what was left of the business and gone back to my life. It's as simple as that. So stop talking about my choices and how you took them away. You offered me a chance to keep what I wanted *and* to clear my name *and* to help you end this evilness that has put a level of fear into this town I've never seen before."

Heat still flared high in her gaze, but along with it he saw something else.

Satisfaction.

Where he'd mistaken her for a woman with little choice or opportunity, he suddenly realized just how wrong he'd been. The situation Bo had put her in—a nearly broke business and a barely functioning home—had actually made it easy for her. She could have walked away from all of it with minimal loss and still taken care of the one thing Bo had valued above all else. Penny.

He'd believed himself holding the upper hand, but all he'd done was provide an opportunity. To fix all Bo had done wrong but also to provide an avenue for her to see that Bo hadn't died in vain.

If the steely look in her gaze was any indication, he'd have a damn time convincing her otherwise. "It's too dangerous. I can see that now."

"Then we face it together."

He tried once more, bringing back recent events in the hope of deterring her. "No. Absolutely not. We're done parading around town. Last night's chase through the parking lot proved that to me."

"We've come too far to back out now."

Where had this stubbornness come from? And why was he even considering—for one small nanosecond considering—going along with what she demanded?

"You can't do this. There are other ways, but we're not setting ourselves up as bait for a killer."

"Cold feet, Finn?"

"That's ridiculous."

"Is it?" She cocked her head, seeming to consider the situation. "Or are you backing out now that we're finally making progress? If that was the Groom Killer last night, hiding out in the parking lot, that means we got his attention. We're too close to stop."

"We're too close to danger."

"So what's the alternative?"

She moved closer and placed a hand on his chest. His pulse was already racing, but the press of her warm palm did the oddest thing. Both calming and exhilarating, the beat picked up even harder, even as he felt a strange sense of peace descend over him.

He'd worked so hard over the past month to keep his spirits up, but he'd be lying if he didn't admit to the fraying he'd begun to feel around the edges. Bo's death—still unsolved—and then a second murder had put a black mark over his department and the men and women who worked so hard to keep the peace in Red Ridge. Add on the general sense of panic in town and the loss of business experienced by so many of Red Ridge's merchants and the murders were taking their toll.

Finn laid a hand over Darby's, the support he felt there going a long way toward reinforcing those flagging spirits. Yet even with her support, he questioned the wisdom of continuing to flaunt their relationship in the hope a killer would pay attention.

"What is the alternative?" Darby asked again.

"We end this now and go back to our lives. If the killer is looking for couples, there will be no need to look at us any longer."

"And what if that makes them go after a different target? One who isn't able to handle himself against a threat like that?"

Unbidden, an image of Michael Hayden lying in a pool of blood at the Circle T filled his mind's eye, his fiancée crying softly inside the restaurant.

"That's not fair."

"None of it is fair. That's why we have to do what is right."

Darby moved even closer, the hand on his chest tracing a path up over his collarbone before settling behind his neck. She placed her other free hand around his waist and pulled him close. "We have to see this through. It's *ours* to see through."

Protest after protest rose to his lips but Finn discarded each and every one. They'd started this and, even if it had begun as a scheme to draw out a killer, it had become a mission for both of them. The time to change course had passed.

So had the time to bail.

They were in this. And while he wished he could go back in time and change the unbelievable hubris that had dragged him down this path in the first place, he had no choice but to play the hand.

The one he'd dealt all on his own.

Chapter 14

Darby took her first easy breath when Finn nodded his agreement. She still wasn't sure when the conversation had shifted—or when she'd begun thinking of the help she was providing Finn as a sort of personal mission—but she couldn't deny the urgent need that now drove her to see this through.

She did have a choice.

He might not see it, but she saw it clearly.

All her choices, both the one she'd made to join Finn in this work and all the ones that had come before, had led her here. She could no more walk away than he could.

Pressing her slight advantage, she leaned into him and took comfort and strength from their connection.

Her earlier thoughts—wondering where they were going and if they had a future—seemed distant and unimportant. Instead she would focus on the moment and take what was here.

In this, too, she had a choice. And she chose Finn.

His lips met hers in a warm welcome and Darby sunk into him. Into the strong arms that reached up and wrapped her in their strength. Into the sexy shift of his mouth over hers. Into the maelstrom of need and want and raw desire that seemed to grip her every time they both got out of their heads long enough to enjoy each other.

This was choice, too.

And for as long as he'd have her, she'd choose Finn Colton.

Darby looked around the squad room, fascinated with the hum of activity. She could only envision it during the week—each desk full, conversation, laughter and likely an insult here or there tossing back and forth across the open space.

Finn's office had been turned into a "war room" of sorts—a place where they could set up their murder boards and hunt for the Groom Killer. He could easily have kept the office for himself, yet he chose to sit in among his men and women.

As one of them.

Did he realize how special he was? She'd watched him as he'd worked with Carson back at the ranch, going over the problem of the killer as well as the questions both had had about Demi. Finn had listened to Carson, probed when he'd wanted to know more and asked for additional clarification as the man argued his points. Finn had then posed his own thoughts and ideas, yet it in a way that was both collaborative and complementary, even when they'd differed. Darby knew she had gotten an inside sneak peek most civilians didn't ever see because of her involvement in "dating" Finn, but it had been fascinating to watch all the same.

Her experience with men, while not nonexistent, had consisted mostly of the years she'd spent with Bo and a few other pockets of dating that hadn't lasted all that long. She and Bo had rarely argued but she'd always had this vague sense that he was humoring her whenever they disagreed on a subject. Almost as if he were hearing her yet not truly listening to what she'd had to say.

She'd had friends at the time who'd expressed similar frustrations about their husbands and she'd chalked it up to one of those things about marriage people forgot to mention. After the vows and the champagne and the cake were done—after you went home and tried to make a life—you had to figure out how to communicate with each other.

And if you got a dud?

Well, that was marriage.

It had seemed terribly unfair. More, it had been a frustration to realize that someone she was trying to make a life with and find middle ground with seemed content to sit on his own personal high ground instead. Worse, Bo Gage had been loathe to share it with her.

"It's sort of a mess right now. We do a massive cleanup twice a year and we're definitely due for it."

"Hmm?" Keying into Finn's words, she shifted her focus to him. "What's that?"

"The squad room. We're a bit of a mess right now. I know how much you like cleanliness and order, and we're a bit short on both at the moment."

She might like order but she liked closed cases better. "I'd rather know you had a messy precinct where everyone worked on shutting down crime than waste one minute worrying about where everything was filed."

"You surprise me. You got so quiet, I figured it was a creeping sense of horror and a desperate urge to flee out the door."

There it was again. That reality that Finn paid attention to her.

"I was actually thinking about marriage," she offered. "Which, if we're being fair, sends some people fleeing for the door, too."

"What made you think about marriage?"

"I was thinking about how you are with your staff. How you listen to them. Take their thoughts into consideration. It's an amazing trait and one not everyone has."

A dull flush crept up his neck. "It's my job."

"No, I don't think so. Your job is running the

precinct and carrying the weight of Red Ridge on your shoulders. That would make anyone think their way was the right way. Yet you bring others into the process."

"I may carry the weight of expectation but the men and women of my squad are out there every day, putting their lives on the line. It would hardly do to forget they have eyes and ears, too. They see things I never will because I'm stuck in here so often. And they're never going to hone their instincts or their ability to think through a problem if I shut them down all the time."

Did he have any idea how rare he was?

Putting Bo and their relationship aside, she'd known a lot of people in her life and few were as emotionally evolved as Finn. From her fussy boss at the diner to the way Hayley Patton had pranced around the K-9 training center, hollering out orders to the staff even though she had no real authority, Darby had observed far too many people who just wanted it done their way.

Without checking the impulse, she tugged on his shirt, pulling him close for a kiss. Every time felt fresh, but something had changed. She saw Finn Colton through a different light than before and it changed everything. The kiss was deeper. More intimate.

And while all that had come before hadn't been even remotely cold or unfeeling, this one was hot.

A loud hoot interrupted their kiss and Darby

pulled back, a big grin on her face. "Sorry. You are at work."

"They'll survive."

"Still." She backed away, bumping into the edge of the desk he'd set up at here in the squad room. The move was enough to have a stack of papers and folders tumbling off the edge along with a loud thud.

"Oh! Oh! I'm so sorry." She hunkered down, reaching for the folders, and saw a small package nestled among the mess of papers. Darby picked up the box, surprised at how heavy it was. A small card was stuck to the top with "Chief Finn Colton" printed in neat script. "This looks like it's for you."

"Where did you find that?"

"It was here. Among the folder and papers. I must have knocked it off along with your files."

"Was it on top?"

She'd seen any number of emotions flicker through his gaze over the past week, which made what she saw now that much more startling.

Traces of fear.

"Finn? Are you okay?"

"Sure. I'm fine."

He took the box from her and shoved it into his pocket.

"What is that?"

"Nothing, I'm sure."

"It looks like something. And, wrapped in red paper, it suggests you have a valentine."

The idea that Finn actually did have a valentine

stabbed at her. He'd told her last week when they'd started their fake relationship that he was unattached. How silly of her to believe him.

And how easy it was to fall back into the same pattern. An attractive man showed interest and in a little more than a week she was right back to the same place she'd been in her marriage. A trusting fool.

"I don't have a valentine."

"It appears otherwise." She kept her tone low and even, praying the quaver she felt tickling her throat didn't come through.

"I really don't. These—" He broke off, a grimace turning his mouth into a straight line. "These gifts keep showing up. They're all anonymous and they suggest I have a secret admirer here in town."

A secret admirer? Was this 1952?

"No one knows who's sending them?" she asked.

"I didn't pay attention at first. And the last few that I did question were brought in by a delivery service."

"Do they know who it is?"

"Someone paid cash."

She wanted to press and probe him as to why he wasn't taking the situation seriously, especially because it was at direct odds with the behavior she'd seen with his staff. Where he focused on them and encouraged their work, his reaction to these so-called gifts to himself seemed to be dismissive.

As if he sensed what she was thinking, he rushed

on. "It was a box of candy, some flowers and a few dopey cards. What am I supposed to do about it?"

"For starters, maybe take it more seriously. Finn, you've been trying for the past week to entice a killer. Maybe you've succeeded."

Finn ignored the discomfort that tightened the back of his throat. "It can't be the Groom Killer. The gifts came before you and I began parading around town."

"That doesn't mean it's not. He or she may be courting a new victim. Did Bo or Michael Hayden receive any presents or trinkets?"

"No. Not that we've found."

"So what if it's some sort of escalation?"

"Darby—" He stilled, her comments sinking in. "You're not half bad at this, you know."

"I watch cop shows."

He frowned at that. "Most of which are loosely based on the truth and dramatized in most parts to highlight a sense of danger. I mean the way you've quickly processed this."

It was just like earlier, when she'd posed the question of breeding her dogs to better detect materials. She was whip quick and, with sudden clarity, he saw a reality of her life.

She'd spent most of it sorely underestimated.

First by her mother and later by her husband.

He thought about Bo's business, his beloved Penny and the future of the dogs he loved so much.

The man might have been a poor husband and un-skilled business owner, but the one thing he'd loved without reservation had been his dog. Finn had to wonder that maybe Bo had known exactly what Darby was capable of and known all along what he was doing. It certainly gave credence to why Gage had never changed his will.

The dead man's faith had been rewarded. Darby was devoted to Penny's welfare and, even without his help or her earlier comments to the contrary, Finn believed she'd have found a way to keep the business afloat even if he hadn't given her the money.

"So why won't you open the gift? See what it is?" Darby asked.

Thoughts of Bo's motivations toward Darby faded as Finn reached for the small package he'd shoved into his pocket. It had a weight to it, whether from what was inside or what his imagination had already created. Setting it on the desk, the small present drew their collective focus as if it were a coiled cobra wait-ing to strike.

He opened the card first, the neat, precise script just as it had been with the other packages. Only, where the comments in the past had all suggested a concerned citizen or a shy admirer, this one was different. The tone was darker and the message, in Darby's words, had escalated.

Roses are red, so is blood.
Mine's true. Is yours?

Finn ripped open the package, only to find a small pewter rose inside. He picked it up, the detail intricate and precise. It was only when he changed hands, attempting to turn it over to get a better look, that one of the lifelike thorns pricked his finger.

"Ow!"

"What is it?"

Finn was careful to handle the piece by the leafy portion to hold it up to the light. A small, sharp needle stuck from the edge of the thorn, sharpening the point that was crafted in pewter.

"You're bleeding."

A small trail of blood ran down his finger and over his palm, and the pad still stung where he'd been pricked.

Darby dug out a tissue from her purse and handed it over, then pulled out another one and wadded it up so she could gently take the rose from his hand.

He wiped up the blood, then kept pressure on to staunch the flow. It stopped quickly, but still stung.

"This is more than just a pointy thorn." Darby twisted the rose in the air, shifting it so he could see what she did. "This looks like it was built to purposely cause pain. Look at that thorn. The third one down."

Finn saw immediately what she meant. The rose had obviously been crafted to do harm, the thorn she pointed to as sharp as a needle. "I wonder if someone had this made. Putting aside how dangerous it is, it's a beautiful piece. The work is so detailed, it could easily be custom."

"Do you have a way of finding that out? And you should have it checked to make sure there wasn't anything on the thorn, like poison."

"I feel okay."

"But have it checked out."

Her concern was touching and while he didn't feel different, he'd make sure the forensics team checked out the rose.

What he was more focused on was finding out who might have sold the flower.

"Fortunately, we do have ways. Believe it or not, tracking something like this is easier than a box of store chocolate or real flowers. The fact that it's so unique makes it an easier find."

"This may be a real break toward finding the Groom Killer. Something that proves Demi didn't do it," Darby said.

"Now you sound like Serena."

"You think Demi did do it?"

Finn considered his cousin and the evidence they'd secured to date. "I don't think we can rule her out."

"But if she is the Groom Killer, why would she send her cousin love notes?"

That was where IDing the person sending the gifts fell apart. If the Groom Killer was his cousin, the likelihood she and Anonymous were the same was highly unlikely. He wasn't close with the other branches of his family but he knew them. In his entire life, there had never been anything but a sort of grudging respect between him and Demi.

Certainly not unrequited love between first cousins. Heck, his family barely did affection.

Which only added to the knot that had settled in his gut the night they'd discovered Bo Gage's body. Was he dealing with two faceless criminals? The Groom Killer and Anonymous? Or, if they were one and the same, was there someone running around Red Ridge who wasn't even on their radar?

He could put out an alert on a known suspect. They could watch for them and put others on alert to do the same. But the not knowing was another matter entirely. Not knowing meant the person could strike again.

And a third strike meant they were well and truly dealing with a serial killer.

"Is it wrong to have a glass of wine?" Serena looked up from her menu, indecision playing around the edges of her eyes.

"One glass?" Darby asked. "I can't see how it will hurt. I'm not your doctor, but you can just dispose of that breast milk, right?"

"You're absolutely right and my doctor told me I could do this." Serena nodded as if decided. "I've been pumping to have extra and so Carson can feed Lora now and again. Which means Mama gets her first glass of wine in a year."

Darby nearly laughed at the look of anticipation and avarice that filled Serena's dark gaze. "Isn't it funny how much more interesting something becomes when you can't have it."

"You know it. I wasn't a big drinker before having a baby, yet at this moment I'm more excited than I can describe. And I get a night out. I love Lora more than I could have ever imagined but I'm looking forward to an adult activity."

Serena's comment only reinforced the earlier thought. Darby suspected Serena had never worried about adult outings before. Yet now that they were scarce, they seemed more exciting.

Sort of like Finn.

She'd been without male company for so long, each time she was with him felt heightened. Special. It had to be the only reason she was so giddy to be out with him. And so determined to make the most of every moment.

Since the reality that their charade would soon be over had begun to fill her with an odd sinking feeling in her stomach, Darby focused on Serena instead. "Who's watching Lora tonight?"

"Finn and Carson made Valeria and Vincent do it. Part of Finn's plans to keep the kids close to home and out of sight."

"Valeria's your sister?"

"Yes, my baby sister. She's madly in love with Vincent, Carson's youngest brother."

Darby remembered Vincent. He'd been a young

teen when she and Bo had started dating. She'd always found him sweet, but could hardly imagine him getting married. "They're only nineteen, right?"

"Yes, and know their own minds. I'm hoping a night with a fussy baby makes them both rethink their marriage plans."

"But Lora's a happy baby."

"Most of the time. Since I think her first tooth is threatening an appearance, tonight is likely not going to be one of those times."

Suddenly, Serena's excitement for the wine and the evening out made even more sense. "You're diabolical!"

"I'm a concerned sister. I love Valeria and Vincent, too. And while I have no hesitation believing they have a love that will last, I'm a bit in my mother's camp on this one. Until this Groom Killer situation is solved, I want them safe. Running around town mooning over each other is the surest way to get on the wrong person's radar."

Sadly, Darby had to admit Serena was right. There were so many unknowns right now, but flaunting a relationship wasn't ideal. And since youth rarely saw itself as anything but invincible, they likely hadn't put the Groom Killer and their own romance in the same category.

Finn and Carson chose that moment to come back to their table. Finn looked so handsome and Darby sent up a silent prayer of thanks he'd run her back to her house earlier to get a fresh change of clothes and to drop off the dogs. It might be silly, but she wanted to look pretty for him.

"Everything go okay?" Serena asked Carson as he took his seat.

"Yep. Backup's positioned just where we planned."

Although it felt like another escalation, Darby knew the precautions were wise. She and Finn had been going out without backup since their charade began and the night before she'd been forced to call 9-1-1 while he'd raced off after a suspect. Between last night's scare and the anonymous present that had arrived for him, it seemed better to be prepared and to put police presence in place.

Finn took her hand, the move a match for Carson and Serena, and Darby was suddenly struck by how hollow his touch really was. Carson and Serena had a future. They were now parents and they were deeply in love. All she and Finn had was that charade.

The endlessly roiling emotions every time she was with him had been manageable up to now. But suddenly, faced with a couple who had not only weathered a personal storm but who had truly found their forever, Darby couldn't deny the overwhelming sadness.

No matter how she spun a fantasy in her mind, she and Finn Colton had nothing.

Finn sensed the change immediately yet couldn't place the reason. Darby's hand beneath his had stiffened when he'd touched her, at complete odds with their time together up to now. He'd gotten used to touching her. To the warmth of her skin and the easy connection they made whenever they were together.

Their waiter arrived to take their orders but it wasn't enough to dislodge the sense that something was wrong. Had Serena said something while he and Carson were securing the kitchen and back entrance?

Or had something else happened?

His sister was normally on point with others, sensitive to their needs and emotions, so he struggled to think she would have said anything that was overtly unkind or hurtful. But what else could it be?

He did a quick scan of the Trattoria, almost convinced he'd find Hayley Patton lurking at one of the tables, but the woman was nowhere to be found among the scattered groups of diners.

"And for you, sir?"

Distracted, Finn hadn't realized it was his turn and he hadn't even looked at his menu. He ordered one of the specials that had sounded vaguely interesting and went back to brooding.

Had he done something? While he'd enjoyed their evenings out alone, the idea to have Carson and Serena join them had seemed like a good one after the arrival of the rose and that clear sense of escalation from Anonymous. It also gave them the chance to flaunt the expansion of their relationship; two happy couples out for the night.

And it had sounded like fun.

Genuine, personal fun.

Finn wasn't sure when he'd begun thinking like that, yet he could hardly deny it. Somewhere along the way, his pretend relationship with Darby had become real. He thought about her when they weren't together and he anticipated getting back to her when they were apart.

And he liked her, damn it. In both the deeply attracted and interested sense as well as the genuine enjoyment and affection for another person.

"Can you believe the winter festival is next Saturday?" Serena asked. She shot him a small wink across the table, only reinforcing his earlier thought that she was on point and aware of others with her deft change to an innocuous subject.

Or a seemingly innocuous one.

"Don't remind me," Carson groaned. "It's all Lorelei has been talking about for two weeks."

"The sweet woman at the front desk?" Serena asked.

"Sweet?" Carson and Finn asked the question at the same time. It was enough to break whatever tension had settled in and Finn relaxed a bit when he heard Darby's light laughter.

"She is sweet," Serena argued. "She's been nothing but lovely to me the few times I've met her."

Carson shot his hands up in a gesture of innocence. "I'm going to choose to believe you. I'd just say my experience with her has been a bit different."

"How so?" Serena challenged.

"She yelled at me at least three times a week the entire first year I worked for the RRPD."

"Finn?" Serena demanded. "Did she do the same to you?"

"Yep. And three a week sounds about right."

"What did she yell at you for?" Darby asked.

"All depends on the day," Carson said. "Some days it was because my lunch smelled. Some days it was because I didn't put paper in the copier despite the fact that I hadn't even used the copier. Other days it was because my shoes squeaked on the floor."

"And after a year?" Darby said it first but Serena had leaned forward, clearly prepared to ask the same.

"She stops yelling," Finn said. "And then she loves you. Elle's about done her penance. Her rookie year's nearly over."

"But she seemed so sweet," Serena said. "She fussed over Lora and was so nice."

"Why do you think she acts that way?"

"Who knows, Darby? Some say it's because she has teenagers, but I started before her kids were that big." Carson sighed. "Once I got over being scared of her, I finally asked her why she does it. She claims it's a test."

Carson was right. Finn might joke about Lorelei—and done his year-one rounds with her himself—but he also respected her instincts. The woman knew the tenacity required to be a cop. Inside and outside the precinct. "If you ask Lorelei, she says it's because she's trying to weed out the cops who won't make it."

"That's her job?" Darby asked, genuinely surprised.

"She's made it her job. And since we're an important department with a K-9 unit, I've hardly argued with her." Finn couldn't resist the smile, an image of Lorelei sending his cousin Brayden off in tears in his first year. "I like to think she not only keeps the place in line, but she adds her own HR services for free."

"Is it working?" Serena asked.

"Without question," Finn said. "And, all joking aside, Red Ridge is better for having her on that desk."

Finn thought about the men and women currently stationed outside the Trattoria, two in the back and two in the front. He trusted all of them with his life. Knew they trusted him with the same. He'd say Lorelei's brand of personnel evaluation was working just fine.

"We're all better for having her on that desk." Carson lifted his glass of soda, gesturing them all forward for a toast. "Adversity makes for determination in those who have the patience to push past it."

As the glasses clinked, Finn couldn't help but take Carson's words to heart. Adversity did make people stronger. If a goal meant enough, hard times assured you'd keep reaching for that goal with even more determination. He'd proved that to himself more times in his life than he could count. So had Darby.

What he couldn't quite shake was the sense that the Groom Killer possessed the same sort of determination.

Chapter 15

As he walked Darby to her front door, Finn still couldn't shake the sense that she was upset. Their conversation over dinner had ebbed and flowed with ease, but something had remained off. She'd smiled and laughed, and the stories about Lorelei had seemed to break whatever tension had gripped the table initially. In the end, though, it hadn't been enough.

Their quiet ride to her house had only reinforced that.

"I'll just get Lotte outside quickly. I want to check the house."

"Of course," she said as she unlocked the front door and pushed it open, then flipped on the hall light.

He hated to leave her but could hardly force her to allow him to stay. The threat that she'd sensed the night before in the restaurant parking lot hadn't manifested into anything and their evening at the Trattoria had been uneventful, as well. He'd confirmed his team would do patrols through her neighborhood but other than taking some sense of calm from that small task, he had no right to tell her what to do.

Three sleepy dogs, their tails thumping in unison when he and Darby walked through the door, only reinforced the sense of safety. He made a fuss over them all as the wagging turned to excitement that they were home. Once they were up and moving, he quickly ushered them all outside to relieve themselves.

The winter sky sparkled overhead as crisp air shocked his lungs, his exhales making thick puffs in the glow of the house lights. The house wasn't deserted but it was set off from the road, the acreage big enough to ensure privacy. Lotte and Lucy had trotted to the far edge of the property, sniffing around as if to check out whether anything had changed.

Only Penny stayed by his side, those big eyes of hers solemn.

"You are a sweet girl." Finn bent to rub at her fur, pleased when she pressed her head against his thigh. "You watch out for her."

He'd always believed that animals communicated. Their inability to speak was only a limitation if you wanted it to be. Their expressiveness and their loy-alty told an entire story if you only paid attention.

Penny's tail wagged as he patted her, light and steady, and he knew she understood him. He also knew that steady movement, back and forth, was her agreement that yes, she'd watch out for Darby. That she was committed to keeping Darby safe.

Just like the patrols, he'd have to take that as enough.

He called Lucy and Lotte to him, the two dogs bounding over the hard-packed snow that covered the lawn. They would happily stay out longer if he'd let them, but it was late and he needed to head home before he made an ass out of himself.

Because he didn't want to leave.

He didn't want to leave Darby alone. And he wanted more.

The sort of more that he had no right to want or to ask for. They had no commitment to each other and he had to own the fact that he'd not asked for one. Yet, as each day went by, Finn couldn't shake the idea that he did want a commitment. He wanted to go out with her in a way that moved past their pretense and toward something deeper.

Toward something more.

He followed the dogs to the door, stomping his feet on the front mat to remove any excess snow. He grabbed the towel Darby kept near the door to rub down the dogs and wipe the snow off their feet, and was instantly aware of her as her light scent and the warmth of her body brushed up against his. "I'll help you do that."

She had an extra towel and worked over Lucy's paws while Finn did Lotte. Lucy bounded off and Darby had already turned to Penny, praising the dog as she rubbed her down. "You were much better than your sister. Only a little bit to dry off."

"She stayed close. Lucy and Lotte took off exploring."

Darby kneeled, coming face to face with Penny. "Not feel like a romp tonight, sweet girl?"

Whatever distance had been between them had vanished and Penny leaned into Darby much in the same way she'd accepted his gentle affection outside. She laid her head against Darby's shoulder and stood still as Darby offered praise and affection.

"Looks like you two have officially bonded."

"Finally." Darby smiled her first real smile of the night as she looked up at him. "You were absolutely right. She did come around."

"She just needed a bit of time to get used to her new reality. To grieve her loss of Bo and to accept that she's safe and loved by her new owner."

Darby ran a tender hand over Penny's soft head. "That she is."

Finn knew he should leave. Knew he should call Lotte over and give Darby space. Yet something kept him rooted to the spot. "Did something upset you tonight?"

"When?"

"At dinner. You seemed—" He stopped, well aware that he was crossing an invisible threshold. Whatever pretense they'd kept up between themselves, if he pressed what was on his mind, there'd be nowhere to hide.

"I seemed what?"

"Upset."

"I was laughing and having a good time."

"I know. But underneath." He sighed, knowing he was making a mess as he fumbled his way through what he suddenly needed to say. "You just seemed upset when Carson and I came back to the table. You were lovely as you always are, but I can't shake the fact that something is bothering you."

"We're not a couple."

"Oh?"

"That was what was bothering me."

When he only stood there dumbfounded, Darby gave Penny a final pat on her head and then stood.

"You and me. It dawned on me as I listened to Serena that she has a real relationship. She has a child. She also has a man who loves her and her daughter without limits. I don't have anything close to that. And now I realize that I've been deluding myself that a fake relationship is somehow a replacement for going out and finding those things in my life."

She took a deep breath, fire burning in her blue eyes as she kept her gaze level with his. "I've become lazy in my personal life since I got divorced and I'm sick of settling. Settling for living a half life, all by myself. So I have you to thank for that. Whatever else this experience has been, it's given me a push I've sorely needed."

Finn took in her words but struggled to understand what she was saying. She wanted to go out and find a relationship? Here he was, hoping to find something with her, and she was ready to look elsewhere?

"I see."

"Do you?"

"I think I do. You have a bright future in front of you and I'm standing in your way."

"No, Finn. You've cleared the path."

It was silly and small, but as he stood there staring right back at her, refusing to let his gaze drop, he had a revelation. Or more a solidification of all he hadn't been able to admit to himself.

She might want a future for herself but he wanted one with her. Or at least a shot at one. And the only way he was going to get that shot was if he put his balls on the line and told her.

"What if I told you I wasn't ready to step off the path?"

"Excuse me?"

"Maybe you're standing in my way." He moved in closer and laid a hand at her waist. "And maybe I like it."

"Me?"

"Yes."

His answer was final, a resounding welcome to

everything he'd been running from in his life. He did want a shot at things with her. At something that went beyond a fake relationship and a hunt for a killer.

But he knew he needed to be gentle. Darby wasn't a woman to toy with. She'd been honest with where she was coming from and what she wanted in her life. "That's what I want. A chance to find out what's between us. I feel a spark. Do you?"

"Yes." She nodded before a small line crinkled her brow. "But I was afraid I was making it up."

"I can assure you, you weren't." That line smoothed out as a small smile edged the corners of her mouth. "So now it's up to you. What do you want, Darby?"

"I'd like a chance, too."

Before he could answer, she closed the distance between them, assuring him she was as on board as he was. "I'd like that chance with you."

They both moved at the same time, her arms around his waist as his wrapped around her shoulders. He'd spent the past week taking kisses wherever he could and all had been delicious, but this was different. The pretense was gone, replaced with the woman who had come to mean so much to him in so short a time.

Her tongue dueled with his, a merging of mouths that would be the precursor to the joining of their bodies. Despite the cold evening air that still lingered in the hallway from the open front door, they quickly generated more than enough heat to battle the lingering chill. But it was the firm actions of her hands that confirmed all they'd still not said.

She dragged his coat off, leaving it to pool at their feet with a thud. Her quick fingers then moved to his waist, tugging the hem of his shirt from his slacks. As her fingers met flesh, Finn sucked in a hard breath at so simple a touch.

It was sweet and seeking and intimate, all at once. And in that moment he wanted her more than he could have ever imagined.

He walked her backward into the hallway, on toward her bedroom. He heard the light tinkle of dog tags and stopped, turning to three witnesses who'd suddenly decided to trail them to the bedroom. With firm command, he stared down Lotte, Penny and Lucy.

"Out there for you three. Keep watch."

He saw the slightest hesitation before acceptance filled three sets of eyes. But it was the wag of Penny's tail as she followed the other two to take up a spot in the living room that suggested she approved.

And that she was more than happy to give them some privacy.

Darby watched three tails disappear around the corner of the hall into the living room and couldn't hold back a giggle. "That's impressive, Colton. It would have taken me considerable cajoling and likely half a box of treats to accomplish the same thing."

He shrugged. "I'm alpha dog."

The funny thing was just how true that statement was. Finn Colton was the quintessential alpha dog. At work and throughout Red Ridge, the man was in charge. In return, he protected everyone in his role as pack leader. Even more than that, he took his role as protector seriously. It was more than a job for him. As she'd come to observe him, she knew it was also his calling.

"I guess you are."

"You guess?"

"No." She shook her head. "I know. You're a protector to your core."

He stilled, his blue gaze crystal in the muted light of the bedside lamp. "You have the same qualities, you know."

Her? "I'm not a protector."

"I think you are. Your commitment and devotion to Penny suggests it, but so does your focus on helping me with the Groom Killer. Your immediate attention and upset earlier over that pewter rose showed it again. Even the way you hold Lora, so close and safe against you. You're a protector, too."

The process of getting to know Finn had been a revelation and it was both humbling and shocking to realize that much of what had been revealed were things about herself. Areas of her personality or the way she was observed by others that she'd never thought of or even considered.

"I want you to know something. Before we—"

She broke off, her glance drifting toward the bed. "I want to be with you, but I want you to know that I have no expectations. Of us."

"I do."

His declaration, so swift and immediate, caught her off guard once more. "You do?"

"For starters—" he pulled her close again, nuzzling her neck "—I expect we're going to have a great time."

She arched her head to allow him better access, her voice going breathy. "I sort of expected the same."

"Good." He pressed a long, lingering kiss there, his tongue finding a pulse point and shooting sensation through her that made her knees weak. "But that's not all."

She tried to focus on his words but the strokes of his tongue against the column of her throat were making it hard to concentrate. "There was something else?"

"Oh, yeah." The hands that had held her in place as he kissed her neck began to move, drifting over her stomach in light strokes. His fingers glided higher, coming to rest beneath her breasts before he cupped her fully with each hand.

And when he did—when his hands settled over her—Darby saw stars. Sparks seemed to flash beneath her skin as all her awareness settled in the glorious way he made her feel and the private cocoon that wove around their bodies.

Here, it was just the two of them. The outside

world and all that was wrong with it had no place between them. For a few short hours, Darby knew, they could both shut it out and the responsibilities they'd both go back to. For now, their only obligation was to each other.

"I also expect that you're going to surprise me. Because you've done it every day since we met and I've found that I like it."

"I'm not very surprising."

"Then I'll be all smug and point it out when you do it again."

His thumbs flicked over the peaks of her nipples and pleasure shot through her with all the force of a rocket. The time for talking and thinking and even dreaming had ended. It was time to take advantage of her chance to be with Finn.

Reaching for the hem of his shirt, she pulled on it, lifting it over his head. The strength she'd already felt through the fabric was on full display, his skin golden in the soft light. A dusting of hair covered his chest, tapering down over his stomach into the waistline of his slacks. She traced the path, pleased when his already impressive stomach muscles tightened beneath her fingers.

Taking full advantage of the moment, she traced the path in reverse, flattening her hands so that she could cover as much area as possible.

Strong and solid.

The muscles that quivered beneath her hands spoke of both and seemed to be the outward sign of what she'd observed in his personality. In his choices and in his life, he was so strong and solid. He had the will to chase after killers and to spend each and every day working to keep Red Ridge safe. He also did it from a position of inclusion, as focused on the work as the men and women of his team. As much a part of things, working with Lotte to catch criminals, as what he asked of his squad.

There was nothing soft about Finn Colton. And as she felt that strength wrap around her, pulling her against the solid length of his body, she gave thanks for that.

In moments, interwoven with long, mind-bending kisses, Finn stripped her clothes from her. As each piece fell, that steady sense that there was nothing but the two of them grew. And once they were both naked, he pulled her down on the bed and covered her body with his.

The intimate press of his body—and the urgency that had built steadily between them—had a streak of shyness weaving through her. Turning her head, she stared at the wall, suddenly embarrassed about what was to come.

"Darby?"

"Hmm?"

"What is it? Do you want to stop?"

Stopping was the furthest thing from her mind, but the sudden embarrassment of just how long it had been since she'd been intimate with a man clawed at her. She wanted this to be good between the two of them and she hardly had a great track record of setting the sheets on fire. Even her marriage hadn't produced a particularly Olympian-like sex experience. Bo's infidelity had put a stop to things relatively early on and other than the first halcyon days of their relationship, her experience was woefully lacking.

All of which only made the moment worse—that she was bringing Bo Gage into bed with her and Finn.

She pressed at Finn's shoulders, struggling to sit up. He moved immediately, giving her the room she needed.

"What is it?" His voice was soft, his touch full of concern where it rested against her back.

"I…um…oh, um, well…" She stopped, the embarrassment growing at the fact that not only had she interrupted what was building between them but she now fumbled over her words. "It's been a while since I did this."

"Okay."

When he said nothing else, she turned to face him. Where she'd have expected frustration or even anger filling his gaze, all she saw in the blue was concern. True, genuine concern.

"It's embarrassing."

"Why?"

"Seriously? Here I am with a sexy man and I'm the shy woman who hasn't exactly been setting the town on fire. Heck, I was so sexy even my husband got tired of me faster than you can say *newlywed*."

As the words spilled out, Darby recognized the truth. She saw it reflecting back in Finn's gaze, but didn't need that reinforcement to know what had truly been festering inside all this time.

Bo's infidelity and casual dismissal of their marriage had done damage. She'd understood it on some level, but believed herself past it. How humbling to realize that it not only still lived inside her, coiled and waiting to strike, but just how little she'd dealt with those feelings.

"I'm sorry. I'm ruining something wonderful and special."

"No, you're not. But can I say something?"

"Sure."

"Bo Gage was an ass."

A giggle bubbled to her lips before she could stop it. "It's not nice to speak ill of the dead."

"Why?"

Her laughter stopped abruptly, cut off by that simple question.

"I'm serious, Darby. Why is it wrong? I'll do right by Bo Gage in solving his murder. He's one of mine and I will see that he gets my very best. But why should I suddenly decide to think well of him because he's dead?"

"I don't know. It's just because you're supposed to do that. We're still alive and he's not. It seems unfair to speak ill of him."

"Sorry, but I don't buy it. Especially from where I'm sitting. You're a beautiful, vibrant, compelling woman who is nothing short of amazing which, to my mind, is the exact reason Bo left you the business. Shame he couldn't have found a way to tell you that, especially because the man has left you feeling less than and alone. If that's not worth speaking ill of, I'm not sure what is."

A sense of joy unlike anything she'd ever known unfurled in her chest. It was warm and sweet and freeing.

So very, very freeing.

With a smile she couldn't hide, she gave him the side eye. "You're not just saying this to get me into bed, Colton?"

"News flash, Gage. I have you in bed."

She looked down at their naked bodies, whatever sense of embarrassment or shame that had stopped her fading. She wanted Finn. And if she truly did believe life was for living, she'd be foolish to let the moment pass them by. "I guess you do."

They turned to each other in unison, their mutual intent clear. And as her lips met Finn's once more, her joy burst through in a big welcoming smile.

Finn lowered Darby onto the bed, his mouth never leaving hers. While he'd not have called their prior moments passionless by any means, something had shifted in their conversation over Darby's past.

The kisses with her were sweeter. Hotter. And considerably more heartfelt. She was an amazing woman and he was determined to make her feel that in every single second they spent together.

With one final press of his lips to hers, he shifted, moving down her body. He spent some time in that sensitive hollow at her neck, enjoying the way her hands grew more urgent at his back, one more point of evidence to how good things were between them. Continuing the journey, he traced a path with his tongue, pressing kisses over her collarbone before coming to her breasts.

She was a small, petite woman, but her curves were lush and gorgeous and absolutely perfect. He plied those curves, pleased when his touch elicited a small moan from the back of her throat before he closed his mouth around one pert nipple. Her moan deepened and Finn felt himself groan as he sank into the moment.

Time passed. Minutes or hours, he had no idea. All he knew was a sense of urgency matched with an unwillingness to rush things. He wanted her— wanted to awaken her to true passion—and his only focus was Darby.

Where had this attraction been lurking, he wondered as he shifted to her other breast, determined to pleasure her for as long as he could before giving in to the demands of his body.

He'd seen her around town. Known who she was. How had he never before noticed how beautiful she was? Or how well they fit together?

Finn pressed on in his sensuous journey. His lips

pressed against her belly button before he dipped his tongue to lightly tickle her. The quiver of flesh beneath his lips let him know he'd done what he'd set out to do. But it was the long, low moan and arch of her hips when he fastened his mouth at the very center of her that had his flesh quivering. He would make this last. Would see that she found pleasure with him, over and over. Even as his body demanded release.

"Finn!"

His name had never sounded sweeter—nor had a woman ever tasted better—as he pleasured her. Long, lush strokes with his tongue. A hot tease of his breath against sensitive flesh. And the addition of his fingers to send her over the edge of pleasure.

He watched her, gratified at the amazing responsiveness, before she pulled him close for a hot, carnal kiss, clutching at his shoulders as she found her release.

But it was the whisper that followed against his ear—half moan, half plea—that let him know he'd not last much longer.

"Now, Finn. I need you. Want you—" she practically purred against his throat "—now."

The sudden realization he'd left protection halfway across the room had him pulling back, determined to reach his pants when she stopped him. "The drawer. I…um…" A blush stained her cheeks, adding to the already pretty flush that painted her skin. "I wanted to be prepared."

Despite the demands of his body or perhaps because of them, laughter bubbled up, swift and immediate. "What was that I mentioned earlier?"

"About?"

"You, Darby Gage." He leaned in and pressed a hard kiss to her lips before reaching for the drawer. "I told you that you were full of surprises. How happy I am to prove you right."

Her smile was bright enough to power half of Red Ridge as he tore open the condom packet and made quick work of putting it on. "I told you I wanted to be prepared."

"Far be it from me to argue with a woman who knows her own mind."

"Good." She reached down to stroke the length of him, guiding him toward her body. As he found her sweet warmth, he sank in deep, shocked anew by how good she felt.

But it was as they began to move, at first tentative then faster as they picked up on each other's rhythm, did the pleasure expand. Build. Grow.

As Darby's release built, his own was nearly upon him. Harder, faster, he thrust, welcomed each and every time by the amazing woman in his arms. His body tightened, his ability to hold on nearly giving out when he heard the change in her breathing. Her arms tightened and her back arched, and Finn felt the telltale muscles intimately sheathing him pull him in, ready to drown him in her body.

Finn gave in then, his release coming on him fast as the crack of a whip and doubly powerful.

All he'd imagined earlier paled in comparison to the real thing and as his body emptied into hers, Finn knew the truth.

He didn't just have more. He had everything.

Chapter 16

Finn ran his hands over her skin as he held Darby close and desperately tried to bury the sense of anger that washed through him. The sensation was foreign and had no place in bed with them, especially after the warm, deep sense of satisfaction that still filled him from their lovemaking. But, damn, if he could let go of the ire or the upset that anyone had caused her a moment of pain or self-doubt.

She was perfect and the fact that Bo Gage had been such an ass to her bothered him more than he could say.

He'd never been happy for a crime committed against one of his constituents—and he certainly wasn't going to start with murder—but it was damn hard to feel any sense of sympathy for a jerk who'd used people and discarded them when he was done. Which was exactly what Bo had done to Darby.

Marriage took two—he knew that better than anyone—but when one behaved in a way that was pure betrayal, it was hard to see the injured party as equally at fault. He and Mary might have had their issues, but he'd remained faithful to her for the duration of their marriage, including the time before their divorce was finalized. He'd made a commitment of fidelity to her and he'd honored it.

"Who are you mad at right now?"

"What?"

Darby's voice was sleepy but her eyes were sharp as she lifted her head to look at him. "I can practically hear the anger in your head. It's got your chest all tight and your arms keep tensing up."

"I'm not mad."

"You are, and you're a crummy liar to boot." She sat up, her hair framing her face in a messy tumble. "What has you bothered?"

"I don't want to upset you."

"Okay. Then I promise not to get upset."

"You will."

"No, I won't."

Finn knew the conversation was too far gone to pull back so he gave himself a moment to prepare his thoughts and hopefully say things in a way that would minimize the pain.

"I'm mad at Bo."

"Why?"

"Before. The way you felt. You're amazing and incredible and beautiful, and the idea that anyone made you question that… It upsets me."

"You're right."

Where he expected something—even if it was a raised voice or a lone tear—nothing manifested. All he saw was complete and absolute agreement.

"And you're not upset?"

"I was before. But right now I feel stupidly happy." She patted him on the cheek, her wry smile loopy around the edges. "Don't worry. It won't last. But while it does, I refuse to ruin it."

And there it was again. Surprise.

"Remember what I said before?" he asked her.

"About?"

"About being full of surprises." When she only nodded, he added, "Look at my smug face and count this as one of those times."

"I'd rather kiss your smug face."

He pulled her down on top of his chest, his hand at the back of her head to guide her to his mouth. He thought that she had a rather smug smile of her own.

"By all means, Ms. Gage. Don't let me stop you."

Finn made a few stops on his way to work on Monday, the memories of the night before going a long way to battle the lack of sleep. Darby had been a revelation and making love to her was more than he could have ever imagined. Better than his most elaborate fantasies, and he'd had more than a few.

Which made the shift in headspace from a gorgeous, responsive woman in his arms to a hunt for a cold-blooded killer that much more jarring.

But no matter how wonderful it was to escape for a few hours with nothing to focus on except Darby, there was still a killer on the loose in Red Ridge.

He and his team had split up all the tips that had come in and he'd followed up on several, canvassing Red Ridge and the surrounding county, none of which had paid dividends. The first two had some merit, suggesting his cousin Demi, had been sighted a few towns over. The next one had been a fishing expedition on the part of a tipper, hungry for information about the case. By the fourth, he hadn't even gotten past the front door, the woman who called it in one of the precinct's "regulars." The woman wasn't a menace, but she was a pest, calling the police out for everything from what she believed was the scent of gas to a perceived slight from a neighbor.

Finn kept his tone stern, even as pity filled him for the slight woman on the other side of her front door. She wasn't that old—a recent check of her license had her in her midthirties—yet she'd developed a strange addiction to calling the precinct. "What was it you wanted to share with us, Lydia?"

"Hello, Chief. I know you've been keeping watch out for Demi Colton. I wanted to tell you I think she's guilty."

This was a new one. Lydia typically complained about neighbors and frequently told him she was prepared to make a citizen's arrest for noise violations. "Oh? Why is that?"

"Please. It's cold out. You're welcome to come in."

He nodded his head but stayed firmly put. "That's very kind of you, ma'am, but I don't want to take up too much of your time. But if you do have information on Demi Colton, I'd like to know about it."

The woman seemed flustered by his kindness and a slight flush crept up her neck. "It's a sense, really. I'd seen her around town before she fled and she's a hard woman, Chief. It would be so easy to see her killing men for sport."

"So you don't actually have information?"

Lydia seemed affronted. "Why, that's information. I'm a concerned citizen making sure I'm keeping the police up-to-date."

"Of course." Finn pulled out his notebook and made a show of writing down what she'd told him. He also made a note to flag the slightly daffy Lydia in Lorelei's files. They'd always respond to a citizen's needs—he refused to ignore someone simply because he or she was a bit off—but his officers needed to go into a situation with their eyes wide open.

He was ready to go when Lydia spoke up again. "Well, I might have something else."

For the briefest moment he could have sworn something sly flickered in her hazel gaze, but the sense was gone as quickly as it had come.

"Your help would be very appreciated."

"I've also seen that Darby Gage around town. Word is that she hated that her ex-husband was getting remarried. It wouldn't be too hard to think she wanted revenge."

Patience at an end, Finn nearly said something, holding back only at the last moment. It was only because of Lydia's long history of contact and the sheer sadness that he felt for her that he held his ground. "Ms. Gage has grieved the loss of her ex-husband. Regardless and based on police work, the precinct has ruled her out as a suspect."

"Oh."

"Thank you for your time, Lydia."

Her hand snaked out and, for a second, Finn thought she was going to take his hand, but she pulled hers back at the last moment. "I know you'll catch the killer, Chief Colton. I have faith in you. From the bottom of my heart, I do."

"Thank you, ma'am." Finn smiled at the odd woman before heading out to continue his work for the day. It didn't take long for the annoying exchange to become a distant memory in his mind.

Darby checked the food in the oven with a meat thermometer, pleased to see her pot roast coming along nicely. She'd spent the past few days in a haze and it felt good to do something in her own house. With no one around to notice the small hearts and cupids floating around her head in circles.

"Or the dopey smile that's likely been riding your face," she added to herself before shooting a look at Penny and Lucy. The dogs had taken up sentinel duty in the kitchen, no doubt praying a fervent canine prayer the oven would open of its own accord and spew its contents in their direction.

"Yeah, you'll get some, too. I can't feel this goofy and happy and not share with you both. Lotte, too, when she and Finn get here."

She'd already anticipated the quiet dinner she and Finn would share. The public dates and show they'd kept up for all of Red Ridge had served its purpose— and she knew they'd be back at it tomorrow night— but she'd made the decision to keep Valentine's Day all to themselves. The mention of a home-cooked meal had Finn quickly agreeing.

Not that going out with the man was a hardship. She'd been cognizant of their pretense in the past, but now all she could feel was the sheer joy of being with him. And of the desire to shout to the rooftops that she was with this man, in every hour either of them could possibly drag free.

Their days were spent focused on their jobs. Hers on Lucy's breeding schedule and making contact with Bo's former clients to see who might be interested in her first litter. Finn's on the continued hunt for the Groom Killer. The lack of clues remained a problem, as did the continued disappearance of Finn's cousin Demi.

But he'd find her. He had to.

Even if it got harder and harder to believe as one day rolled into the next. What was Demi hiding? And if she really were innocent, why didn't she believe the RRPD could protect her?

Darby questioned the woman's motives as she finished up a few website updates at the kitchen table. She wasn't the world's best web designer, but she'd played around with a few programs and had given the site for the breeding business a nice makeover. That and the pot roast and she'd call it a damn productive day.

Both had also kept her mind running in the background with thoughts of how to help Finn.

She'd lived in Red Ridge all her life. Surely she had enough knowledge of her fellow citizens to be of some use beyond the public ruse of dating Finn. But because of knowing the townsfolk all her life—or maybe in spite of it—she couldn't shake the mystery of Demi Colton, no matter how many ways she twisted and turned the puzzle over in her mind.

Darby knew firsthand how infuriating Bo Gage could be. And while she hadn't been pregnant with his child, she had been married to him. So if you compared life choices, she and Demi had at least a common frame of reference. Even if she mentally added the even deeper importance of a child to the mix, she simply couldn't see being mad enough to kill the man. Angry, yes. Disappointed, absolutely.

But murder?

Even with time to think about it and consider

Demi as the one who'd put a bullet into Bo, the woman just didn't seem like a match for the crime. That only became more true when you considered the second victim. Demi might have a personal motive against Bo, but that flew out the window when Michael Hayden was added to the mix.

Killing Bo would be personal. Killing Michael would be twisted and sick. Had Demi just snapped and was going around killing grooms on the nights before their weddings? All because Bo had broken their engagement after a week? When they'd only been together a few months anyway?

But they hadn't discovered anyone else with motive, obvious or otherwise. Two dead bodies and next to nothing to go on. Even with the new direction Darby and Finn's relationship had taken, and the enjoyment of their time together, the endless questions haunted him. She saw it in his eyes and knew it kept him awake long after she'd fallen asleep in his arms.

Which was why she'd demanded that Valentine's Day be private and just for the two of them. The meat-and-potatoes meal she'd crafted—pot roast and Idaho reds—was as down-the-line "man food" as you could get. The appreciative smile he gave her a few hours later when he and Lotte walked into the kitchen reinforced his interest in the food—a sure sign she'd selected correctly on the meal.

"That smells amazing."

"Thanks. Penny and Lucy have lain around the kitchen all afternoon, basking in the smell."

"I don't blame them." He kissed her, a sound, smacking smooch on the lips, before he bent to pet both dogs. Their immediate offering of their bellies suggested the pot roast wasn't the only thing in the kitchen that had them happy and she enjoyed watching the ease with which he won over the ladies of the house.

Worn circles filled the creases beneath his eyes and Darby considered asking him about the case. Since it was his time to relax and take a break, she filed it away, promising herself she'd find a way to bring it up later.

He pulled her close for another kiss, long and lingering this time, and she let the thought flit away, content to sink into him and the quiet moment between them. It had been like that since Sunday, the easy, generous lover she'd taken showing his affection and consideration in a million different ways.

It was humbling to realize how quickly she'd come to crave that. The soft, yet deliberate, touches and the easy way of being together.

She'd already set the small, drop-leaf table for dinner and pointed toward the wine on the counter. "You still on duty or would you like a glass of wine?"

"We're in for the night. I'll open it up."

Finn focused on the wine and she pulled dinner from the oven, their domesticity yet another element that was easy. Companionable.

And with that realization came another.

She was in love with Finn Colton.

The pan tilted in her hands as she bobbled the pot roast, nearly answering the dogs' prayers.

"Easy there, Darby. Do you have it?" He'd moved next to her, his hands nearly to hers before she side-stepped him.

"Yes!" she squeaked before gripping the pan harder. "Don't touch."

"You okay?"

"Of course. I just don't want you to get burned."

He snagged a few hand towels off the counter and helped her settle the pan on the stove top. "I'm fine. Are you sure you're okay?"

"Of course." Her heart pounded in her throat and she could have sworn they heard her heartbeat three towns over. "I'm fine. Just a bad grip. It's fine."

"The pack over here is disappointed your hands are so steady." He pointed to Penny, Lucy and Lotte, all intently focused on the stove.

Darby fought for some sense of equilibrium and grabbed at the silly conversation about the dogs. That was normal. Simple. And had nothing at all to do with love or feelings or an inappropriately needy response to the man you'd been sleeping with. "They've been hoping for a taste since before I put it in."

Oblivious to her upset, Finn snagged a roll she'd left covered on the counter. "Our opportunistic room-mates. It must be hell not to have opposable thumbs."

The silly comment was enough to have her laughing and she vowed to push the thoughts of love from her mind. She'd pull them out later, when Finn wasn't around and she could truly analyze them. It was Valentine's Day, after all. She was feeling fanciful and silly.

That was it.

It had to be.

Finn finished loading the dishwasher at Darby's insistence that no one cleaned dishes in the sink on a holiday. And since he'd equally insisted the one who cooked the meal wasn't stuck cleaning it up, he'd sent her into the living room while he worked. His stomach was full and the meal, shared with an amazing woman, had been one of the best of his life.

So why was he still so riled up? Was he giving off vibes?

Whatever weird moment had gripped her earlier, when he'd first gotten to her place, had passed. Their meal had been fun and lighthearted, with both of them talking about some of the funny and lovable dogs who hadn't made it through K-9 training.

There was Buster the black Lab, who was even now enjoying life on a farm two counties over. And Sinclair, one of the rare German shepherds not to graduate from the program. He'd been adopted by a teacher at the high school and, through a random act of leash twisting, wrapped her up during lunch one day in the park with one of the mechanics from the Red Ridge Tire and Lube. The three of them now lived happily ever after in an apartment over the garage.

It had been fun and silly and had conjured up memories of Buster and Sinclair and a host of other dogs he'd been happy to see adopted so they could go on to a future that was exactly right for them.

It had also been the antidote to the bad mood he'd walked in with. The gift that had come to the precinct that afternoon had gotten to him and he hadn't fully shaken it off. He'd own it and admit that, finally, his anonymous gift giver had rattled him. Finn knew he should tell Darby about it, but he hadn't wanted to spoil the evening.

But now that dinner was done and he wasn't a liar—or even an omitter—on principle, something urgent nagged at him to tell her.

"Dishwasher is on." He walked into the living room, amused to see Penny curled up next to her on the couch, the dog's head in Darby's lap. "What was that you were saying about her coming around?"

"I guess she has."

Sheer delight filled Darby's face at Penny's closeness. Her smile was warm and inviting, and he felt himself being drawn even deeper into the living room.

Finn didn't want to break the spell with something ugly and unpleasant, but he also wanted to share it with her. Wanted her opinion and her thoughts.

Wanted her comfort.

"Can I show you something?"

"Of course."

He crossed to his bag and pulled the heavy box from where he'd buried it in the bottom. The inside of the box was coated with fabric over a layer of protective foam and from it he pulled out the glass heart.

"That's beautiful." Her smile vanished, replaced with a frown. "But it's another gift from Anonymous, isn't it?"

"Yes." He handed her the heart—the lab had already done a quick overview and confirmed no prints—so he'd felt comfortable taking it with him.

Darby shifted Penny slightly before taking the heart and turning it over in her hands. "It's not as dangerous as the rose. Nothing sharp or out of the ordinary." She ran a fingertip over the glass. "It's smooth. Heavy, too. And expensive, by the looks of it."

"That was the lab's assessment when I ran it over."

"Did they say anything else?"

"Only that there weren't any prints they could find. One of the techs is going to look into the manufacturer to see if they can find anything. It is Valentine's Day. Any number of stores could be selling something like this."

She held it up to the light, turning it back and forth before shifting her gaze once again. "Did a card come with it?"

"Yes."

He pulled that out of his bag, as well, and held it up. Just like the other gifts, it followed a pattern. The writing was neat and it had been anonymously sent. But, like the rose, there was a sense of escalation in the message on the card.

A heart is fragile, take care with it.

Finn handed over the card.

"How do you take care with something, or someone, in this case, if you don't know who they are?"

"That's been the mystery from the first."

"It doesn't make sense. If the Groom Killer wanted to taunt you, you'd think there would be a better way. There's no ownership or bragging over the murders."

Yet again, her sharp intelligence shone through and he was caught up in the wonder of Darby. He and Carson had discussed the situation, and as trained professionals had come up with the same conclusion.

"It also doesn't make a lot of sense that my cousin Demi would be sending something like this." He wasn't ready to rule Demi out, but it was one more point of incongruity in trying to pin the Groom Killer details on her.

Assuming the two were related.

"No one's seen the delivery person?"

"Lorelei's been on the lookout but this was delivered in a stack of packages and it wasn't until after the delivery man had gone that she even realized it was addressed to me. She followed up with the service but they had nothing."

"That's even weirder." Her hand shook slightly as she handed back the card. "This doesn't feel right."

"I know."

"Do you really?" She gently moved Penny's head from her lap and resettled the dog on the couch before standing and coming to his side. "Does this scare you as much as it scares me?"

"I'm a big manly man. I don't scare easily." When the bad joke failed to make her smile, he went with the truth. "Yeah, it does. More than I want to admit."

"What are you going to do about it?"

"Keep doing what I've been doing. While it may not be related to the Groom Killer at all, I need to follow this lead. Demi is still a suspect and we're chasing down whatever we can, but she's poofed. These gifts are from someone who's actively taunting the chief of police. I need to work with that."

"And continue putting yourself out there as bait."

"Yes."

It was both statement and agreement. And right now, it looked like his only chance to catch a killer.

The watcher moved through the center of Red Ridge like a wraith. That's how she'd always seen herself. Neither here nor there, just a spirit that most people weren't even aware of.

All her life, that's how it had always been.

Until she'd met police chief Finn Colton.

He was so magnificent. He kept the town safe—kept *her* safe—and she owed him a debt of gratitude for pulling her from the abyss. No longer did she lie alone at night in bed, afraid of what lurked in the shadows. Her mom had taught her to be afraid of what hid there but the chief had slowly helped her come into the light.

There was a big world and if the right man was there protecting it, everything would be okay.

He was even going to catch the Groom Killer. He might be short on clues now but she'd been keeping watch for him. She'd pay attention for any changes in town and she would tell him. A concerned citizen.

The only problem was that Gage woman. She put the chief at risk. Made him turn his head away from his responsibilities, and it had to stop.

The watcher drifted to the edge of the town square. Work had already started on the booths and stages for the winter festival. She usually hated the festival. It came right on the heels of Valentine's Day—a holiday that never favored her—and was always a celebration full of happy families, sappy couples and people out in groups enjoying themselves.

Her mother had called them heathens and it was a term that had stuck. The Red Ridge Heathens. It happened every year, a beacon the town looked forward to in the middle of winter. Because what it really was, after all, was a chance to drink in public and make a lot of noise and ruckus.

Images of those people enjoying themselves made her think again about the chief. He'd been squiring that Gage woman around town and she knew she had to expect he'd come there with her.

Didn't he care there was someone out there who only wanted his happiness? Who loved him? She'd sent the heart to show him how much she cared. Maybe that would be enough to make him think twice about Darby Gage.

She hoped so.

She continued on down Main Street, the lights from the restaurant windows spilling out onto the street. They weren't all crowded for Valentine's Day—another side effect of having a killer on the loose—but there were people out. Couples staring at each other across the table. A few families out enjoying being together.

If the chief would only pay attention to her gifts, they could be sitting there, staring at each other, too. If he only knew how much he mattered to her.

She'd put herself squarely in the Groom Killer's sights for a date with the chief.

Her gaze caught on the town square once more and she considered what she'd do. The festival would be the place to make her move. To let him know how important he was. To show him they should be together.

She could do it. She could be a heathen, too. Her mother might not approve, but Mother wasn't here any longer.

It was time to step into the light.

Chapter 17

Darby came awake, the angle of the light shining in the window a surprise. This wasn't her room.

Where was she?

Before the question could register, a large male arm tightened around her stomach, a lethargic groan emanating from the back of his throat as he pulled her close in his sleep. And then she remembered.

She and Finn had put on their love show for all of Red Ridge since Valentine's Day. Big, flashy outings around town including a snowball fight he'd initiated at the edge of the town square the night before that had ultimately gotten what seemed like half of Red Ridge involved. By the end, they'd had a laughing pile of people, tired from tossing snowballs and melting snow dripping off their winter caps. Finn had used the moment to his advantage, tackling her in front of everyone and kissing her senseless in the middle of the town square.

Which should have made her embarrassed but had only left a warm, rosy flush to her skin every time she thought about it.

After last night's snowball fight and dinner at the diner with the rest of the snow battalion, they'd come back to his place and made love.

Which only made her more rosy and even more flushed as she thought about sex with Finn.

He was amazing. He'd unlocked something inside her that she knew she had been missing, but hadn't realized quite how much. Yet now that he was here, in her life every day, she couldn't deny how welcome he was.

Which took her right back to being in love with him.

She'd managed to put it out of her mind since Valentine's Day, but like those erotic flashes of making love with Finn that kept her company off and on throughout the day, her feelings popped in and out, as well. A few days to consider how she felt and let it sink in hadn't changed her mind. Nor had it gotten much easier to digest.

She glanced down at the large forearm that rested over her stomach, tracing the length of corded muscle with her gaze. He was a powerful man—impressively so. But his strength came not only in the physical but in his ability to practice restraint in equal measure.

He was unfailingly kind to his constituents. Any number of people had stopped him over the past few days and he'd been cordial to all of them. Even his family members who clearly believed it was wrong of him to keep looking toward Demi as a suspect had earned his kindness and respectful, affable conversation. Even his ranting uncle Fenwick—an unexpected visitor to their table the other night as they'd shared a steak dinner—had been met with Finn's easy manner and efficient competence.

Which only shows how far gone you are, Darbs.

Willing her gaze off the sexy length of his forearm—and, seriously, obsessing over his forearm?— she forced herself to look around his bedroom to distract herself from her thoughts. The warmth spreading through her chest, reinforcing all she'd eagerly observed, needed to be squashed.

Or, at minimum, contained.

For all the time they'd spent together he hadn't indicated he had any thoughts about something longer term. He said he wanted to try a real relationship, which had been wonderful so far, but what did that really mean? Would he still be with her by spring? Or summer? And what happened once he caught the Groom Killer?

She'd heard stories of how heightened danger could make a person feel intense feelings that couldn't possibly last. What if that was true for Finn?

While she knew her feelings were genuine, what if his were of the moment? How would she ever survive what would no doubt be a major heartache if what was between them suddenly vanished once the lingering threat of a killer was contained? Ignoring the hitch in her throat the thought induced, she focused on his bedroom instead.

Like the rest of his condo, it was small but comfortable, with more than enough room for a single man. He lived in a complex near downtown Red Ridge, which he'd mentioned he'd chosen for the easy access to work.

The warm, overstuffed furniture in his living room was welcoming and lived in, and his condominium felt like a home. A bachelor pad, evidenced by the limited supplies in the fridge and the layer of dust on his bookshelves, but a comfortable home all the same.

"And you accuse me of being a loud thinker." Finn punctuated his sleepy comment by shifting onto his side and tightening his hold at her waist. He pulled her close in one smooth move, his mouth finding a particularly sensitive spot on her collarbone.

"Good morning."

"That it is." He smiled against her skin. "The sun is shining and I've got a beautiful woman in my arms."

"You sweet talker, you."

He lifted his head, a wry smile tilting his lips. "Is it sweet talk if it's true?"

She snuggled closer. "I don't see why not."

They spent several quiet moments, kissing and touching, wrapped up in each other, when Finn let out a quiet curse.

"What is it?"

"I've got an urgent paw in my back that doesn't care about our make-out session. She wants to go out."

Darby sighed, knowing Penny and Lucy would need to do the same. Finn rolled out of bed and as she stared at his incredibly attractive—and entirely naked—backside, she acknowledged how morning routines worked at his place. "I guess it's a bit different having a dog in a condo than letting them out into the backyard."

That smile was back, deeper and naughtier this time. "My neighbors prefer I wear pants. Since I feel the same way about them, it works nicely. But, yeah, it's not as easy as just opening the door."

"I'll let you get to it, then, and I'll put coffee on."

"Deal."

He dressed quickly and Darby couldn't quite persuade herself to get out of bed. She watched him pull on an old sweatshirt and gym pants, fascinated by the stretch of muscles before that magnificent chest disappeared under thick cotton. Finn shot her a wink before rounding up the dogs, and she realized he'd been well aware of the show he'd put on.

Their quiet interlude at an end, she sighed and got out of bed. Dragging on the sweater and jeans she'd worn the night before, she padded out to the kitchen in the wake of Finn and three dogs. It didn't take her long to find coffee in his fridge and filters in a drawer. In short order the pot on his counter was up and running.

Her gaze caught on his workbag, nestled in one of the kitchen chairs. The box holding the glass heart peeked out of the top and she considered it from where she stood. Like a coiled snake, it became her sole focal point as she stared at it across the kitchen.

Although she had nothing to go on, the entire situation suggested a woman. Which was irrational and likely territorial, she acknowledged to herself, but there it was.

The anonymous notes, the deliveries and even the types of gifts. Whatever Finn might be dealing with, Darby instinctively believed Anonymous was female.

She was also certain the sender wasn't Finn's cousin Demi. Not only did the presents have an underlying sense of something sexual, which would be odd from a family member, but all Finn's comments up to now suggested that he and Demi weren't close. And if they did follow the supposition that Demi had killed Bo in some sort of lover's rage, why would she suddenly become attracted to her cousin?

Which was when it all clicked.

Hard.

The presents hadn't seemed to have anything to

do with the Groom Killer because they *weren't* about the Groom Killer at all. They were about Finn.

If the escalating notes and gifts were any indication, he was possibly in more trouble than either of them had suspected. Finn and his team were on the lookout for a killer with a gun and a grudge.

But what if the real threat came at him from a direction he'd never even considered?

Finn laughed as he coaxed Penny into the hallway of his building. Although he had a small fenced patio off his first-floor unit, which he allowed Lotte to use in a pinch during bad weather, he believed it was his responsibility to get her outside to deal with her needs every day. Penny and Lucy deserved no less.

Lotte had long gotten used to a common entryway, but Penny seemed overly intrigued with the setup. Between the smells entering the hallway from his neighbors—including the tantalizing scent of Saturday morning bacon—and the perpetual layer of noise from the elevator, she hovered in a confused haze of activity. She'd raced inside as soon as they'd all finished their outside business, sniffing everywhere she could find and then trotting back and forth from the elevator bank to the hallway and right back again.

"Come on, girl. Let's go see what Darby has."

Penny reluctantly followed, her training and obedience taking over, but he didn't miss the look she shot the hallway over her shoulder.

"Poor thing. Pot roast on Wednesday. Bacon on Saturday. It's a crazy world." Those soulful eyes looked up at him in agreement as they walked into his condo.

Penny's attention shifted immediately and she barked as she ran over to Darby. The swift change in behavior had him following on the dog's heels into the kitchen. "What's wrong?"

She leaned against the counter, her arms folded over her stomach, her face pale.

"Darby?"

"The heart. I think I get it."

"Get what?"

He followed her gaze and saw the box holding the glass heart. He'd been carrying it around, hoping he'd find out where it had come from. But his canvassing of Red Ridge stores, the closest mall in the county and an outdoor shopping district in Spearfish hadn't turned up a single clue.

Or anyone who even recognized the glass piece.

Several shop owners had commented on its quality and one had even suggested a few possible manufacturers, but other than that, he had nothing.

Except an object that made his bag far heavier than its weight suggested.

"What do you get?"

Darby pushed off the counter. Her skin was still pale, but determination rode her gaze. "You've been targeted."

"By the Groom Killer?"

"What if the Groom Killer is a convenient distraction? What if there's someone else who wants to do you harm and all this chaos in the midst of the murders has given them a chance to strike?"

He knew she spoke from concern, but couldn't fully keep that in the forefront of his thoughts as anger shot through him. "You're telling me I've got another problem on the loose in my town? 'Cuz I'm having a hard enough time keeping up with one."

"Face facts, Finn. These 'gifts' and messages have escalated. What if this person is looking to do you harm?"

Face facts? Wasn't that what he did every damn day? "Then we catch them. It's that simple."

"But they're on the loose."

"A fact I'm well aware of." He crossed the short distance to the table and pulled the box from his bag, shifting it from hand to hand. "You think I don't understand what this means? Or that I'm oblivious to the danger?"

"Are you? Because you seem to think you can handle this all, but how are you going to go up against a crazy person with a gun? Or possibly two?"

He had no right to be upset in the face of her concern, but all he'd wanted was a quiet morning with her and the dogs. A chance to shut out the world and the noise and focus on something other than blood and death. Yet, here she was, pushing it in his face and suggesting he didn't understand what was really going on in Red Ridge.

Or, more to the point, what he'd somehow ignored as it had built and grown and *seethed* beneath the surface of his quiet little bucolic town.

He owned that.

Was responsible for it.

And since Bo Gage's death, he'd been forced to accept that his ability to keep law and order was waning at best.

"I know what I can handle."

He saw recognition fill her eyes. Saw the moment she understood that her pushing had gone from a discussion about a killer to a discussion about him. And he hated himself for it.

"This isn't about you, Finn. Surely you can see that? It's about people with problems. With an inability to see or understand that harming others is wrong."

"And there you go again. We should consider hiring you for the force. Your detective skills are bar none. Should I now add psychology to the list?"

Her pale skin and wide eyes had vanished, heat flushing her cheeks and blue fire sparking in her gaze. "Be mad at me if you want. Take it out on me, even. I won't shatter like that glass heart. But don't tell me you're oblivious to the danger."

"I'm not oblivious to anything."

"Could have fooled me."

She pushed off the counter and stomped out of the kitchen. As he stood there and watched her go, he made no move to stop her.

* * *

Laughing, happy people surrounded her as Darby worked her way through the Red Ridge town square. The winter festival was in high gear, in spite of the biting cold and the snowstorm that threatened to end things early. Space heaters had been set up at varying intervals to ensure people could warm up; adding those to thick coats, heavy mittens and hands full of cups of hot chocolate, the hearty residents of her town seemed fairly good at staying warm.

She and Finn had reached a tentative truce as the day had worn on and he'd finally acquiesced and let her go home for a few hours to get a few things done. The time away had done her good and had given her a chance to clear her head a bit.

When Finn had met up with his team, she'd told him she was going to wander off to explore and say hi to a few people. He'd attempted to argue but broke off at her protests that she'd be fine at four in the afternoon in and around several hundred fellow residents.

She loved him. All her inward protests and mental gymnastics couldn't change that. Or, more to the point, wouldn't change it. But she also wasn't his punching bag, willing to sit around while he brooded over his job and his town and the problems that lay beneath.

Finn was a good cop. But being a good cop meant that he was going to run up against people who defied logic or understanding. That wasn't his fault, or his doing, and the reality that he'd begun to think that the presence of a killer in his town was evidence he wasn't doing his job was a puzzle.

She headed for the hot-chocolate table to pick up a cup and got in line behind a family. A child of about five stood with her parents, her hand wrapped in her mother's. She chattered happily about a booth where she could win a stuffed dog and how she was going to sink a golf ball into a bowl to win.

Darby had passed the booth earlier and knew the game was rigged to ensure every child got a prize, even if it wasn't the large stuffed toy that hung from the top of the booth, drawing the eye and beckoning people over. She thought about Lora and how in a few short years she'd be here, ready to do her own ball toss.

As she waited, her thoughts tumbling one over the other, Darby let her gaze roam the crowd. Was a criminal here? Whether it was the Groom Killer or the sly, swirling threat from Anonymous, she filtered each person she saw through the lens of potential criminal.

And realized that it was considerably more interesting to look at the excited five-year-old and contemplate her happiness at winning a stuffed dog.

What changed people? How did one go from happy at five to disillusioned at thirty-five? Forty-five? Older? And how had she been lucky enough to escape that?

Her mother had spent her life disillusioned. Convinced the only thing the world gave was drudgery and misery, her mother had toiled away without ever finding joy in anything. While not as outwardly dangerous as the Groom Killer, it wasn't a way to spend a life.

Why could she see it yet Finn couldn't? He felt responsible for his town, which she understood. But he couldn't take any responsibility for the choices his townspeople made.

She stepped up to get her cup of hot chocolate and wondered at the sudden chill that whipped through her. Tension ran the length of her spine and she turned at the sudden awareness of being watched. Taking her cup, she stepped to the side of the table and made a show of blowing on the hot liquid as her eyes scanned the crowd.

More families. A few couples; one that she recognized from the diner. And a few of Finn's deputies spanned the perimeter, watching the proceedings. Darby continued her scan, running over the same set of faces again, slowing as she got to a lone woman, standing at the edge of the festival square. She didn't know why she stopped—or why the woman drew her attention—but as Darby stood there she caught the woman's hard glare.

Was the woman watching her?

And why did she look so weird, standing there alone?

It was an unfair thought, Darby knew. She was alone. She'd spent the past hour contentedly walking around the grounds and didn't think twice that she didn't belong or that she should leave.

Yet something was odd about the woman.

She'd just begun to walk over when large arms wrapped around her from behind, warm lips quickly finding the sensitive spot beneath her ear. "You look better than that hot chocolate."

She whirled in Finn's arms, the menace of that quietly stoic figure fading in her mind at his arrival. "It's delicious and I'm not sure I'm sharing."

His arms widened enough to allow her to turn, but he didn't break his hold. "I deserve that."

"You do not—"

He squeezed her and pressed a quick kiss to her lips, effectively cutting her off before he lifted his head. "I do. I was a jerk and, worse, I was a jerk to you."

"I don't fault you for caring about your community. For being frustrated over your work. But I don't understand blaming yourself."

"Funny. Carson said something similar a few minutes ago. I believe his words were a bit different though. More pragmatic, too."

"Oh?"

"He told me to get my head out of my ass."

"Sound advice." She handed over her hot chocolate, offering him a sip. "Have some hot chocolate. It'll give you a head start."

Pain, white-hot and sharp, stabbed at her. As forceful as knives, Lydia nearly doubled over in pain as she watched Finn Colton wrap his arms around that Gage woman.

She'd seen him earlier. Had even gotten up her courage to pass by him and brush her arm against his. He'd been distracted by his meeting with his officers, but she knew he'd sensed it.

Had known he'd felt her love.

Yet here he was, flaunting his relationship with that woman in front of her. In front of the whole damn town.

She slapped a hand over her mouth, holding back the rising bile as the chief bent his head to kiss that woman. That should be her. He should know how she felt. He should be with her.

Only, he didn't. He wasn't. He'd ignored her gifts and had brushed off her attempts to draw his attention with her information about the Groom Killer.

As she stood and stared at him, watching how he wrapped his arm around Darby Gage's shoulders, Lydia knew the devastating truth. Finn Colton would never be hers.

But as she stood there, gathering herself in the cold, Lydia made a vow. Her chief wouldn't be anyone else's, either.

Finn carried a small stuffed dog under his arm as he and Darby crossed the last block to his condo. The winter festival had been a success, the townsfolk seeming to enjoy themselves through another cold February night. He'd waited through shift rotation, when a new set of deputies came on duty and, after making one last turn around the grounds, had left the last hour of the festival to them.

"I can't believe you got the dog in one try."

"I'm a good shot."

"No, you let that little girl win the big dog." She reached over and ran a fingertip over the head of the small toy. "And you got me the little one instead. Very heroic of you."

"All in a day's work."

"For you, maybe." She stood on her tiptoes and pressed a kiss to his cheek. Finn wasn't sure if it was relief that they'd moved past their argument or just the joy of being with her, but her words and her kiss made him feel ten feet tall.

He let them into his unit and took his first deep breath since they'd left. The festival was a success and no one had been lurking in the shadows, waiting to cause trouble. To add to it, he'd had a chance to make up for his earlier crappy behavior and was satisfied to see a smile once again curve Darby's lips.

The dogs greeted them with a few barks and three rapidly wagging tails. He gestured them out the door. "We'll be back in a few minutes."

Darby surprised him by pressing another kiss on him, this one hard and urgent against his lips. "I'll wait for you."

The kiss and the promise of the woman waiting inside carried him back down the common hallway and out the door. The lightest strains of music echoed in the distance, his condo close enough to the town square that he could still hear the festivities. He smiled again and would have whistled if he could, considering how much better he felt.

He'd hated fighting with Darby. Worse, he hated the fact that he'd attacked her when all she'd tried to do was help. It didn't speak well of him, but it was a revelation to realize that she hadn't held it against him.

And very different from his experience when married.

For as gentle as she seemed, Mary had been more than willing to fight dirty. An argument between the two of them, regardless of who started it, usually resulted in a few days of deliberate silence, even if he apologized. Which had made it that much more surprising when Darby had not only forgiven him but had welcomed him back with a warm kiss and a sexy smile.

Nothing had lingered. She'd been her bright, beautiful self and if he hadn't been a part of the fight, he'd never have known they'd had one.

It was funny how his marriage had been on his mind lately. For something he'd managed to bury for the past five years, it had been quick to surface with the reality of Darby in his life. It had been an even shorter leap to compare her to Mary. And, with it all, he found Darby a wonder at every turn.

Whether it was the thought of his marriage or sim-

ply the feelings that had grown without him even realizing it, Finn had to acknowledge the truth.

He was in love with Darby.

It had happened so easily and so simply.

He'd always imagined falling in love again would
be a hard-fought war. A dark slide back into a relationship where his head battled his heart for domi-
nance. Only it hadn't taken a battle at all.

It had taken one feisty woman with a sharp mind,
a bright smile and a sense of determination that never
failed to humble him. He should be unsettled—ratio-
nally he kept waiting for that feeling to kick in—yet
as he stood there, watching the dogs romp along the
shrub line, Finn knew nothing but peace.

Penny's sharp bark pulled him from his thoughts,
but the warning was too late to do any good. Sharp
pain radiated through his skull as something heavy
hit the back of his head.

Before he could even register an attack, the world
went black.

Darby puttered in the kitchen, the scent of the
pound cake she'd won at the cake walk wafting toward her now that it was open. She'd just begun hunting for a knife to cut the rich treat when she heard
the knock on Finn's door. In the rush to get the dogs
out, she figured he must have forgotten his keys.

She had the door open before she could even register that neither Finn nor Penny, Lucy or Lotte stood
on the other side.

Instead a small, slim form rushed inside, driving into her body with surprising force. Darby whirled backward, her arms pinwheeling as she tried to fight off the assault.

"You bitch!" the woman screeched.

Quickly shifting to the reality of what was happening, Darby struggled against the small body trying to pin her to the chair. Screams ripped from the woman's throat, expletives and sobs in equal measure.

Darby pushed at the manic form, unable to believe the woman's strength. She shoved and kicked, screaming in some hope of getting attention, if not from Finn then from one of his neighbors.

A hard bark echoed in the air, muted through the screen door that led to Finn's small patio. Darby didn't want to take her focus off her attacker, but the bark registered as possible help. Shifting her gaze to the door, she saw Penny up on her back legs, bumping her body hard against the glass. Slowly an idea filled her and Darby shifted her focus from fighting off her attacker to using the woman's momentum to get them moving.

With a deliberate shift in her weight, she slid off the back of the chair, using the force of their bodies to rush them toward the door, the woman screaming the whole time. "He's mine! You don't understand!"

Darby's arms tired under the continued assault and she weighed letting go of the steady pressure against the manic gleam in the woman's eyes. Darby had no doubt the woman had come there to kill her.

That knowledge had her pushing harder, digging deeper for the strength as she back-walked them a few more steps toward the patio door. Penny's barks grew more frenzied and Darby pushed one more shot of strength into her body, shoving as hard as she could at her attacker.

The force did little to stop the woman's forward momentum, but it was enough to give Darby a chance to tug on the door. She pulled on the knob, wrenching hard on the handle only to find it stuck. A hard sob fell from her throat as the woman leaped on her from behind, fingers clawing at Darby's face and neck.

The sob turned into a scream as pain registered from her attacker's assault. Darby kicked out from behind, scoring a slight hit when the heel of her boot connected with a shin, even as another round of pain radiated against the tight hold on her neck.

The kick was just enough to have the grip on her neck loosen and Darby grabbed blindly for the lock, flipping it and dragging on the knob.

Penny fell into the room in a rush of barks and growls and leaped on the woman, immediately stemming the assault and going to battle. Incoherent screams turned into shrieks as Penny pinned down her quarry.

Lotte and Lucy leaped over the low patio fence, their barks and growls a match for Penny's. In moments they'd surrounded the woman, a phalanx of protection holding her back and away from Darby.

They were there. They'd come to protect her. The knowledge had her legs wobbling. As Darby fell to the floor, she heard the sirens. Shouts wove in between the mechanical screams and two officers raced through the patio door on the heels of the dogs.

But it was Finn's haggard features, a trail of blood running down his forehead, that had her dragging herself off the floor in a renewed burst of strength. He stood on the other side of the patio fence and she raced to him, wrapping him in her arms.

"Are you okay?" she asked, shocked to feel how cold he was.

"Never better." His arms went around her, his innate strength still evident beneath the shaking of his limbs as he pulled her close.

Finn huddled in a thick blanket, Lotte on one side and Lucy on the other. Darby came next on the couch and Penny lay on her other side, her head in Darby's lap. Several RRPD members still managed the scene inside his house but Finn had been given strict orders to sit still while he held an ice pack to his forehead. He kept the pack on but refused to let go of Darby's hand with his free one.

He'd come so close to losing her. Just when he'd found her and discovered the depth of his feelings.

"Do you know who she is?" Darby's voice was hoarse but steady.

His town crazy woman, Lydia, had been removed a few minutes earlier. The medics had moved her, dealing with the bruise she'd sustained when Penny had knocked her over. Surprisingly, Penny had avoided biting the woman, using her strength to hold her still until Lotte and Lucy had added their support.

"Her name's Lydia. She lives in town and is a nuisance. Always calling the precinct for something or other. I never imagined she was dangerous."

"She's been sending the gifts?"

Finn nodded, confirming the details one of his deputies had managed to get from her. "I had no idea. I never would have suspected her."

"How could you?" Darby turned to him. "How would you ever know she was so dangerous? Or so deranged."

He couldn't. That was the simple fact. But it had been his choice to drag Darby into this mess in the first place. "There wasn't a way of knowing. But I should have thought before bringing you into this. Before parading you around town as my girlfriend and making everyone think we were a serious couple. Instead all I did was show you off in the face of a deranged woman with an agenda."

"I entered this with open eyes."

"And you've more than kept up your side of things. But I can't believe I almost lost you."

She squeezed his hand, drawing his gaze to hers. "I can't believe I almost lost you, too. Which is why

I have to tell you I love you. I don't care if you don't feel the same, I just need you to know."

The haze of pain that muddled his mind cleared in the face of her news. "It's funny you mention that. Something dawned on me just before I got bashed over the head outside."

"What's that?"

"I love you, too."

Joy filled the pretty blue of her eyes, a match for the warm, welcome smile that painted her face. "What are we going to do about it?"

Finn looked at their joined hands, their assembled huddle of dogs and the team of people that tromped through his condo. His life was crazy and complicated and he still had a killer to catch.

But none of it seemed impossible with Darby beside him.

"I say we keep being in love and figure out the rest as we go."

Finn wasn't sure who moved first—the room had begun spinning again—but it didn't matter the moment their lips met.

She was here. She was safe. And she loved him.

Best Finn Colton could tell, life didn't get a whole lot better than that.

Epilogue

"The rabbit died."

Finn's eyes widened, his shock clear as he stopped midway to tucking his napkin on his lap. "We're having a baby?"

Darby glanced at the dog that even now lay next to the stove, her gaze pointed upward at the meat loaf sitting in a pan on top. "I meant Lucy, silly. We had a successful breeding. The vet confirmed it today."

"Wow. Of course. That's great."

Something flickered deep in his gorgeous blue eyes.

Did he think she *was pregnant?*

Darby wondered if she should say something, nearly discarding the words before she admonished herself. That was the old Darby. The woman who held back or felt like she couldn't express her true self.

All that had changed since Finn had come into her life. It had been reinforced again a month ago when that deranged woman had attacked her in Finn's apartment.

Life was meant to be lived. And part of living was saying what you wanted and what mattered to you.

Finn mattered to her.

Their future mattered to her.

"Would you like to have a baby?" she asked.

"Wouldn't you?"

"Of course—" Darby broke off, trying to find the right words. "I mean, for a long time I'd put it out of my mind. I wasn't with anyone and dwelling on it wasn't going to get me very far. But now? With you? With how I feel about you?" She nodded. "I think about it."

"I think about it, too. I see the way you are with Lora and all I can imagine is you holding our baby."

"I imagine it, too."

Finn laid his napkin down and got up out of his chair. He came around the side of the table, dropping to his knee. Something dropped out of the bottom of her stomach as the gesture registered.

Something delicious and exciting, like the first dip of a roller coaster.

"I love you, Darby Gage. I love being with you and I love imagining a future with you."

"I do, too."

"Then let's make that future real. I want to be with you. I want to marry you. And I want to make a heap of babies with you."

She leaned forward and pressed a kiss to his lips, that roller coaster starting its next big ascent. Oh, how she wanted that future, too. More than she could have ever imagined.

But no matter how much she loved him, some things hadn't changed. "There's still a killer on the loose."

He nodded. "I know. But I'm not going to stop living my life. Living our life."

"I don't mean that. But we already drew the attention of one crazy person. Maybe we can keep our future to ourselves for a while?"

"A secret engagement?" He wiggled his eyebrows, his smile going bright. "Like a covert op?"

"Something like that."

"I like going under covers with you."

She laughed at the innuendo and kissed him once more. "Me, too."

"So, it's settled? You will marry me?"

The roller coaster crept higher. "Yes."

"And you'll have babies with me?"

It ascended a few more notches, reaching the peak. "Yes."

"Can we do that under covers thing?"

Darby laughed and stood, pulling him to his feet as the bottom dropped away once more. "I can't see any reason why we can't get started right now."

Finn tugged on her hand and nearly had her out the door when she pulled him back.

"What's wrong?"

She pointed to their plates. "If we leave that meat loaf on the table, it won't be there when we get back."

Finn shot a stern look at the dogs. "Lotte's well trained. She won't touch it. And Penny and Lucy are equally good."

"Lucy's eating for seven now," Darby reminded him. "It's hardly fair to tempt her like that."

Finn had the plates back on the counter and his hand around hers quick as a flash, dragging her toward the bedroom.

"You don't waste time."

"Not when I see what I want."

"And what's that?"

"You, my secret fiancée." Finn pulled her into the bedroom before stopping to pick her up. He whirled her around in his arms before pulling her against him, his lips pressed to her ear. "Only you."

Darby pulled him close and knew she'd received far more than she ever could have imagined. In two short months her life had changed in ways she'd only dreamed of. As she pulled Finn close, she reveled in their secret. And in the future that spread out before her as she waited to become Mrs. Finn Colton.

A future that was bright and shiny and sure to be absolutely wonderful.

* * * * *

**IF YOU ENJOYED THIS BOOK
WE THINK YOU WILL ALSO LOVE**

HARLEQUIN
ROMANTIC
SUSPENSE

Danger. Passion. Drama.

These heart-racing page-turners will keep you guessing to the very end. Experience the thrill of unexpected plot twists and irresistible chemistry.

4 NEW BOOKS AVAILABLE EVERY MONTH!

HRSXSERIES2020

She lunged forward, slamming him against the brick wall
at his back, her forearm against his throat. "Who are you?"
she snarled.

Stunned, he didn't resist her. Clearly, Rachel had some
serious self-defense training, which only furthered his
certainty that this was a woman who believed herself to be
in mortal danger.

"I told you," he rasped past her forearm. "I'm Marcus Tate."

"That's your name. Who are you?"

"I don't understand—"

"How did you follow me without me spotting you? How
do you know I look in shop windows to check my six? For
that matter, why are you here? Why did you think you could
take down some bad guy who might be following me?"

Ah. He didn't usually talk about his job, and certainly not
with civilians. But this situation was not usual in any way.
"I'm a soldier," he gasped.

All of a sudden, the pressure from her arm was so heavy he couldn't breathe, and he abruptly feared she might actually crush his larynx. Urgently needing to breathe, he reached up in reflex and pinched the pressure point in her hand between her thumb and fingers.

She yelped and jumped back from him, settling into a fighting stance with her hands in front of her and her weight lightly balanced on the balls of her feet.

"I mean you no harm, I swear," he said desperately. "You were just cutting off all my air."

"Who. Are. You," she bit out.

"Lieutenant Marcus Tate, US navy SEAL."

She hissed in sharply at that. Welp, she knew who the SEALs were. More to the point, she wasn't thrilled he was one. Which was weird as heck. Most people would be jumping up and down for joy that a SEAL had their back.

He continued doggedly. "I messed up my shoulder a couple of months ago. Had surgery on it a few weeks ago, and I'm here in Sunny Creek to rehab it. I'm staying with my old teammate, Brett Morgan, at Runaway Ranch. He'll vouch for me and everything I've just told you."

Speaking of which, his shoulder was screaming in protest at all the exertion he'd just put it through.

"If you don't mind," he said carefully, "I'd like to walk back to my truck and get some ice for my shoulder. It hurts like a sonofa—" He broke off. "It hurts a lot."

"You can walk in front of me. I'll follow behind you," she said grimly.

Don't miss
Her SEAL Bodyguard *by Cindy Dees,*
available May 2022 wherever
Harlequin Romantic Suspense books and ebooks are sold.

Harlequin.com

HRSEXP0322

Love Harlequin romance?

DISCOVER.

Be the first to find out about promotions,
news and exclusive content!

 Facebook.com/HarlequinBooks

Twitter.com/HarlequinBooks

 Instagram.com/HarlequinBooks

Pinterest.com/HarlequinBooks

You Tube YouTube.com/HarlequinBooks

ReaderService.com

EXPLORE.

Sign up for the Harlequin e-newsletter and
download a free book from any series at
TryHarlequin.com

CONNECT.

Join our Harlequin community to
share your thoughts and connect
with other romance readers!
Facebook.com/groups/HarlequinConnection